British Summer Time

LIZ GWINNELL

First published in paperback by
Michael Terence Publishing in 2023
www.mtp.agency

ISBN 9781800945685

Michael Terence
Publishing

For Mum and Dad
Because you loved the Summer

There are two flames burning in the human heart all the time:
the flame of anger against injustice and
the flame of hope you can build a better world.

- *Tony Benn*

This story is based on true events.

Any resemblance to persons alive or dead, except where public figures are specifically mentioned, is entirely co-incidental.

Three Weeks Before

Chapter 1

August 1984

High up on the bank on the north side of the A64, a middle-aged man dressed in a grey raincoat raised a pair of binoculars to his eyes.

"Are you sure they're coming Sir?" the man standing next to him said. "I didn't think the festival was starting for another three weeks."

"Of course they're coming Peters," Commander Clive Taylor barked. "Don't ask stupid questions."

Sergeant Ray Peters blew on his hands. Dorothy had warned him it would be cold in Yorkshire, even in August. She had packed three handknitted jumpers and two pairs of Argyle socks into his suitcase, just in case. He wished he'd put on one of the jumpers this morning. It was bloody freezing. A shout from the Commander cut into his thoughts.

"Here they come Peters!" he said. "Here they come."

Peters squinted to his left and saw the first vehicle in the procession appear in the valley below them.

"Make a note of every number plate you see," Taylor barked. "Every bloody one of them."

Taylor lowered his binoculars and watched as the Peace Convoy approached. Coloured flags and pirate flags waved from the roofs of every lorry, truck and van and the sound of a klaxon broke the silence of the morning. The vehicles were old, their paint faded and peeling as their engines struggled to cope with the slight incline of the road.

Taylor clenched his fists, feeling a mixture of irritation and triumph that the Convoy had finally arrived. He could have done without being sent to the ass end of the Universe but as one of the Met's four specialist commanders, there was no one more capable of heading up Operation Raymond than him. Clive Taylor prided himself on getting a job done and wouldn't rest until he had removed every piece of scum from this earth including striking miners, long haired drug smoking hippies, football fans who rioted on the terraces, IRA bombers and last but not least, the Peace Convoy.

Suddenly Taylor dropped the binoculars.

"Bastards," he said. "Do they think we want to see their hairy asses?"

Sergeant Peters followed his gaze and tried not to smile.

"It's not on Sir is it," he said. "What sort of people show their bottoms to police officers?"

Taylor snorted.

"Scum bags that's what," Peters said, staring after the Convoy as it snaked away to their right. "These sorts of people are capable of anything Peters," he said. "Anything. Remember that Peters, remember that."

Chapter 2

There was a happy, high feeling on the Love Bus as it travelled north along the A64 towards West Yorkshire. Bob Marley music blasted out of the speakers on the upper deck where girls with long hair swayed to the music and men with dreadlocks passed around joints and played Canasta.

Downstairs, Grendo Blake gripped the black steering wheel of the converted London bus. The muscles in his upper arms rippled and his long grey hair was tied back in a ponytail. They had been driving for miles without seeing any road signs and all he could do was hope they were heading in the right direction. As the lead vehicle in the Peace Convoy, he had to get it right. The 140 vehicles following him in a quarter of a mile procession were depending on him.

Standing to his left, Carl Lamb, known in the Convoy as Shepherd, looked out of the window at the heavy grey skies of Yorkshire.

"Any idea?" Grendo asked him.

"No," Shepherd said, shaking his head. "But look over there Grend. Look over there."

Grendo turned his head in the direction Shepherd was pointing and saw two men standing at the top of the grassy bank which sloped down to the road.

"Pigs," Grendo said, as he stared at them. "I thought they'd pop up sooner or later. Can smell 'em a mile off I can."

Shepherd ducked his head to get a better look.

"They've got binoculars," he said. "The bigger man. He's got binoculars."

Grendo flexed his arms and gripped the wheel more tightly.

"Cheeky bastards," he said. "But nice of them to turn out and welcome us to Yorkshire. Let's show our appreciation shall we Shep?"

Shepherd grinned.

"Yes," he said. "Too fucking right."

Shepherd swung along the poles away from the driver's cab and ran up the stairs.

"Convoy salute!" he shouted. "Pigs to our right!"

The men threw down their cards and the girls stopped dancing and rushed over to the long window on the right hand side of the bus where they dropped their trousers and lifted up their skirts to moon at the men standing on the bank as the bus passed by.

"That'll give them something to think about," Shepherd grinned as he re-zipped his flies. "Boys in blue we salute you!"

A girl with long brown hair moved towards him, holding on to the back of the seats to steady herself. She was the only one who hadn't mooned at the roadside.

"What if they ain't coppers?" she said. "I mean what if they're just normal people like hitch-hikers or something? What if we get arrested again?"

Shepherd smiled and hooked her hair behind her ear.

"We won't get arrested," he said. "I promise."

"We got arrested for stealing milk last week and it wasn't even us."

Shepherd sighed.

"We won't get arrested Rose," he reassured her. "So stop worrying and go and do some more dancing. I've got to go downstairs and help Grendo work out where the fuck we are."

"I love you Shep," she said, her blue eyes a little out of focus.

"Aye and I love you too," he said. "So go and do some dancing. Ok?"

"Ok," she said, smiling up at him. "Ok."

Chapter 3

Commander Taylor stomped back towards the gold Ford Cortina parked in the layby. He walked so quickly that Ray Peters had to run to keep up with him.

"When we get back to the station, I want you to put out an alert warning every force in Yorkshire that they've arrived," Taylor said, glaring at Peters across the roof of the car.

"Little bastards," he added, yanking open the passenger door. "They'll regret doing that."

Taylor got into the car and tugged the seatbelt across his stomach.

"Hurry up and get that heater on Peters before I freeze my balls off."

Peters swallowed.

"I'm afraid there isn't one Sir," he said. "This was the last car in the garage and they let me have it at a discount because the heater's broken."

Taylor clipped in his seatbelt and sighed.

"Why am I not surprised," he sighed, looking out of the window. "We're in the arse end of the universe after all. Godforsaken place."

Peters eased the car out of the gravel car park and on to the main road.

"And make sure you tell them they're armed," Taylor said. "When you put out the alert."

Peters glanced in the rear-view mirror and swallowed.

"But Sir we don't know for definite that they're armed. I didn't see any guns."

"Of course they're armed!" Taylor barked. "Don't question my judgment Peters or you'll be back arresting prostitutes in King's Cross before you can say Jack Rabbit."

Ray Peters knew better than to say anymore. He had worked with Clive Taylor for five years and his reputation in the Met was legendary. He had had men demoted if he didn't like the tone of their voice. There was a joke in the control room that his wife took obedience classes in the village hall while the dog stayed at home.

"Put your foot down Peters can't you?" Taylor said after a moment. "My wife drives faster than you."

Peters nodded and eased his foot down on the accelerator. He had no idea what lay ahead but he had a feeling it was not going to be all Yorkshire tea cakes and James Herriott as Dorothy had suggested.

Chapter 4

Roger Appleby was just the sort of lilly livered police officer Clive Taylor couldn't stomach: soft like his name with no backbone. When were these backwater bobbies going to realise that times had changed and that policing wasn't Dixon of Dock Green anymore? What was needed these days was tough guys doing a tough job; a more aggressive approach to contain the pockets of civil unrest and disorder breaking out across England.

"Tell me Appleby," Commander Taylor said. "Were you at Orgreave in June?"

They were sitting in the office allocated to Taylor at Droxby police station. The door opened on to the control room and Taylor didn't like the way that was set up either, with all ranks drifting around, smoking cigarettes, drinking tea and reading newspapers. It was sloppy, that's what it was: sloppy.

Appleby put his tea down on the table between them. Taylor felt a prick of irritation at the way he carefully lined up the bottom of the cup with the indentation in the saucer.

"No," he said. "No I wasn't. There weren't many local police there."

"Thought not," Taylor grunted, knocking back his tea in one gulp. "We learned a lot of lessons about policing at Orgreave Appleby," he said. "A lot of lessons. And that's the sort of scenario we're looking at here."

Appleby cleared his throat.

"Surely not Sir," Appleby countered. "I mean a festival is very different from a miners' strike. There was a one day festival at Ambrell in '82 and there wasn't any trouble."

Taylor eyed him coldly. It was just the sort of wet comment he'd expect from this man.

"Well it's going to be different this time," he said. "Number one, the Convoy didn't exist in '82 and number two, intelligence suggests thousands of them are on their way to Ambrell and when you get thousands of travellers arriving in one area that means only one thing. Do you want a bunch of dirty drug smoking hippies upsetting the locals, pissing in their front gardens and selling drugs to their children? They could even be armed this time."

"Armed?" Appleby repeated. "You mean guns?"

Taylor sighed.

"Yes. Armed. Guns. Chain saws. Spears. Axes and so on and so forth. We have to be prepared just like we were prepared for Orgreave."

"But they were flying pickets," Appleby countered. "And this is a music festival."

Taylor stood up and started to pace around the small room with his hands in his trouser pockets. He was beginning to feel claustrophobic.

"Anarchy is anarchy whatever name you call it," he said. "These sorts of people are the same the world over. Rebel rousers. Troublemakers. It's about time you local forces realised that if you sleep on the job you will wake up to a nightmare."

"We're deploying twelve officers," Appleby countered, defensively.

"Twelve?" Taylor snorted. "Twelve?"

"It's all the manpower we can spare," Appleby said. "We're not expecting trouble. There was good rapport with the organisers in '82. We're hoping it will be the same this time."

Taylor placed the palms of his hands on the table and leaned across to stare into Appleby's face.

"This is a *pop* festival," he said in a low, controlled voice. "A festival where they take drugs, run around naked and get up to God knows what. And there is a separate field for the Convoy. I presume you know about that? A field where the Convoy will be staying; where they will be openly allowed to sell drugs and break the law?"

"I was aware of it," Appleby said. "We tend to turn a blind eye to the drugs. If there's no trouble," he added hastily.

Taylor stared at him for a moment and then straightened and turned away.

"I want your men to be vigilant," he said. "I don't want headlines criticising the police for not doing their job properly. I want searches – of people, tents, vehicles and I expect you to find the guns and the weapons and confiscate them. Do you understand me?"

Appleby nodded.

"I do Sir. Yes Sir. I understand perfectly."

Taylor stared around the room.

"Good," he said. "One more thing Appleby."

"Yes sir?"

"Is this your office?"

"Yes," Appleby nodded. "Yes it is. Was."

"I thought so," Taylor said, taking a vase of flowers off the windowsill and handing them to him. "Take these away," he said. "I'm not getting married."

"Yes sir," Appleby said, taking the vase and holding it in both hands.

"That will be all," Taylor sighed. "Now get out of my hair. I've got work to do."

Chapter 5

Usually they travelled in Idlewild, the 1970s camper van he'd nicked from his old boss in the best coup Hartlepool had ever seen. Today she was being towed by one of the trucks further back in the Convoy after the radiator sprung a leak near Birmingham. So they'd hitched a lift with Grendo and his wife Janey on the Love Bus and they'd fix Idlewild when they stopped to set up camp.

Since they'd joined the Convoy three years ago, Shepherd had never been happier. He had always hated getting up at the crack of dawn in the freezing cold to work at the garage. He had never liked the vicious cycle of wages-rent-wages and scratching enough of a living to pay the rent and get food in the fridge. Now, with the Convoy, he felt he was living, not just existing and Rose was happy too. It was a bit hairy at the time but they'd done it hadn't they? They'd done it.

"Camp up ahead!" Grendo called over his shoulder. "Prepare to land!"

The bus indicator flashed orange and Grendo pulled her off the main road down an uneven lane. Rose made a face at Shepherd as they bumped along and held on to the back of the seat. They had every confidence in Grendo. He had driven through hedges to get into fields and negotiated the trickiest of terrain. He'd been in the Army once, driving trucks in the deserts and foothills of Afghanistan and done a tour of Northern Ireland too. No lane or byway defeated him despite the size of the decommissioned London bus. Grendo just steered her with his big muscular tattooed arms like the captain of a pirate ship negotiating the roughest of seas. Once it had taken passengers to and from work; now it was a cosy home softened with scatter cushions and rugs and lined with shelves of books. And sitting on the shelves and hanging from macrame baskets nailed to the ceiling was a profusion of leafy cannabis and tomato plants.

"The boys in blue can't tell the difference," Janey once told him. "I've lost count of the number of tomato plants they've taken off me. I'd like to see their faces when they try to smoke the leaves. Well," she'd shrugged. "They're all at it aren't they? We've all sold drugs to coppers, haven't we Grend?"

Grendo had converted the back seat so that it folded down into a bed. Thrown across it were blankets Janey had knitted and cushions and pillows she had sewn on the old Singer machine she kept in a wooden box under one of the seats. Grendo had stripped the bus and made wooden panels and doors. It was just like home and Shepherd loved it. All of the vehicles in the Convoy had once been something else just like their occupants had once been someone else. Now they had all been given new life and, in a way, he had too, Shepherd reflected, as they bumped across the uneven ground of the field and came to a sudden halt.

Chapter 6

Katie May loved Van Morrison. She knew everything about Van the Man there was to know and the walls of her sixteen year old bedroom were a perfect shrine to the unassuming singer from Northern Ireland. Last year, on his birthday, which she marked every year in her diary in red pen, she and Juliet had danced round her bedroom to *Brown Eyed Girl* and eaten cheese sandwiches. And now, now he was playing at a music festival five miles away.

"Hugo Davis has got tickets," she confided as they sat by the river one late July evening. It was the summer holidays and they were bored. There was nothing to do around here, nothing.

"Hugo Davis?" Juliet said. "The boy from St. Clair's?"

"The one and only," Katie said. "He's asked me to go with him."

"To a festival?" Juliet said. "Hugo Davis has asked you to go to a *festival?"*

"No to the public toilets," Katie said, rolling her eyes. "Of course to a festival. And guess what? Van Morrison is playing."

Katie looked at Juliet, her eyes shining, waiting for her to congratulate her on her great good fortune.

"So why does Hugo Davis want to take you?" Juliet said suspiciously. "Those public schoolboys usually look down their noses at us lot."

Katie shrugged.

"He says he's fancied me for months."

Juliet was silent for a moment.

"I saw him kissing Myla Mayers at the bus stop last week."

"Oh they finished," Katie said, airily. "Ages ago. She's a bit stuck up. That's what he said anyway."

"What does your dad say?" Juliet said, plucking at a dry blade of grass. "About you going to a festival?"

Katie shrugged.

"He doesn't know and I'm not going to tell him. I'll say I'm staying at yours for the Bank Holiday weekend."

Juliet looked at her with wide eyes.

"But what if he comes looking for you?"

"He won't," Katie said. "He'll spend Saturday afternoon in front of the telly watching the horse racing and then he'll go down the Club. I'll be back before he's noticed I've gone."

Juliet looked at her.

"You will be careful won't you? Aren't there a lot of drugs and stuff at festivals?"

Katie shrugged. Sometimes Juliet was so annoying.

"That's just what the papers say," she said, not really knowing if there were or if there weren't and repeating the answer Hugo had given her when she'd asked exactly the same question.

"But you hardly know him!" Juliet said. "Where are you going to sleep?"

"In a tent of course," she said.

"With Hugo?"

"He's bringing two," she said. "And we're getting a lift," she added. "Before you start going on about hitch hiking."

"I wasn't," Juliet said, her tone a little wounded. "I wasn't going to say anything about hitch hiking."

Katie stood up. She had expected Juliet to be envious of her date with Hugo and going to see Van Morrison but instead she was acting all prim and proper and bringing doubt into the sparkles in her mind.

"You will be careful won't you?" Juliet said, looking up at her friend.

"Oh for God's sake," Katie rolled her eyes. "You should be pleased for me instead of worrying about it all."

"Sorry," Juliet said. "I am. Pleased for you. Really I am."

"So you'll cover for me then?"

"If I have to," Juliet sighed. "If I have to."

"Thank you," Katie said, leaning down and kissing her on the top of her head. "You're the best friend ever."

Chapter 7

Lady Caroline Oxley woke at lunchtime with the taste of last night's wine in her mouth. An old moth-eaten fur coat was thrown across her and daylight peeped through the curtains of the Orange Room. Munro, her shaggy Irish wolfhound, sat up and licked her face.

"Oh don't do that darling," she said pushing him away gently. "It's far too early for that sort of thing."

Caroline threw off the coat and swung her legs from the couch to the floor and walked towards the window. As she pulled back the curtain, she could see men in the grounds below scurrying around like ants. The stage where the bands would play at the festival was already constructed and tents and marquees were dotted across the fields.

Lady Caroline felt a surge of excitement run through her.

"If this is anything like 1982 Munro," she said. "This is going to be a wonderful festival. What do you think eh?"

Munro barked as the door opened and her butler, Sowcroft, came in with a tray on which there was an ornate silver teapot and a china cup and saucer.

"I thought m'lady might like some tea," he said.

Lady Caroline smiled at him.

"Why Sowcroft how very thoughtful of you," she said, sitting back down on the couch as he set the tray on the occasional table in front of her.

"Will m'lady be coming down to start discussing the plans for the straw structure?" he asked.

"What?" she said. "Oh yes. Yes. Of course. What time is it?"

"It's a little past midday m'lady. I thought I'd let you sleep."

"Well you let me sleep far too long," she said crossly.

"Robert Oaks is waiting for you when you are ready," he said. "I made him remove his footwear before entering. And I'm afraid I have to report a fresh leak in the ceiling of the Charleston Suite. I've put a bucket under it for now."

Lady Caroline lifted her teacup to her lips. Bloody house! Always springing a leak somewhere.

"Get someone to fix it Sowcroft would you?"

"And who might you suggest m'lady?" he said politely. "You let most of the staff go last year if you'll remember. There's only me and Robert and some farm workers left."

"Well get one of them to do it, I don't know," she said.

Honestly, did she have to think of everything? People might think it was fun to own a great big pile of a stately home like Ambrell but the reality was very different. It sucked in money and it swallowed it. It was one of the reasons she'd decided to hold another pop festival. Money was always in short supply.

"Sorry Sowcroft," she said. "I'll think of something. Tell Robert I'll be down in ten minutes."

"Very well m'lady," he said, bowing as he left the room.

It was ridiculous really, she thought, as he left her alone to her thoughts and her tea, rattling around this old pile with an ancient butler. Even Sowcroft's suit was shabby but he still acted like he was serving a great family in a great house even though it was just her and Munro with half of the house shut up and the contents of the 14 rooms shrouded in dust sheets. It made her head hurt to think about it.

Her mood brightened at the thought of the festival. Leaks in the ceiling and the lack of staff could wait. It was time to start building the straw palace. She'd been dreaming of it for weeks.

Chapter 8

Shepherd loved it when they came off the road and made camp. He joined a working party tasked with digging the latrine pits and chopping down trees for firewood and when he finished, the sun was setting in the west as he joined Rose by the fire. She took hold of his hand as he sat down and Janey stirred an iron pot of stew nestling in the flames.

There were about twenty lorries and vans caravans parked in the field. The Convoy had divided and sections of it had driven on to other locations because 600 people in 140 vehicles wasn't easy to accommodate.

Locks came in from his right and poked a smoking, fat joint under his nose.

"Have some of this Shep," he said, sitting down next to him and stretching his long legs out in front of him. "Finest Leb. Makes the sunset wild."

Shepherd took the joint from him as Grendo and some of the others came to sit by the fire. It was so peaceful, Shepherd reflected. Somewhere he could hear sheep bleating and, in the distance, the rumble of the traffic from the A64. Children ran around splashing each other with water, dogs ran in crazy circles and Shepherd pulled on the joint and felt a deep sense of contentment.

Shepherd looked around him. They were a mixture of all sorts here. Fugitives from the depression that hung over England like a dark suffocating blanket making it difficult to breathe, find work, be heard. There were anarchists, fortune tellers, people who had lost their way, people who had found their way; spiritualists, pontificators, radical types and dreamy types. They were all bound by one thing: life on the road. For some, life had driven them there. For others, like Grendo who had been travelling for years, it was a lifestyle choice.

"Where the fuck are we anyway Grendo?" Locks asked, breaking the silence.

"Fucked if I know," Grendo said. "There weren't any road signs. All I know is we're in Yorkshire."

Another man came along and took a seat by the fire. Shepherd didn't know him that well, he'd just seen him around from time to time. All he knew was his name was Butcher, a quiet man who said little. It didn't matter in the Convoy: no one asked questions and everyone was welcome in this big patchwork of a family. There were rumours that some of the Convoy were men on the run from prison or worse and that had spooked Rose to start with until Shepherd had reassured her.

"The police might be looking for me too," he'd told her when she voiced her concerns.

"Btu you only nicked a van," she said. "You never killed no one."

That was when he'd shown her the axe under the bed.

"Don't worry," he said. "No one's going to mess with me."

In reality, it wasn't men on the run they needed to worry about. Their enemies were the forces of law and order and a government that was determined to get everyone off the road, rounded up and corralled behind the barbed wire fences of respectability.

"We're not far from Ambrell," Butcher said, breaking into his thoughts.

Grendo looked up from the joint he was rolling between his fingers.

"Oh aye," he said. "Know that do you?"

Butcher looked away at the hills and the trees and the setting sun beyond.

"We used to come here when I was a kid," he said after a moment. "Family holidays."

"Oh aye," Grendo said. "And where was that then?"

"Scarborough mostly," Butcher said. "We went to loads of places. I can't remember them all now."

Butcher shook his head as the joint reached him and he let it pass to the next person in the circle.

Grendo stared at him for a moment.

"Perhaps you can navigate us to Ambrell if you know the area like."

Butcher looked uncomfortable.

"What," Grendo teased him. "Rumours about the Love Bus making you jittery? They're all true, you know," he said, pausing to lick the paper of the joint. "All of them. Orgies. Drugs. The lot. You name it. It all happens on the love bus."

The others gathered around the fire laughed but Butcher looked embarrassed. Janey took the pot off the fire and started to dish out stew into mess tins.

"Leave him alone Grend," she said gently. "Not everyone's got the same sense of humour as you."

Later that night, Rose turned to Shepherd as they lay in bed.

"Why does Grendo always challenge Butcher?"

"Grendo?" he said. "I hadn't noticed. You know what he's like. Dry sense of humour."

"That Butcher's a strange one."

"Why do you say that?"

In the darkness, Rose shrugged.

"I don't know," she said. "It's just a feeling I get."

Shepherd sighed and turned away on his side, pulling the blankets over his shoulder.

"You read too much into things," he said.

"But I'm never wrong am I?" she said, sitting up and looking down at him.

Shepherd sighed.

"Don't start all that spooky stuff now," he said. "It's late."

Rose lay back down and stared at the ceiling. Shepherd closed his eyes and reached for her hand in the darkness. Tomorrow was going to be a challenging day. Tomorrow they were going to fix Idlewild.

Chapter 9

This year, she thought, this year she was going to recreate the Palace of Versailles.

"The what?" Robert Oaks said when she told him, scratching his head and looking puzzled.

"The palace built by Louis Quatorze," Sowcroft volunteered. "Versailles."

"Oh," Robert said looking even more confused. "A palace? Made out of straw?"

Caroline ignored the doubt in his voice. She had it all pictured in her head. The fairytale turrets, the chandeliers she'd get out of the cellar and hang up inside. She didn't know how they would run electricity from the house but Sowcroft, despite his outward appearance as a respectable and law-abiding butler, knew all sorts of things about extracting electricity which had both surprised and delighted her at the last festival.

"We've only got three weeks," she said abruptly. "And I want it to be perfect Robert. Perfect."

Robert stared at the ground and kicked at it with the back of his heel.

"You won't be able to build it here," he said.

"Why not?" Caroline said. "I thought it would be perfect just to the left of the stage."

"Marsh land," he said. "If it rains, it's curtains. Now if you was looking at the travellers' field, that's different. That's chalk that is."

Caroline stared at him and sighed.

"What *is* he talking about Sowcroft?"

"Marsh land," Sowcroft said, standing in the field in his butler's outfit. "Things sink on marsh land. Especially if it rains."

"Oh dear," she sighed. "And I so wanted it to be by the stage."

"We can build it in the travellers' field," Robert said.

"Can we?"

"Yes m'lady," he said respectfully. "Yes."

"If I get a book from the library I can show you what it looks like."

"Yes m'lady," Robert said, nodding his head. "You do that and I'll create it."

"Thank you Robert," she said, turning on her most beguiling smile. "I knew I could rely on you."

She wandered back to the house and on the way, passed through the kitchen garden. When she was a child and her mother had been alive, it had been a thriving cornucopia of fat marrows, ripe tomatoes and giant plants that had both scared and delighted her. Now it was a mess, a veritable jungle of chaos and neglect. The pear and apple trees looked sick and shrivelled and the espaliers that supported them were broken and rotten. The grass was so long it came up to her knees and the land was full of stinging nettles and weeds rampaging over what had once been neat little beds supplying fruit and veg to the house and the families who worked there.

Sowcroft, in the manner of all good butlers, appeared silently from nowhere and cleared his throat.

"Begging your pardon m'lady," he said. "You have a visitor up at the house."

"Oh?" she said. "I'm not expecting any visitors. Who is it Sowcroft? That nice festival organiser with the blue eyes?"

"No m'lady. It's a man calling himself Commander Taylor. He says he's from the Metropolitan Police."

Lady Caroline frowned.

"The Metropolitan Police? What on earth is he doing in Yorkshire?"

Inside, her heart sank. Was he here about Tim? Was there news, finally?

"He says he wants to speak to you about the festival," Sowcroft said. "I've shown him into the library and put a bucket in the corner under the leak."

Lady Caroline sighed.

"Thank you Sowcroft," she said. "Thank you."

Chapter 10

They'd spent all day fixing Idlewild and the last thing Shepherd needed was Rose getting all weird on him. There was a peaceful happy feeling in the camp tonight and Shepherd just wanted to chill out.

"I want to go home," Rose said as they sat on the grass by the steps of Idlewild. "I've got a bad feeling about this festival."

"Oh for fuck's sake," Shepherd sighed. "Can't you just relax and enjoy yourself?"

"I saw trouble," Rose said. "In the cards. The Tower. The 9 of swords. Those aren't good cards Shep. They ain't good at all."

Shepherd squinted his eyes against the evening sun. Someone was juggling coloured balls over by the fire and two members of the Convoy were kneeling on the grass writing on a board in big red letters.

"You read too much into those cards sometimes," Shepherd said. "We're at a music festival. What could go wrong?"

Rose shrugged.

"I don't know," she said. "I've just got a bad feeling that's all."

Shepherd looked up at the sky.

"Let's go and sit by the stream," he said. "Take the guitar."

Rose shook her head.

"I don't want to sit by the stream Shep. I want to go home."

"Don't be daft," he said, getting to his feet and holding out his hand to her. "Come on. We'll pretend we're by the sea. Remember how we used to sit by the sea?"

Rose reluctantly let Shepherd pull her to her feet. With his guitar slung over one shoulder and his other arm looped around her, they headed towards the woods.

"Think about what you'd go back to," he said as they walked. "I mean you don't really want to go back to all that do you? Your stepdad? Living in a house? The unemployment queues? Hartlepool? Aren't you happy?"

Rose shrugged and didn't answer and they walked on in silence.

They stopped when they reached the trees; ancient, old white willows with thick dark trunks dipping their branches into the stream that ran alongside them.

Rose sat down on the bank and dipped her feet in the water.

"There," Shepherd said, sitting down beside her. "Feel better now do you?"

Rose hadn't spoken for a while and Shep wasn't sure what she was thinking. He was never sure. Rose was deep, sometimes beyond him, but usually he could bring her back. Tonight was proving more difficult.

Shepherd knew better than to talk too much when Rose was like this. If he said too much about not going in one direction, she'd go there. Better to just let her speak when she was ready. Women were curious. You lived alongside them, slept with them and shared all of life's intimacies with them and then they came out with a blinder like that, something out of left field you didn't see coming.

Shepherd pulled his guitar on to his lap and started to pick out a song on his guitar. It was one of Rose's favourites: Paul Weller's *English Rose.*

Behind them the sound of children playing in the camp drifted on the breeze and birds sang high in the trees as the orange sun slipped down behind the hills. It was idyllic, Shepherd thought, this life. He was 26 years old and he'd spent most of that life caged in a run down seaside town on the East coast of England which had seen better days by far. Why would Rose want to give up the freedom they'd found and return to dreary grey skies and men shuffling along the pavement in the dole queue?

"Feeling better?" he asked after a while, breaking the silence.

Rose turned and smiled at him. Shepherd felt a sense of relief. Crisis over. He put his guitar down and leaned over and stroked her long dark hair.

"You wouldn't want to leave your Shep would you?" he grinned.

Rose smiled up at him as he leaned over and gently kissed her on the mouth. He shifted his weight and pulled her down on the ground so that they were both lying on their sides and Rose reached up and looped her arms around his neck. Shepherd trailed his hand down her back and pulled her in towards him. He moved his other hand to her breast and Rose moaned and closed her eyes. Suddenly she stiffened and sat up.

"What was that?"

"What was what?" he said, his eyes closed, as his hand circled her breast.

"That noise," Rose said. "I heard something."

"No you didn't," Shepherd said, kissing her neck. "Lie down."

Rose pushed him away.

"There!" she hissed in a loud whisper. "Didn't you hear it?"

Shepherd sighed and sat up.

"I can't hear anything," he said.

Rose got to her feet staring across the stream into the shadowy trees beyond. Darkness came swiftly on an August night and had ambushed them before they'd noticed it.

Shepherd groaned and sat up, looping his arms around his knees. Trust Rose to get all weird on him now right at the moment when he wanted her more than anything.

A twig cracked and Shepherd turned to look behind him. Two men were standing there and one of them had a gun. And the gun was pointed straight at him.

Chapter 11

Sowcroft had brought that dreadful old teapot again. The Commander didn't seem to notice and was staring around him at the Old Masters hung on the walls of the Library. He looked strangely out of place in his police uniform in this dusty, cool room where the bookshelves groaned with works penned by Dickens, Chaucer and D.H. Lawrence. Lady Caroline had never read any of them. They were dreadful dull old things but they were Mummy's books and she couldn't bear to part with them.

Clive Taylor put his cup down on the saucer, his chunky fingers looking clumsy against the delicate Coalport china.

"So Commander," she said sweetly, her calm tone belying her thumping heart. Was he about to tell her they had found Tim? Was he about to impart dreadful news or good news?

"What brings you to Ambrell? I would have thought you boys in blue would be far too busy to pay a social call, what with the Miners' Strike and the flying pickets and all these things going on around us."

Taylor sat upright, his back ramrod straight, in an attempt, she thought, to assert his authority in a house he could never dream of owning in a world where he didn't belong.

"I'll get straight to the point," he said. "This isn't a social call although it is a pleasure to meet someone of such good standing and pedigree."

Lady Caroline flinched at his clumsy attempt at flattery.

"I'm on special secondment from the Met," he continued. "And I've been sent up here to police the festival."

"You've come all the way up here because of a festival?" she said, feeling relief and disappointment flood through her that this wasn't about her brother. "Don't you have better things to do in London?"

Taylor cleared his throat.

"We have nothing against the festival itself," he said. "It's the field allocated to travellers that's our concern."

Lady Caroline looked at him. Munro was sitting at the side of her chair watching Taylor with bright eyes and his tongue hanging out. She got the impression the Commander was nervous around dogs from the way his eyes kept darting towards him.

"In what way is it a concern Commander?" she asked. "We didn't have any trouble in '82."

"Our concern is the Convoy," he said. "They arrived in Yorkshire last week."

"The Convoy?"

"The Peace Convoy. To put it as nicely as I can, it is a travelling community largely made up of anarchists, drug dealers and those who have no respect for the law. They travel around in old clapped out vehicles from festival to festival in a very large… well… convoy. We've been tracking their movements for some time now. Mrs Thatcher is particularly concerned about them."

"Ah, I see," Lady Caroline said. "Well we can't have our venerable PM having sleepless nights can we?"

Taylor looked at her. He had a feeling she was laughing at him but he wasn't quite sure.

"It's important not to underestimate who they are and what they are capable of," he said. "We have intelligence which suggests they have weapons: axes, chainsaws, you name it. And then there's the drugs. These people think nothing of selling drugs to children and sticking two fingers up at the law."

Lady Caroline paused, watching the man filled with such self-importance sitting opposite her.

"Tell me Commander," she said after a moment, lifting her teacup and holding it to her lip. "Do you believe people should enjoy themselves?"

He looked confused by her question for a moment.

"Because you see," she continued. "I'm happy to hold the festival and have a travellers field. After all, if you shut all the other festivals down, where are all these people going to go? I hear Reading and Glastonbury aren't happening this year. I also hear that Reading was going to be re-arranged at Lilford Park but the licence was refused. So where are all the young people supposed to go to play their music and listen to music?"

Taylor looked like she'd hit him in the face with a wet fish. Lady Caroline stifled the urge to laugh.

"You seem to know a lot about it," he said, recovering himself.

"I make it my business to know about it," she said. "I'm organising a music festival. It's my business to know such things. These are such glum times, it does people good to let their hair down once in a while don't you think?"

Taylor stared at her.

"As I said," he continued. "It's not the festival that concerns us. It's the Peace Convoy. You come from a good family Lady Caroline. Do you really want these sort of people on your doorstep, dancing around with no clothes on and selling drugs to children?"

"Is there any evidence they do that?" she asked coolly.

"Yes," he said. "Plenty."

Lady Caroline leaned forward, uncrossed her legs and placed her cup and saucer carefully on the table.

"So let me get this right Commander," she said, leaning back in her chair. "You're saying that people *might* do dreadful things and you want to stop them doing dreadful things before they've even done dreadful things?"

He took a moment to process her words and then he got to his feet and reached for his hat which was lying on the table beside him. Munro barked as he fitted it on his head. Lady Caroline watched him. She'd hit a nerve.

"There will be a significant increase in police numbers in this area over the next few weeks," he said. "Please think about what I said."

"Oh I will, I will," she said, ringing the little brass handbell shaped like a milkmaid that sat on the table.

"The Commander is leaving," she said as Sowcroft entered the room. "Do see him off the premises."

Taylor nodded his head at her.

"Thank you for your time Lady Caroline," he said.

"Oh it's my pleasure," she smiled. "My absolute pleasure. Do call again won't you?"

Sowcroft opened the door and stood to one side as Taylor walked past him and out into the corridor.

After he had gone, Lady Caroline leaned back in her chair and looked up at the ceiling as Munro laid his shaggy head in her lap. Absent mindedly she patted his head, her thoughts drifting. She hadn't told the Commander the real reason she'd wanted a travellers field again this year. The real reason was personal, private, and not to be shared with the Met. Lady Caroline closed her eyes and let her thoughts drift back down the years to a time when there hadn't been holes in the roof and weeds strangling the kitchen garden.

Chapter 12

"Don't shoot," Rose begged. "Please, don't shoot."

Shepherd felt his heart pounding as he stared at the man holding the gun.

"Stay where you are," the man said, raising the barrel. "Don't come any closer."

Shepherd rolled his eyes up at the sky.

"Can't you put that fucking thing down?" he said. "You're freaking out my girlfriend."

The man lowered his gun and made a signal with his arm for the two men behind him to come forward. Rose had gone very quiet and Shepherd took hold of her hand to reassure her.

"What are you doing out here in the woods at this time of night?" the man with the gun said. "No one comes to the woods at this time of night."

Shepherd sighed.

"Ever heard of the Peace Convoy?" he said. "Well, we're part of it. We've come for the festival. Go over and look at the field if you don't believe us. Hundreds of us there are, hundreds."

"That festival don't start for another three weeks," one of the men said. "You could be lying. You could be coppers."

Shepherd signed and dropped his arms against his thighs.

"Do we look like pigs?" he said. "Well? Do we?"

The three men stared at him for a moment.

"Hard to say," the one at the front said. "Coppers come in all sorts of disguises."

"We ain't coppers," Shepherd said. "So can we just go back to camp? Honestly man this is a fucking joke."

A flicker of a smile played across the man's face.

"So you won't report us?"

Shepherd frowned.

"Report you? What for?"

"Poaching," one of the men said. "Only we haven't been poaching have we John? Haven't shot a thing all night."

"More's the pity," one of the others grumbled. "Starving I am. Kids ain't eaten for three days."

Shepherd's ears pricked up.

"Are you miners?" he said.

"We might be," the man at the back said. "Who's asking?"

"I'm asking," Shepherd said. "Look, we were just sitting down by the river, me and Rose, my girlfriend. We don't care if you're poaching or planning a revolution."

"Well we're not, we was just out for a walk like."

"Oh aye," the second man nodded. "Yes. Out for a walk."

"With guns?" Shepherd asked.

"Are you hungry?" Rose said, cutting into the conversation.

"Oh aye we're hungry alright lass. We been hungry for days, weeks, months."

"We've got food back at the camp," she said. "Why don't you come with us and have some?"

The men exchanged glances.

"We don't take charity," the man at the front said. "We ain't beggars."

"We didn't say you were," Rose continued. "But if you *were* hungry, you'd be welcome to join us."

The men exchanged glances.

"Can't do no harm," the one at the front said to the other two. "We could go and have a look. We don't have to eat nothing if we don't want to."

Shepherd listened, measuring their responses.

"It's this way," he said. "Follow us."

Shepherd and Rose headed back to the camp with the three men following them. As they came out of the trees onto the periphery of the camp, the fires burned brightly and some of the dogs barked and came running over to sniff at the men's shoes. They bent down to pat them on their heads and Shepherd led the men over to the fire where a group were sitting around in front of the orange flames.

"We found these men in the woods," he said. "They're miners and they're hungry."

Grendo raised his head and stood up.

"Hungry eh?" he said. "Well we don't do hungry round here. Sit down. Make yourselves at home. Is that a Browning X-Bolt?" he said, nodding at one of the guns.

"Yes it is," the man said, holding it out. "It was me father's. Right proud of it he were."

Grendo stared at the gun and ran his finger gently along its barrel in wonder.

"Sit down, sit down," Janey said, gesturing with her hands for the men to join them. "We've got stew, jacket potatoes, tomato soup and bread. There's plenty for everyone. Dig in."

The men murmured greetings and nodded at the group and sat down on the chairs Grendo and Shepherd pulled up to the fire. Their clothes were rough working men's wear and their faces were swarthy in the firelight. Shepherd sat down opposite the man who had done most of the talking in the woods as Janey brought dishes and handed them to Grendo who filled them up with stew.

The men ate with rough working hands, holding their plates under their chins, shovelling the food into their mouths. The rest of the circle sat silently as they ate, stoking up the fire, passing around a spliff with a glowing tip. It didn't take the men long to devour what was on their plates.

"More?" Janey said, watching them.

"We don't want to be greedy…"

"Nonsense," Janey said, ladling more stew on to their plates. "We've got plenty. You're welcome to share."

The men set to work demolishing the food and this time they ate more slowly. Shepherd watched them, amazed at how hungry they were. When they had finished and lay their plates down on the grass beside them, Grendo was the first to speak.

"So you're miners then?"

The big man wiped his hands on his rough trousers and held one out.

"Sorry," he said. "We're forgetting our manners. John," he said. "And this is Danny and Marko. And aye, yes, we're miners. Striking miners mind. Striking."

Everyone around the fire shook hands. Except Butcher, Shepherd noticed.

"We're from Arlett," John said. "A village on't other side of river."

"I'm Grendo," Grendo said and in turn, each member of the Convoy introduced themselves.

"So what are you doing here?" John asked. "This a camp is it?"

"We're travellers," Grendo said. "We're on our way to the festival at Ambrell. You know it?"

"Ambrell Priory?" John said.

"Aye," Grendo said, blowing a ring of smoke up at the night sky. "That's the one. Buggered if we know how to find it though. Some bastards have taken down all the road signs."

"Aye they do that, the pigs," Danny said. "They done it to stop us."

"Stop you?" Shepherd asked. "From poaching?"

"We wasn't poaching," John said. "Or alright, maybe we was a bit. But what would you do if you had no money coming in? If your wife and bairns were starving?"

"Poach," Grendo agreed nodding his head. "With a Browning X Bolt."

John smiled.

"We're pickets," he said. "The police have taken down all the road signs to stop us picketing other mines and stop the flying pickets coming here. They forget we was born and bred here. Know this area like the back of our hands we do."

"They took down the road signs?" Janey breathed. "The pigs?"

"Aye and the rest," John said, nodding his head.

Grendo nodded at Janey and she got up and came back to the fire holding a clutch of Carling Black Label cans.

"Fancy a beer?" she said.

The men took the cans she offered and opened them.

"Thank you," John said. "We ain't eaten or drunk like this for months have we boys? Not since March anyhow. That's when the strike started like."

The men pulled open the ring pulls and drank thirstily with their heads tilted back.

"Ah," John said. "That's good that is. That's good."

The group were silent for a moment. Twigs on the fire crackled and snapped and sparks shot up into the air as Janey poked the fire with a small spear.

"You're not far from Ambrell," John said after a moment. "About ten mile I'd say wouldn't you Danny?"

"Aye," Danny nodded, from the opposite side of the fire. "About that, aye."

"Still want to be careful mind," John said, a note of caution creeping into his voice. "Don't dig up any potatoes. Me and some of the boys, we put signs up we have, warning people about the potatoes."

"The potatoes?" Janey repeated. "What about the potatoes? I saw them growing in a field on the other side of the stream earlier. I thought I'd go and get some tomorrow."

"Aye well don't," John said, draining his can of beer and peering in the keyhole left by the ring pull. "Some of the farmers are in league with the police see and they've put poison down. The police are hoping they'll either kill us or starve us to death."

Grendo snorted.

"Bastards," he said.

"Aye," Danny nodded. "They know we're hungry. They reckon they can starve us back to work but we're not going. We're not going back until the government agrees to keep the pits open and guarantee our jobs are safe."

"Is it that bad?" Janey asked in a soft voice.

"Aye," John said, nodding. "Aye. Worse than bad it is to see your kids hungry and to rely on hand outs. It's hard for men like us who've worked down the pits and made an honest living all our lives. But like Danny says, we won't be scared off so easily. I was at Orgreave in June and I ain't see nothing like it. Corralled into a field like cattle we was and the pigs, well, they was brutal, swiping their batons and charging their horses and blaming it all on us. Bastards they are, the lot of 'em."

"They're not that keen on us either," Grendo smiled. "Seems like there's a lot of fugitives in this green and pleasant land of ours."

Shepherd had been quiet, listening to all that was said, hardly believing that men like this were so down and out, so down on their luck, so out of Society. They'd been invisible until the Strike started, men who spent their lives underground in the dark hot mines digging coal for the fires that warmed homes and powered power stations and then, suddenly, when they raised their heads to protest at what the government wanted to do, they became public enemy number one. Something wasn't right somewhere. Something wasn't right.

"Aye well," John said, getting to his feet. "Best be getting back or missus will think I've run off with Arthur Scargill. You been more than generous and I don't know how we can thank you. If we can ever return the favour we will. I don't know how, but we will. Ambrell isn't far from here. Turn right out of here, continue for about three mile, go through Arlett and out t'other side. You'll see Ambrell on the right. Can't miss it."

"Thank you," Grendo said, standing up and shaking John's hand. In the light of the fire, Grendo's grey hair hung thick and wavy to his shoulders, the red bandana he wore around his head dark in the firelight.

"Remember to watch out for them potatoes," John said. "Or you'll get more smash in your mash than you bargained for."

Janey appeared from the darkness carrying a tower of bread and fruit cake piled up under her chin.

"Here," she said. "Take these back for your families."

The men looked at her, their eyes full of emotion.

"Thank you love," John said. "Thank you."

Shepherd watched the men trudge away towards the trees, their rifles on their shoulders, until they were shadows, until they were gone. And only then did he realise Rose was no longer sitting beside him.

Chapter 13

Lady Caroline still looked for Tim everywhere, even now, five years after he had disappeared. She'd wandered through the crowds at the last festival in '82, hoping his face might suddenly appear in the crowd. He had vanished without a trace and all she knew was that he had joined a travelling community. And so having a travellers field at this festival was laced with hope, hope that it might just tempt him home again.

The idea of building a straw palace modelled on Versailles was for him. Tim had always loved Paris with its kings and queens and glamour and glitter and spangles. He'd once dressed in a Charles Worth evening gown that belonged to their mother and Caroline had clapped her hands and laughed in delight as he appeared at the top of the stairs and struck a pose. Her father, the Earl, had not shared her amusement. He had called him every name under the sun and despite Tim being sixteen at the time, had whipped him with his brown leather belt. Caroline had tiptoed into his room afterwards and sat next to his bed, holding her brother as he cried.

What would he make of it all now she wondered, with Ambrell falling down around their ears and Daddy in a nursing home? Tim wouldn't recognise the father who had terrorised him throughout his childhood. The Earl was now a man who had trouble remembering which slipper to put on and his once bright mind which had, in its glory days, been one of the best of his naval generation, was now broken and confused.

Lady Caroline sighed and moved slightly in her chair. She knew she ought to get up and find a book about Versailles to show Robert what her dream palace looked like but the visit from the police had set her mind down a road she didn't often travel. She had always felt so protective of Tim. He didn't fit into the world they were born into and try as he might, the Earl couldn't make him. This had resulted in so many clashes between them that one day Tim had just up and left. She remembered how she had run through the house calling his name, opening door after door and when she couldn't find him, she had gone to bed and cried herself to sleep.

Caroline had always felt protective of her younger brother, ever since their mother had died when she was ten years old. In some ways she was glad he wasn't here because he didn't know what a sorry state Ambrell was in. He didn't know about the finances or how much in debt they were. She had felt physically sick when she found out how the Earl, so outwardly respectable, so locally revered, had speculated on risky businesses and gambled away much of the family fortune. Now, three years later, she just felt disappointed, resigned to it.

The door opened and Sowcroft came into the room.

"Penny for them m'lady?" he said.

"Oh," Lady Caroline said, tossing back her long blonde hair. "I'm not sure they're worth that much Sowcroft. I've allowed myself to dwell and sometimes that's not a good thing."

Sowcroft frowned at her.

"Well in that case m'lady may I suggest something to take your mind off whatever you've been dwelling on. I found this," he said, stepping forward with a hard back book in his hand. "It tells us everything we need to know about Versailles. I believe it belonged to your mother."

Lady Caroline took the book from him and looked at the cover.

"Thank you Sowcroft," she said, looking up at him with shining eyes. "Thank you."

Chapter 14

"I can't find her anywhere," Shep said as he returned to the camp and met Grendo coming in the opposite direction. "I can't find her anywhere."

Grendo put a comforting hand on his arm.

"She'll be back," he said. "She can't have gone far. We're in the middle of nowhere for fuck's sake. A woman can't just disappear."

They'd been looking for Rose for hours with torches and fire sticks; in the woods, down by the stream, even on the other side of the river, following the direction the poachers had come from.

Shepherd returned to Idlewild. It felt empty without Rose. Where had she got to? They'd never been apart, not in the three years they'd been in the Convoy and not much in the two years before that either when they'd lived in the flat by the seafront in Hartlepool. God they'd had a laugh in that flat! Maybe he had pushed her too much, maybe she hadn't really wanted to go on the road as much as he had. Maybe she'd just gone along with it because she knew it was what he wanted to do although to be fair, there weren't many other choices at that time.

Shepherd sat down on the bed and pulled his guitar towards him.

She'd be back soon, he told himself as he picked out Bob Marley's *Redemption Song* on the strings. She'd be back soon.

Chapter 15

Robert scratched his head and turned the book upside down and then the right way up again.

"I'm not sure about them Ironic pillars," he said. "Pillars is difficult. They can fall down, see. Fall down on top of people."

Lady Caroline was becoming increasingly frustrated. Clouds were gathering in the west and they were about to get well and truly soaked in a typical British summer downpour and all Robert could do was scratch his head and turn the book this way and that.

"It's Ionic Robert," she corrected. "Not ironic. Surely all you have to do is turn the bales on their side? That would work wouldn't it?"

Her voice was edged with exasperation. They had three weeks to create Versailles. Ok so it had taken Louis XIV forty years to construct the real one in Paris but she wasn't asking for a real one. She was asking for a simple palace made out of bales of straw. Was that too much to ask? Judging by Robert's perplexed expression, it seemed like it was.

"We could do it without ironic pillars," Robert said as spots of rain began to fall.

"No we can't Robert," Lady Caroline said, clutching the neck of her Barbour more tightly around her throat. "The Palace of Versailles has pillars and I would like it to look like the Palace of Versailles not something from a theme park in Blackpool."

"Leave it with me your ladyship," Robert sighed. "I'll speak to Dave. He done some nice wooden rafters over at Cottleby last year. He might know."

Lady Caroline decided that saying anymore would be useless.

"Just get the pillars sorted Robert," she said. "Please."

Robert nodded.

"Right you are your ladyship," he said. "Right you are."

Lady Caroline went into the house with Munro trotting at her heels just as the rain clouds burst.

She sighed and headed to the scullery where the spare buckets were kept. Time to check for new leaks.

Chapter 16

Shepherd couldn't sleep. He'd had a joint earlier and that had helped him to drift off but now he was wide awake again with Rose on his mind, waiting for her to walk in the door.

Shepherd threw off the blankets, felt around for his heavy boots, pushed a hand through his shoulder length hair and opened the door. It was dusky outside, the time on an August morning, just between the dark and the light when the world is still touched by magic. A misty veil hung over the fields and the dogs in the camp were quiet, sleeping with their heads on their paws as he left Idlewild and walked quietly past the dying embers of the fire they'd sat around earlier. Over in the woods, an owl hooted and Shepherd headed towards the trees, not really knowing where he was going but anything was better than lying in the van trying to sleep and thinking too much.

The woods were dark and shadowy at that time of the morning but he liked it that way. He didn't really think he'd find Rose in the woods but the act of being up and about and searching for her quietened the thoughts racing around his mind.

Shepherd stepped slowly through the trees. Twigs snapped beneath his feet and the bracken rustled with invisible creatures. The wood smelt earthy, of decaying leaves and rich soil and he breathed in the smell, marvelling once more at how he had never walked in or seen a wood until he'd joined the Convoy. Rose could go one better: she had never seen a cow until they got on the road and saw a group of them huddled in a field. At first she was frightened of them and when Shepherd had stopped laughing, he managed to reassure her that no, they didn't have big teeth and no, they couldn't run very fast.

Shepherd smiled at the memory. There were so many of them. They reassured him that they had something, that she wouldn't stay away for long. Rose loved him and he loved her. It was as simple as that. One couldn't be without the other.

Shepherd knew he was close to the main road because he could hear cars swishing past and as he approached the perimeter of the wood where the trees thinned out and the light filtered through, he saw a Ford Cortina parked in the layby with its headlights switched off. Two men stood next to it.

Shepherd moved behind a tree and held his breath. The men were talking in low voices but from their gestures, he could see they were quite animated and that the man in the raincoat was doing most of the talking. The other man had his back to him and so he couldn't see his face. Shepherd was about to turn away when the man turned and a passing car lit up his face with its headlights.

Butcher. Butcher from the Convoy. Butcher taking a thick brown envelope from a man in a raincoat in a layby.

Chapter 17

A light rain started to fall as Shepherd retraced his steps through the wood to the camp. He felt miserable. He hadn't found Rose and he had no idea where she was. He was worried too. She didn't know the area. Anything could have happened to her. All he could think about was Rose. He was so concerned at not being able to find her, that what he had seen in the layby went right out of his head. Shepherd decided that he would wait until it was light and then he'd go over to the Love Bus and see if Grendo had any ideas.

Shepherd sat down on Idlewild's steps and unlaced his muddy boots. Rose always insisted he take his boots off before he went in. She liked to keep things clean. She was good at keeping things clean and tidy.

Shepherd stood up, opened the door and switched on the light. And then he saw her, sitting on the edge of the bed.

"Rose!" he said, his heart lifting. "Where've you been baby? Where've you been?"

Shepherd went over to her. She was home. Home.

"I'm not staying Shep," she said, turning her face away as he tried to kiss her cheek. "I came to say goodbye. I couldn't leave without saying goodbye."

Shepherd felt his optimism of moments earlier draining away.

"What do you mean you're not staying?" he said. "You're here aren't you? You came back?"

Rose looked at him and her eyes filled with tears.

"No Shep," she said. "I'm not staying. My step dad's coming to fetch me. I wanted to talk to you before I left."

Shepherd sat down next to her feeling a little dazed by her words.

"But why?" he said. "You're happy aren't you? With me? With the Convoy?"

Rose nodded.

"Yes I'm happy," she said, letting him take her hand. "With you. But this isn't the life I want Shep. I've enjoyed the adventure and we've had lots of fun but I want to go home to a house where there's hot water and a bed, get a job and stay in one place long enough to know where I am."

"Do you want me to come with you?" he said, not sure, even as he said it, that he could.

"No," she shook her head. "You're happy on the road. I wouldn't want you to give that up for me. You'd be miserable."

Shepherd realised, with a deep sadness in his heart, that it was true.

"So you've made up your mind?" he said.

Rose nodded.

"Yes. I'm sorry. I'm sorry Shep."

Part of him wanted to make her stay, part of him wanted to say every word under the sun to persuade her not to go but in his heart, he knew it was over and knew that there was no use trying to get someone who wanted to go to stay.

They sat in silence for a moment.

"When are you going?" he said.

"In about half an hour," she said, glancing at her wristwatch. "I came back to get some stuff. And to see you before I went."

"That was good of you," he said more sharply than he'd intended.

"Don't be like that," she said, tears shining in her eyes. "I still love you Shep… and maybe one day… you know… maybe."

Shepherd pulled her to him and felt the warm closeness of her and they sat for a moment not saying anything with his chin resting on top of her hair. It smelt of flowers, of fresh air, of the magic that infused her soul.

"You know," he said softly. "One of the things I've learned from being in the Convoy is to let go, to let people be free, not try to bend them to your point of view."

"I know," Rose said, her voice muffled against his chest. "You're a good man Shep. It's not you. It's me."

Shepherd held her away from him by the upper arms and they smiled sadly at each other.

"Right then," she said more brightly, standing up. "I won't drag this out, I'll get me things."

"Help yourself," Shep said. "Most of it's yours anyway. You know I don't hold with material possessions that much."

Rose moved around the camper van picking up the crocheted blanket she'd made last winter and her spare pair of boots.

"Don't you want the Fat Mirror?" he teased her as she walked past the mirror propped on the draining board.

"No thanks," she smiled. "You can keep that. It always makes me look…"

"Fat," they chorused, smiling despite the heavy sadness they both felt in their hearts.

"I'll walk you to the edge of the field."

"Ok," she said. "Ok."

For a moment he was tempted to tell her what he'd seen in the layby earlier but then he decided not to. Rose was leaving and he wanted to spend every last moment he had with her breathing her in, hearing her voice, capturing and storing her away for the empty times he was sure lay ahead.

When Rose had finished packing her bag, they stood on the steps outside for a moment.

"Goodbye Idlewild," she said, softly, patting her bright green paintwork. "Take good care of the man won't you?"

Shepherd took her bag as they walked across the field. The sky was getting lighter in the east as the new day dawned.

"Don't take any shit from him will you?" he said as they waited in the layby for her stepfather's car to appear.

"He's mellowed," Rose said. "Apparently he had a heart attack last year. A bit of a wake up call. Mum says he's a changed man. I mean can you imagine him driving all this way from Hartlepool a year ago?"

Shepherd wasn't sure. What was that old saying about leopards and spots? From the little Rose had disclosed about her family life, he knew her relationship with her stepfather had been difficult, violent even. That was one of the reasons she had agreed to move into the flat with him. And because she had loved him.

"Do you still love me?" he asked her.

Rose looked up at him, her tote bag trailing on the ground.

"It's not about love," she said. "It never is."

A Ford Granada approached and slowed down, its indicator flashing orange.

"Here he is," Rose said, lifting her bag from the ground.

Shepherd had never met her stepfather and wasn't sure he wanted to. What did you say to a man who had beaten your girlfriend's mother, locked your girlfriend in a cupboard and burned all her clothes? He just hoped Rose was right and that the medical wake up call had changed him for the better.

"I'll be off then," Shepherd said. "Be good Rose. Don't let the world change you."

Rose stretched up on tiptoe and planted a kiss on his cheek.

"And you," she said. "And don't burn the toast."

Shepherd smiled and ran his finger lightly down her cheek and as the car door opened, he turned and walked briskly towards the woods.

He didn't want to watch her go. It was easier that way.

Chapter 18

When Shepherd got back to the camp it was daylight and people were up and about packing up. He hadn't meant to stay out walking for so long but he'd needed to walk, needed to get things straight in his head before he went back to the Convoy.

"What's happening?" he asked Grendo who was loading wood into the back of the Love Bus.

"We had a nice little visit from the farmer," Grendo said. "And he kindly asked us to leave. We could sit it out for eight weeks and wait for the eviction notice but seeing as how we only stopped here on the way to Ambrell, everyone's decided we should head off. We've got our very own travellers' field waiting for us there. Everything alright?"

Shepherd looked down at his boots, not sure if he could trust himself to speak.

Grendo put a firm hand on his arm.

"She'll be back," he said. "Women always gets these ideas in their heads. Janey's left me hundreds of times. Always comes back though. Can't keep away from the Love Bus."

Shepherd looked up.

"Did you know?" he said. "That Rose was leaving?"

"No," Grendo said, turning away and loading more wood into the bus. "But there ain't much I don't see. Saw you two going off across the fields this morning and I says to myself I says, Grend, something isn't right there. And then you came back without her so I don't need to be Columbo to work that one out."

Shepherd sighed.

"You know you think you know someone and you don't," he said, bending down to help Grendo with the wood.

"Ah the sweetness of life," Grendo said. "My view is to take everyone as you find them but expect them to bite at some point. Flash!" he called, as a man with long blonde hair loped past. "You covered up the latrines?"

The man called Flash grinned and nodded and the moment of quiet intimacy was over.

"So," Grendo said. "My advice to you is this: go and put your dancing shoes on. We got a party to go to."

It was only when he got back to Idlewild that Shepherd remembered Butcher and the man in the layby. He'd tell Grendo later. There was no time to go it now: they had a festival to get to.

Two Weeks Before

Chapter 19

Lady Caroline had few visitors these days and so the sound of car tyres crunching on the gravel drive was unusual. Moments later, she heard a door slam and men's voices floating up to the window.

Lady Caroline sighed, put down the magazine she was reading and left the Orangery. She'd been having such a nice relaxing Sunday afternoon. If it was that police officer again she wasn't going to get the best china out. He could have a porcelain cup from the kitchen and lump it.

Munro trotted along behind her as she walked down the stone flagged passageway to the front door. Where was Sowcroft? What was the point in having a butler if you had to open the front door yourself? As she reached it, the door flew open and her father walked in, disgruntled and dishevelled in an old tweed dressing gown. Sowcroft hurried in behind him making faces at Lady Caroline.

"Daddy!" Lady Caroline exclaimed as he pushed past her and headed down the stone passageway towards the kitchen.

"The taxi driver needs payment m'lady," Sowcroft said. "I'm afraid the Earl has ventured forth without any finance."

Caroline sighed and fished in the pocket of the Barbour jacket hanging by the front door and took out a five pound note.

"What's he doing back here?" she said, handing the money to Sowcroft.

"I'm not quite sure m'lady," Sowcroft said. "I believe he thinks he's on shore leave. The taxi driver said he picked him up from Summerfields where he insisted on returning home to fetch his slippers."

"Didn't the home try to stop him?"

"Perhaps they were unaware m'lady," Sowcroft said. "You know what the Earl's like when he gets an idea in his head."

"Oh heavens," Caroline said. "All he had to do was telephone me if he wanted his slippers. Go and pay the driver Sowcroft and I'll go and find Daddy."

Caroline hurried down the corridor and opened the kitchen door. Her father was sitting at the table spooning cereal into his mouth. Milk was slopping out of the bowl and on to the table and he looked up and glowered at her.

"Let this place go a bit Caroline haven't you," he said, sucking milk off the spoon with loud slurping noises. "I knew this would happen. I knew it."

Caroline felt the years slip back until she was six years old again. She had always feared her father's rages and black moods and it was like she was back there all over again, being told off for swimming in the river or making a mess in her bedroom. Slowly she sat down on a wooden chair to his left and adopted a calm approach.

"I wasn't expecting you Daddy," she said softly. "You should have telephoned to say you were coming."

"Telephoned?" he said. "What do you think I am? A common tradesman? I live here."

"Of course you do Daddy," she said, placating him. "It's just I could have got a nice joint of beef in. You'd like that wouldn't you? Roast beef and Yorkshire pudding was always your favourite."

"Stop patronising me," he said. "I'm not a child. Any tea going on around here? They make the most disgusting tea in Italy. I couldn't wait to get back to England. Mind you we had a terrible crossing, terrible. Standards are slipping Caroline. Standards are slipping right across the board."

Until he'd mentioned Italy, Lady Caroline had found him frighteningly normal. The mention of Italy however, reassured her in a strange sort of way that this wasn't her father speaking. This was the dreadful disease that had taken over and invaded his mind.

She stood up and placed the kettle on the Aga.

"And worst of all," he continued. "They will insist on poking and prodding you all night to see if you're awake. I don't know why they do that. I never used to do that on my Watch. Leave the men to sleep I say. Leave the men to sleep."

Lady Caroline felt a deep sadness creep into her soul. Her father's mind was all jumbled up with the now and the then and all she could do was keep him relatively calm until she could get him back to

Summerfields. What a dreadfully synthetic name that was: deliberately designed to coat the bitterest pill with artificial reality.

Suddenly he stood up so abruptly that the wooden chair tipped over behind him and crashed against the stone floor.

"I need my bed," he said. "Bloody people keeping me awake all night. Wake me up when it's my turn to take the wheel will you? And don't leave it to the last minute like you usually do."

Caroline turned from the Aga and looked at him. He was so old and pale and fragile. She hurried over to him and righted the chair. She had the terrible urge to cry but she fought it down. Sentiment wasn't needed in this sort of situation. Calm strength was the thing.

"Oh dear," he said, sinking back down on to the righted chair. "I get so confused don't I? What am I talking about, the Watch? I'm here aren't I? At Ambrell?"

"Yes you are daddy," she said, turning away to hide the tears in her eyes as she poured boiling water into the old brown teapot. "Yes you are."

"Is your mother in?" he barked. "Or is she out gallivanting again?"

She could hardly keep up with him. His mind was all over the place. It was the reason she had taken the hard decision for him to go to the home two years ago. She had felt guilty ever since but when she saw him like this, it made her remember, made the decision seem justified.

"But I can't Sowcroft," she had cried at the time. "How can I send him away from his home?"

Sowcroft had been a tower of strength even when he was officially off duty at two o'clock in the morning. The police had just brought her father home again for the fourth time that week and she got the feeling that whilst they were sympathetic and kind, they were running out of patience.

"You don't want a tragedy on your hands m'lady," Sowcroft had said in his wise, steady voice. "And that officer did say he had no clothes on when they found him by the river."

"Oh don't, don't," she had said. "I can't bear it. I can't bear to think about him doing that."

"Well maybe we should think about it in the morning," he'd said. "When things aren't quite so dark and raw. Things always look better in the morning m'lady."

And so that is what they had done: thought about it in the morning and later that day, her father had been welcomed into Summerfields where he had his own room, painted yellow, with flowery curtains at the windows and the number 17 on the door.

The Earl got to his feet, swaying a little and looked around the kitchen as if he had never seen it before.

"A sleep," he said. "Yes, a sleep. That's what I need. I'll probably feel better after a sleep," and he wandered off out of the door and down the flagstone corridor.

Chapter 20

The miners had been right, Shepherd reflected. It hadn't taken long to get here once you knew where you were going. The last bit of the drive had been a bit hairy down the country lanes leading to the grounds of the big house but Grendo had expertly navigated them and now the vehicles were parked up in what had been designated as the travellers field.

"What the fuck is that?" Shepherd said as he and Grendo stood by the side of the Love Bus looking up at the bales of straw looming high above them.

"Fucked if I know," Grendo said, scratching his chin. "Maybe they're storing it here."

Now decanted from their vans, trucks and buses, the members of the Peace Convoy scurried around, putting up tents and benders and carrying planks of wood on their shoulders. Two white goats nibbled at the bales of straw, a small group of children played with a bright orange frisbee and from the top deck of the Love Bus, Bob Marley's *Is This Love* blasted out.

"Better go and get some wood for the fires," Grendo said, opening the back doors of the Love Bus and pulling out a chain saw.

They had just started to walk towards the trees at the far end of the field when they heard a woman's voice behind them.

"Excuse me!" EXCUSE ME!"

They both turned and saw a blonde woman, in her early thirties, hurrying towards them in a Barbour jacket, Wellington boots and a blue headscarf. An Irish wolfhound loped along beside her. Some of the travellers' dogs wandered over to have a sniff and the Irish wolfhound wagged his tail and reciprocated.

Grendo and Shepherd stopped and waited for her to catch up with them.

"Uh oh," Grendo muttered. "Looks like trouble."

"Are they your goats?" she said in a shrill voice, pointing back at the wall of straw.

"They are," Grendo said politely. "May I introduce Brenda and John. Our mascots."

The woman stared at them.

"I don't care what their names are," she said. "I want them to stop eating the straw. And move those vans. You've parked far too close to the palace."

"Palace?" Grendo repeated. "I don't remember seeing no palace."

The blonde haired woman rolled her eyes and jagged her finger at the straw.

"*That*," she said, "is a palace and you have parked far too close to it."

Grendo turned his head and looked up at the towering wall of straw.

"It don't look like a palace to me," he said. "It looks like bales of straw."

"The Palace of Versailles is under construction," Caroline said, irritability puncturing her voice. "And I would appreciate it if you would kindly move your vehicles and control your goats."

Grendo exchanged a look with Shepherd.

"On who's say so?"

"On my say so," she said. "I'm Lady Caroline Oxley and I own this land."

"Ah," Grendo said. "In that case we beg your pardon," he said, bowing. "We had no idea we was in the presence of royalty."

Shepherd wanted to laugh but kept his face straight.

"What? I'm not royalty. Now just move that, that *bus* would you?"

"Right you are," Grendo said. "Right you are."

Lady Caroline stormed off the way she had come and the two men watched her go.

"All the same that lot," Grendo said. "All the same. I'll catch you up," he said, handing Shepherd the chain saw. "Once I've moved the Love Bus and caught the goats."

Shepherd headed towards the row of trees which divided the travellers' field from the festival field. Through the gaps, he could see men crawling around the scaffolding erected around the stage. He'd have a wander over there later and have a look around. There were some good bands coming including Phil Lynott's *Grand Slam* and Marillion. He enjoyed the festivals the Convoy visited. In May they had gone to the Silver Moon Festival in Cumbria and someone had chased a pig through the camp in the middle of the night. Before that, it had been the Green Moon Festival, completely washed out by a violent thunderstorm with hailstones as big as rocks. The tents had been washed down the hillside and a stream had changed course. He still remembered how the ground had sparkled with semi precious stones, washed out of the old lead mines beneath their feet. Rose had sunk to her knees and let them run through her hands believing they'd found buried treasure.

Shepherd smiled at the memories. He had loved those festivals and he was sure Rose had too. Why would she choose to turn her back on it all and go back to normal life? It baffled him. She had never said, until last night, that she wasn't happy with the life they were living. She had never said anything at all.

Shepherd got to work with the chain saw, nodding at several other members of the Convoy who were also cutting down wood. He could feel autumn coming, the early evening chill of late August hinting at the mists and turning leaves to come. Purply blue sloes and blackberries hung in the hedgerows and the elder and hawthorn berries were green, waiting to burst into crimson life. Rose would have filled buckets with blackberries and sloes and made jam and wine out of them.

Shepherd willed himself to focus on the task at hand. Thinking about Rose all the time wasn't doing any good.

Chapter 21

Clive Taylor wished he hadn't had the cheese omelette for lunch. Now waves of acidic indigestion rose at the back of his throat and his chest burned. Canteen food was suspicious at the best of times and he rarely ate it in London. But Droxby police station was in the ass end of nowhere and you couldn't just nip out to the local pub for a pint and a sandwich.

Droxby, he reflected, was like a village stuck in the 1950s and the police officers weren't much better. No wonder they couldn't control the miners. No wonder they'd had to send in the riot police at Orgreave. He bristled at the thought of it. He had been one of the commanders in charge of that operation back in June and he wouldn't forget what those pickets did. Luckily the Press had been on the side of the police; portraying the miners exactly as they were: a bunch of anarchic trouble makers who needed to wake up to the fact it was 1984.

And now, as a result of his ability and performance at Orgreave, he had been sent back to Yorkshire to sort out the Peace Convoy. The *enemy within* was what Margaret Thatcher called them and he was with her all the way on that. If you asked him, Margaret Thatcher was exactly what this country needed when she was elected Prime Minister in 1979: picking it up by the scruff of its neck and shaking it and she was still shaking it. He was proud to serve under such a valiant, brave leader, even though she was a woman. For far too long the government had given in to strikers and anarchists and now, the Iron Lady was cracking the whip and about time too.

Roger Appleby came into the canteen with his hat under his arm, smiling and nodding at some of the lower ranked officers who were hunched over tables stuffing food into their mouths. Taylor felt irritated by the gesture. You didn't gain respect by smiling and nodding at the lower ranks. No, you lead by example, by authority. These Yorkshire police needed to get tough. They needed to stop trying to please everyone and get on with the job.

"Appleby," Taylor nodded as Roger Appleby took hold of the back of a wooden chair and scraped it backwards. The noise grated on Taylor's nerves: he hadn't slept well in the bed and breakfast the night before and he felt tense and irritable. The bed was soft and lumpy and he had to share a bathroom with Peters which he wasn't happy about. A man of his rank and importance shouldn't be expected to share a pisser with a sergeant.

"Hello sir," Appleby said, sitting down. "Enjoying our canteen food?"

"Hardly enjoying," Taylor said irritably. "My dog has had better meals."

"Have you tried the bread and butter pudding?" Appleby continued. "Marge makes it herself. It's rather good."

Taylor stared at him.

"I didn't come here to discuss bread and butter pudding Appleby. Are you aware the Convoy has arrived at Ambrell Priory?"

"I wasn't aware of that Sir, no."

Taylor sighed. Did he have to do everything round here? Spoon feed the West Yorkshire police as well as keep an eye on anarchists and law breakers?

"We've been a bit busy with the road blocks," Appleby said. "Our priority is to stop the flying pickets. Especially after that business at Orgreave."

"Surely you have enough man power to do more than one thing at once?" Taylor snapped, raising an irritated eyebrow.

Appleby reddened.

"It's not easy…" he said. "We have a lot officers off sick."

"The Convoy arrived two days ago," Taylor continued, ignoring Appleby's tales of woe. "When do your officers intend to visit the site?"

Appleby stared at him.

"We weren't planning to," he said. "The festival doesn't start for another two weeks."

Taylor folded his arms, leaned across the table and lowered his voice.

"I realise that sergeant," he said. "But I specifically told you we have intelligence to suggest the Convoy is armed, possibly dangerous and in possession of a large amount of drugs."

Appleby held his gaze.

"And I believe I mentioned to you Sir," he said. "With all due respect, that we tend not to get involved unless and until there's any trouble."

Taylor stared at him.

"So are you telling me that the people who live near the site – decent, honest, hard working people – could all be murdered in their beds because the West Yorkshire Constabulary can't be bothered?"

"It's not that Sir…" Appleby stuttered. "It's… it's a manpower issue… you know how it is."

"No I don't know *how it is,"* Taylor said, feeling the acid swirling and burning in his stomach. "But what I do know is that if you don't remain alert, these sort of people will creep under the radar and ambush you before you know it. And then what will you do Sergeant? Then what will you do?"

"We don't have them down as a serious threat to law and order," Appleby countered. "There were no issues at the festival two years ago, in '82."

Taylor leaned forward on his folded arms.

"That's because the Peace Convoy wasn't present two years ago. Tell me Sergeant, are you aware of what our Prime Minister thinks of the Convoy? What most of Great Britain think of the Convoy? Do you know what a threat they present to law and order?"

"I'm aware they are not the most popular section of the public if that's what you mean Sir."

"Margaret Thatcher," he said, savouring the magical cadence of their great leader's name. "Margaret Thatcher was re-elected as prime minister last year and we, as officers, must ensure that we stand by her and stand up to these so called peace groups. They are not necessarily promoting peace Appleby. That is a cunning disguise. Many believe they are a front for far more subversive activities, backed by Russia, infiltrated by communists, ready to rise up and overthrow all we hold dear. In short Appleby, they are not people like you and me. They are not human beings."

Appleby shifted in his chair.

"Will that be all Sir?" he said. "Only I've got a strategy meeting in ten minutes about policing the pickets at Cortonwood and Bulcliffe Wood."

Inspector Taylor sat back in his chair and sighed.

"Did you hear anything I said Sergeant?"

"We'll visit Ambrell when the festival starts Sir," he said. "I'm afraid that's all I can say at the moment."

Chapter 22

Evening, Shepherd reflected, was probably the best time of day. It was time for the sun to rest, time for the birds to roost and time for people to lie down by fires. They had been at Ambrell for two days now and although he was making a conscious effort not to think of Rose, it was hard to live in Idlewild without her.

Shepherd picked up his guitar and left the van. He found more solace from his thoughts when he was closer to nature, sitting with his back against a tree and just quietly observing and absorbing the sights and sounds around him.

As he walked across the camp, he smiled at the hand painted board someone had put at the entrance to the travellers' field.

BRENDA AND JOHN PRESENT…

THE TIME OF YOUR LIFE!

Some of the tents had chalk boards propped up outside them offering every type of oblivion possible: Red Leb, Black Moroccan, Hash cakes, Nepalese Black, Acid, Mushrooms. If you were looking for the ride of your life, you'd find it here.

Shepherd headed out of the field and turned down the lane that ran past the side of Ambrell Priory. It was a magnificent building: all gothic chimneys and red brick. He couldn't imagine living somewhere like that. It was a far cry from the houses he'd grown up in or the flat he and Rose had shared on Hartlepool seafront before they joined the Convoy.

Shepherd had walked around the site quite a lot in the previous two days and noticed a path leading between tall hedges which he hadn't yet had time to explore. He was pleasantly surprised to find it led to a river with bullrushes on the banks and birds singing in the ash and elm trees. The evening was peaceful with just the music of the birds and the flowing of the river. Once again Shepherd's thoughts turned to Rose. How could she turn her back on all this and return to a grey town without hope?

He felt a splash of rain on his hand and looked up at the sky. Heavy clouds were gathering and looked like they were threatening a whole lot more. Shepherd turned right and headed along by the river. He never minded a bit of rain but getting soaked wasn't on his agenda. Rose couldn't stand the smell of wet clothes drying in the van.

A little further along he found a wooden hut on the river bank. Shepherd thought it must belong to the big house, maybe a summer house or, a boat house perhaps. He tried the door and it opened inwards. The smell of damp and moss and kerosene and apples greeted him. Outside, the rain began to fall more heavily. No one would mind if he took shelter for a minute or two.

Shepherd stepped inside and sat down on the wooden bench that ran along the back of the hut. There were coat pegs to his right higher up on the wall and a white towelling bathrobe hung from one of them. Shepherd listened to the sound of the rain on the corrugated iron roof. He loved that sound. It was the sound that had brought him much comfort as a child as he moved from one foster home to another. At that time, rain had seemed to be the only constant in his life, that and the suitcase that was brought out from under whatever bed he'd been sleeping in, indicating that his time in that particular bedroom was over. Maybe that was why he adapted so well to life on the road, he reflected. Always moving on, never staying in one place long enough to put down roots. He liked it that way. Apart from the two years they'd lived in the flat in Hartlepool, he'd never lived anywhere for long.

Shepherd propped his guitar on his knees and felt for the strings. He closed his eyes and picked out random broken chords which started one song and then drifted into another.

The day they'd left it all behind was a Friday. Payday. He'd woken late, grabbed the alarm clock and shot out of bed in a panic calling to Rose that they'd slept in and were late. Rose was working in the hairdressing salon at Better Bake which was probably the only factory in the world that gave its female employees a regular shampoo and set. He had hardly had time to say goodbye to her that morning, just grabbed his keys and ran out to jump on the bus and get to the garage.

When he got there, the doors were locked and bolted and the other mechanics were standing around outside smoking and looking up at the windows.

"What's going on?" Shepherd said.

"He's locked us out and gorn AWOL," Mazza told him. "Wait til I get my hands on that bastard."

To start with, Shepherd genuinely believed there must be some mistake: that perhaps Mr Hastings had slept in and would come along any minute in his old camper van. They'd done it up for him good and proper last year when he'd brought it home from the car auctions in Birmingham but if he owned a garage, Shepherd reflected, he'd drive a BMW or a Porsche, not an old 1960s Volkswagen camper van.

"You mark my words," Mr Hastings had said as they renovated the green van. "One day people will pay thousands of pounds for one of these."

They didn't believe him, they'd just got on with repairing and fixing the cars and vans that were brought to the garage and collecting their wages from the office in little brown envelopes every Friday afternoon.

When Mr Hastings hadn't turned up by 10.30am, some of the lads decided to go to his house. Shepherd wasn't sure at first, but what else were they supposed to do? Apart from anything else it was payday and jobs were hard to find. You only had to look at the length of the dole queue in Hartlepool town centre on a Thursday morning to realise that.

So Shepherd went along with them to the red brick terrace in Primrose Gardens. When they got there, the curtains in the bedroom and downstairs windows were closed and the green camper van was parked outside. Who kept their curtains closed at this time of day?

"Lazy bastard," Mazza said as he looked up at the house. "Reckon we should give him an alarm call don't you boys?"

The other men grinned and nodded as Mazza broke away from the group and walked down the weedy path. When he reached the front door, he banged his fist on the peeling paint and stepped back, looking up at the bedroom windows. Shepherd watched, expecting the bedroom curtains to open at any moment and Mr Hastings's face to appear from behind them.

When it didn't, the men continued to stare at the bedroom window.

"He's done a runner," Gary said. "The bastard. He's done a runner."

"He wouldn't leave the van here if he'd done a runner," Mazza said.

"He would if he had to leave town quickly," Gary said. "You saw them men what come in last week. They was practically having a punch up in the office. You was the one who said they looked like enforcers."

Shepherd knew all about the enforcers. They roamed at night in packs, and sometimes in the daylight hours as well: men sent through unofficial channels to collect money and debts. No one went through the legal channels when money was at stake. There were knocks on doors in the middle of the night, beatings down alleyways and men who muscled their way into houses and carried off furniture and anything else they could find.

"Well," Gary said. "He ain't asleep that's for sure. He ain't in there Maz. He's gone."

"Bastard," Mazza said, still looking up at the bedroom windows. "What the fuck do we do now? The Missus will cut me balls off ah go home without me wages."

"Let's go back to the garage," Gary said. "Something will turn up."

The three men sat outside the garage waiting for Mr Hastings for most of the day. Shepherd felt unsettled. What would he do if he lost this job? They were already behind on the rent. He'd seen the dole queue snaking around the block on a Thursday morning. He was a good mechanic but there were loads of good mechanics in that queue, old and young. There were three million unemployed in this country.

"Nowt goin' on round here," Gary sighed after they had sat on the pavement for two hours. "Reckon I'll be off."

"Aye me too," Mazza said. "And if ah see that bastard ah'll knock his teeth out."

They drifted off, leaving Shepherd sitting alone on the pavement as the street lamps came on casting an eerie glow across the locked up garage.

Shepherd stood up, aimed a frustrated kick at the door and then, with his hands thrust into his pockets, started to head home.

Although it was early on a Friday evening, the town centre was deserted. Shepherd walked past empty shops and men huddled on street corners towards the flat he shared with Rose on the harbourside. He could remember the days when he'd run through these streets as a young boy, ducking through the legs of the workers who came off shift from the steel plant and cheeking the gangs of men pouring out of Gray's shipyard when the bell went. Where had those men gone? Where had the ships gone? Hartlepool was a deserted shit hole, a ghost town just like the one The Specials sang about a few years ago.

Shepherd lit a cigarette and as he turned the corner of the harbour, he saw Rose sitting on the doorstep outside their flat, surrounded by black bin liners.

"What's happened?" he said, stopping in front of her.

Rose looked up and her hair fell around her face as she shook her head.

"The landlord threw us out," she said, her face wet with tears. "It was horrible Shep, horrible. Hee only gave me ten minutes to get all our stuff. I had to leave loads behind."

Shepherd threw his cigarette away and crouched down beside her, putting his arm around her shoulders.

"Come on now," he said. "Come on. It'll be alright. It'll be alright."

Rose looked up at him, her eyes blurred with tears.

"How will it be alright?" she sniffed. "We've got nowhere to go."

Rose looked up at him, her eyes wild and liquid. She was looking to him for answers, looking to him for solutions.

Shepherd thought for a moment and then got to his feet.

"Wait there," he said. "I won't be long."

"Where are you going?" she said, wiping at her nose with the back of her hand.

"Stay there," he said, facing her as he walked backwards and away from her. "I'll sort it Rose. I will. I'll sort it."

Chapter 23

It wasn't difficult to hot wire a camper van. Shepherd had learned a lot of things hanging around the streets when he should have been at school. Within minutes, the Volkswagen engine was purring and drubbing with life. Shepherd jumped up into the driver's seat and glanced up at Mr Hastings's bedroom window. The curtains were still closed and there were no lights on behind them, no sign of life at all. Shepherd pressed his foot down hard on the accelerator and drove off without turning the headlights on.

Rose was still sitting on the steps when he came round the corner and pulled the van into the kerb. He left the engine running, jumped out of the driver's side and slid open the side door.

"That's Mr Hastings's van isn't it?" Rose said, getting to her feet. "Did he let you borrow it?"

"Sort of," he said, picking up the bin liners and throwing them in through the side door. "Help me get this stuff in," he said. "We need to get out of here."

"You nicked it didn't you?" Rose said, smoking a cigarette. "You nicked it."

Shepherd sighed.

"Just get the stuff in Rose," he said. "Get the stuff in."

Rose ground out the cigarette under the sole of her Doc Martens and started handing the bags to Shep. When they had finished he opened the passenger door and Rose climbed up inside.

"Are we on the run?" she asked him as he banged his door shut and sped off down the road with the headlights off.

"Sort of," he said, looking straight ahead. "Sort of."

Chapter 24

The rain had stopped and it was dark outside. Shepherd had been so lost in his thoughts and reminiscences that he'd spent far longer in the little wooden hut by the river than he'd intended. He seized the neck of his guitar and stood up, ready to walk back along the river and home to the camp. Suddenly the door opened and a woman walked in.

A woman who was completely stark naked.

Chapter 25

"What the bloody hell!"

Lady Caroline had not expected to find a man in the boathouse. Sowcroft was always warning her about taking evening dips in the river and reporting sightings of "oddballs" wandering along the river bank.

"Sorry!" Shepherd said, looking down, looking up and turning his back towards her. He saw the hanging bathrobe and whipped it off the peg, holding it out behind him in her direction. She grabbed at it and pushed her arms into the sleeves and tied it around her waist. Shepherd caught a faint whiff of wood smoke probably, he thought, drifting over from the camp.

"What the bloody hell are you doing in here?" she demanded. "And who the hell are you?"

"Carl Lamb…" he said, addressing the wooden wall. "But my friends call me Shepherd."

The woman sighed and when she spoke again, her voice was slightly calmer.

"Do you make a habit of doing this sort of thing?" she asked, rubbing at her long blonde hair with a corner of the towelling robe. "Hiding in boat houses and half scaring women out of their wits?"

Shepherd raised his eyes and looked up at the wooden roof.

"No," he said, wishing the ground would swallow him up. "No. I came in here to play my guitar. It started to rain," he added, thinking how foolish he must sound.

"Ah," she said. "A guitar player. Is that something you do often? Wandering by the river and playing your guitar in the rain?"

Shepherd sighed.

"No," he said. "I'm from the Peace Convoy. We're camping in the field. For the festival like."

"Ah," she said. "The Peace Convoy. I had a nice little visit from the police earlier this week about the Convoy. Oh do turn around. It's very difficult having a conversation with someone who's got their back to you."

Shepherd turned around and recognised the woman immediately.

"You're the lady from the big house aren't you?" he said. "The one who told us to move the Love Bus when we arrived."

"Oh please," she said. "You'll be tugging your forelock next. I'm Caroline Oxley. From Ambrell Priory. I'm sure you've seen that great big ugly ruin of a house."

Caroline fished in her pocket and brought out a packet of Rothmans cigarettes.

"Want one?" she said, offering them to him.

Shepherd took out a cigarette and bent his head as she lit a match.

"Thanks," he said, stepping back and blowing the smoke up at the ceiling. "And I wouldn't call that house ugly by the way."

"Wouldn't you?" she said, blowing a perfect smoke ring up into the air. "That's because you've never stepped inside it. Ugly and falling down," she said. "But we all have our crosses to bear don't we?"

Shepherd stared at her. It seemed surreal to be standing in a wooden hut with a half naked woman talking about a stately home.

"I always have a swim in the river in the evenings," she said. "More so since my father decided to have a little holiday from the nursing home. He can be a bit demanding," she added in a softer voice. "Trouble is they're refurbishing, whatever that means, and so it looks like he's here for a little while longer."

Shepherd didn't know what to say. He wasn't used to conversations with people from outside the Convoy let alone ladies of the Manor. In a way they were outlaws, like Robin Hood and his Merry Men, and they had little contact with the outside world unless they were chastising them, chasing them or evicting them.

"I'd best be getting back to camp," he said. "Sorry I frightened you."

"Pity," she said. "I thought you might play me something on your guitar. I do like a man who can play the guitar."

Her blue eyes twinkled and Shepherd suddenly felt hot and uncomfortable.

"Maybe some other time," he said, feeling a strong urge to bolt and get back to camp. "I'd better get back."

"As you will," she smiled. "As you will."

As he opened the door, the smell of the woodsmoke he'd noticed earlier grew stronger and as he looked to his right, he saw plumes of black smoke rising up into the sky.

"Have you seen this?" he said. "It looks like something's on fire."

She came up beside him and looked up at the sky.

"Dear Lord," she said, pulling the dressing gown more tightly around her. "Dear Lord."

Chapter 26

Shepherd put his guitar down on the slatted bench and ran like he'd never run before. He burst through hedges, jumped a small brook and ran up the sloping lawn behind Ambrell Priory. Smoke billowed from the roof of the garden room tacked on to the back of the house and he could hear opera music coming from inside. Shepherd pulled open the French windows. The heat from within made him step back for a moment. Pulling the hem of his t-shirt over his mouth and nose, he ducked his head and went inside.

"Hello!" he called. "Hello! Is anyone in here?"

Shepherd felt his foot come up against something on the floor and he stopped as he realised there was a man lying there.

"Fuck," he whispered. "Fuck."

Shepherd squatted down and patted the man's face.

"Can you hear me?" he shouted through his t-shirt and above the opera music. "Are you ok? Can you hear me?"

The old man groaned and his eyes flickered open.

"What? Who are you? Are we abandoning ship?"

"The house is on fire," Shepherd shouted. "We need to get out of here! Are you hurt? Can you walk?"

The man looked dazed, his fluffy white hair standing up in tufts on top of his head. Shepherd noticed he was wearing a tartan dressing gown.

"No need to shout," he said. "All you have to do is give the Order."

Shepherd took hold of his hand and tugged him into a sitting position.

"Come on," he said. "Time to go."

"Is it?" the man said. "Is it time to disembark?"

The room was misty with smoke and suddenly the lights went off, plunging them into darkness and silence. A large piece of wood fell from the ceiling and landed in front of them, missing them by inches. He heard a woman's voice call out and moments later, Caroline appeared through the smoke.

"Daddy!" she said, rushing forward and dropping to her knees. "Daddy get up! There's a fire! We need to get you out of here!"

The man blinked and looked at her.

"What have I told you about wandering around the house in your dressing gown Caroline? It won't do, it won't do at all."

"Oh for goodness sake Daddy shut up!" she said and then raised her eyes to Shepherd. "Can you help me get him up?"

Shepherd bent down and together they managed to get him on his feet. They ducked their heads under his armpits so that his arms were across their shoulders and hurried him to the door. Outside, they negotiated him down the slope and sat him on a stone bench at the far end of the lawn.

"Thank you," she said, breathing heavily. "I'm afraid he doesn't know where he is or who he is half the time. He could have stayed in there, oblivious."

Shepherd looked at her.

"Is he your dad?" he said.

"Yes," Caroline said, swallowing. "He used to be one of the best officers in the Royal Navy. And now, and now…" she looked away but not before Shepherd saw tears in her eyes.

"Where's Sowcroft?" she said abruptly, standing up. "And my dog? Munro! Munro!"

Flames danced out of the windows and roof of the garden room and danced with orange defiance against the darkening sky.

"Don't!" Shepherd said, putting a hand on her arm. "You can't go back in there."

"But my dog!" she said. "I must rescue my dog!"

"I'll go," he said, his heart sinking as he said the words. "Just stay with your dad. Who's Sowcroft?"

"My butler," she said. "He lives on the first floor. There's a telephone in the hall if you can get to it."

Shepherd looked at the burning building. From his inexperienced eye, the fire looked like it was restricted to the back of the house. The rest of it was sturdy, built of heavy old stone and that wasn't going to capitulate so easily.

"Stay here," he said, trying not to look down the front of her dressing gown.

Shepherd hurried back up the sloping lawn. Smoke was billowing in thick black clouds up to the sky and Shepherd hoped and prayed that someone had seen it and called the fire brigade.

Shepherd circled around the back of the house. He couldn't risk going back through the French windows and he had to find another way in. He walked down the side of the house and found a door halfway along. Shepherd shook the handle and it opened. Holding his t-shirt over his mouth and nose, he stepped into a dark, stone flagged passageway which led to a huge kitchen. Shepherd hurried across the room in the dark, tripping over something on the floor which clanged and rolled across the stone tiles. He yanked open the door at the other end, hurried along another passageway and came out into the hall. An ornately carved wooden staircase rose to his right and a wide, vast hall opened out in front of him.

"Hello!" he called. "Hello! Anyone in here?"

A dog barked and moments later, an Irish wolfhound came bounding down the stairs.

"Hello," Shepherd said as the dog came towards him and sniffed at his legs. "Stay with me boy," he said. "Stay with me."

Shepherd looked around and saw a black Bakelite telephone sitting on top of an ornate hall table. He picked up the receiver and dialled 100, keeping his eye on the dog who sat in front of him with his tail swishing.

"Operator," a clipped British voice announced. "Which service do you require?"

"Fire brigade," he said. "And hurry. Ambrell Priory is on fire."

"Hold the line please caller. Hold the line and I'll try to connect you."

Munro barked and Shepherd raised his eyes to the staircase above him.

Coming down the stairs was a man holding a shotgun. And the gun was pointing straight at him.

Chapter 27

This was the second time in less than two weeks, Shepherd reflected, that he had been at the end of a gun.

"Are you Sowcroft?" he said, the phone buzzing in his ear as he stared at the gun.

"I might be," the voice behind the gun said. "Are you a burglar?"

"Don't be daft," Shepherd said sounding braver than he felt. "There's a fire man. At the back of the house. You need to get out."

"I haven't heard that one before," Sowcroft said, keeping the gun trained on Shepherd. "You burglars are inventive, I'll give you that."

Shepherd glared at the man.

"There's a fucking fire man!" he said. "And if you don't believe me, go into that room at the back of the house. I've just got the old man out."

"The Earl?" Sowcroft said, looking shocked. "Is he alright?"

"As alright as he'll ever be," Shepherd said. "Now do us both a favour and take the dog and get the fuck out of here!"

Sowcroft hesitated, not sure whether to believe him or not. Shepherd rolled his eyes and turned his back on him as finally someone from the Fire Brigade answered the phone.

Sowcroft came slowly down the stairs, keeping the gun pointed at Shepherd.

"Ambrell Priory," Shepherd said into the receiver. "Yes that's the one. There's a fire. At the back of the house. No, I don't think there's anyone left inside. Except me. And a butler. And a dog. Yes I know we need to get out. I know."

Sowcroft disappeared down the corridor but was back within minutes.

"Good God!" he said. "Good God! The garden room is almost completely engulfed by flames!"

Shepherd replaced the receiver.

"Is there another way out?"

Sowcroft stared at him, looking pale and shocked.

"For fuck's sake man," Shepherd said. "Put that bastard gun down!"

Sowcroft seemed to recover himself.

"There's no need to swear," Sowcroft said, lowering his gun. "It is my duty to stay with the house. I've been with the Earl for over forty years."

Shepherd ran his hand through his hair.

"Oh for fuck's sake," he said. "What is it with you people? There's a fucking fire!" he said. "Can't you drop all this bollocks about Queen and country just for a moment?"

Sowcroft looked suitably shocked. He probably hadn't been spoken to like that before but it was too bad. He wanted to get the fuck out of here, get the dog back to its owner and fuck off. He'd had enough for one night.

"Right you are," he said. "If you'll kindly follow me."

Chapter 28

As they hurried around the side of the house, thick plumes of black smoke rose up to the night sky punctuated by showers of sparks and orange and yellow flames.

"I think I owe you an apology," Sowcroft said as he hurried along behind Shepherd, holding the gun down by his side. "It's just you can't be too careful these days."

Munro bounded across the lawn as if he knew exactly where his owner was and Shepherd saw the shadowy figures of Lady Caroline and her father sitting on the bench where he'd left them.

"The fire brigade's on the way," Shepherd said as they reached them. "Is he alright?"

He nodded at the elderly man who was sitting on the bench staring at the house.

"Yes, thank you," Caroline said, reaching forward to pat Munro. "I don't think he really knows where he is," she said sadly. "Or what's happening."

"I wanted to light a candle," the Earl said suddenly. "It was our wedding anniversary. Claire wore a blue dress. That's when I first saw her. Outside the opera house in Vienna. Wearing a blue dress."

"My mother," Caroline whispered to Shepherd.

"She loved that dress didn't she Daddy?" she said in a louder voice.

"10th August 1948. Best shore leave I ever had."

Sowcroft pointed over at the trees to their left.

"I believe the fire brigade have arrived m'lady."

Munro sat back on his haunches and barked.

Shepherd turned to look at where he was pointing. In the dark he could see shadowy figures emerging from the trees.

"That's not the fire brigade," he said, as Grendo strode towards them.

"They're travellers. From the Camp."

Grendo stopped in front of the bench breathing heavily.

"Shep," he said. "I didn't realise you was here. Is it the big house? There's smoke all over the camp."

Caroline looked up at him.

"I'm sorry about this," she said. "Unfortunately it seems my father decided to light a candle with somewhat disastrous consequences."

Grendo looked down at her, his chest heaving with the exertion of running.

"Grendo," he said, holding out his big meaty hand to her. "We'll help you. My wife's organising a bucket chain. We're getting water from the river."

Caroline shook his hand and looked to where he was pointing. A chain of people were passing buckets along a line running from the river to the house.

"We haven't got enough buckets," he said.

Caroline sighed.

"Oh dear. All the ones I have are positioned inside the house catching drips from the leaks in the ceiling. Not that there's any need for that tonight."

"I've got buckets," Shepherd said. "Rose kept a load under the van. She had a thing about buckets."

"Who's Rose?" Caroline said.

"My girlfriend," Shepherd said a little awkwardly because what did he call her now?

"It's a long story," he said, turning away. "I'll go and get the buckets."

Shepherd ran to the lane and on to the camp. It was deserted at this time of night with just a few people wandering round. Those who weren't forming the chain to the river were sleeping in their vehicles despite it being relatively early. There were larks as well as night owls in the Convoy.

Shepherd looked over at the Love Bus. Was that a light in the window? He peered through the darkness and stopped. It was a light. A faint beam of a torch. And it was moving around inside.

Chapter 29

"What the fuck are you doing in here?"

Butcher turned and straightened up. Whatever he was doing Shepherd had caught him red handed. Shepherd felt a flicker of anger inside him. It was completely against the rules of camp to go inside someone else's bus or truck.

"I was looking for a book," Butcher said, keeping his face composed and friendly. "Grendo's got so many."

"Did he say you could?"

"Not exactly," Butcher looked awkward. "But we all share everything in the Convoy don't we? And… well… It's a bit delicate."

Shepherd stared at him.

"How can looking for a book be *delicate?*" he said. He wasn't sure about this Butcher man and finding him in Grendo's bus had brought his mistrust to the surface.

Butcher sighed and sat down on the edge of the bed.

"I suffer from depression," he said, looking up at Shepherd. "It's not something I broadcast to the world. I've been feeling very down lately: black moods and all that. Grendo mentioned having some books about it."

Shepherd stared at him.

"Is that why you met that man in the layby last week? The one by the main road? I saw you talking to some bloke in a raincoat. Who was that then? Your psychiatrist?"

"No," Butcher smiled. "My step father. He came to tell me my mother's been sectioned."

"Not having much luck lately are you?" Shepherd said, eyeing him coldly. "You better get out of here before Grendo finds you. Have you seen the dog chain he wears on his belt?"

A flicker of something crossed Butcher's pale face but in the next moment, it was gone.

"You won't mention this will you?" he said. "Only it's so… so *embarrassing.*"

Shepherd stared at him.

"Get out of here and I won't," he said. "But if I catch you in his van again I will."

Butcher squeezed past him with his back to the wall and left by the open door. Shepherd stared after him for a moment and then let it go. He didn't have time to think about it now. Ambrell Priory was on fire and he had to find buckets.

Chapter 30

It was exhausting work and there were moments when Shepherd wondered if it was hopeless, hopeless, this chain of men throwing buckets of water at such a beast of a fire. But then the fire brigade arrived and the tide seemed to turn as their hoses shot strong jets of water at the house, finally getting the fire under control. From what the fire fighters said, the fire was limited to the back of the house, eating up and destroying the garden room. There was going to be one hell of a mess once it was finally put out.

The Earl was lying on the grass, fast asleep. Sowcroft had fetched a stripy deck chair and sat beside him like a daytripper on Brighton beach. Lady Caroline sat on the bench with Munro at her feet. Shepherd broke away from the group gathered on the back lawn and went to sit beside her.

"Ok?" he said.

Caroline nodded.

"It's a strange thing watching one's house burn," she said, her eyes fixed on the firefighters. "I might complain about the old monstrosity and how it eats money like a cash starved monster but it's home. There are so many memories tied up in there. I'm just hoping the fire hasn't reached the main part of the house. I couldn't bear it if the library was damaged."

Shepherd followed her gaze. The flames had been extinguished, replaced by dark clouds of steam and smoke rising into the night sky. Caroline turned to look at him.

"I'm so grateful to you for getting Daddy and Munro and Sowcroft out," she said.

"Don't mention it," Shepherd said, leaning forward and clasping his hands between his knees. "It was the least I could do."

Caroline sighed again.

"It isn't what I needed," she said. "Not with the festival in two weeks' time and Daddy being home again. There seems to be so much to do at times it's quite overwhelming."

Shepherd thought he heard a catch in her voice and turned to look at her. Caroline raised her hands to her face and wiped at her tears impatiently.

"Oh don't mind me," she said. "I'm just feeling a bit sorry for myself that's all."

Shepherd reached into his pocket and handed her his handkerchief.

Caroline laughed through her tears.

"I didn't have you down as the sort of man who'd carry a handkerchief," she said, taking it from him and dabbing at her face. "This is a night of surprises."

Shepherd leaned forward, staring at the house and the firefighters milling around on the lawn.

"What's there to do?" he said. "For the festival like? The site looks pretty much up and running to me."

"Well there's the stage to finish and then there's the Portaloos," she said. "The last time I heard anything about them they were stuck on the M6 in Manchester. And then there's the straw palace. Oh! I wish I'd never started that thing! It's more trouble than it's worth."

She smiled bravely through her tears and Shepherd had an urge to comfort her. If it had been Rose or any other woman from the camp he would have pulled them into his arms but this was Lady Caroline Oxley and he wasn't sure if you applied the same strategies to women like her.

"Perhaps we could help," Shepherd said. "We might look like a bunch of hippies and Margaret Thatcher may hate our guts but we're ok. Really we're ok."

Caroline smiled and wrapped her arms around herself, shivering slightly in the cool night.

"I know," she smiled. "I know. I mean look what you've done for me tonight. You even gave me your handkerchief."

"Oh that's nothing," Shepherd said. "You should see us when we really get going. Rescuing maidens from dragons 'n all sorts. And if you speak to us really nicely, we'll turn back tides. But only on Sundays."

Despite herself, Caroline laughed.

"So I should think we could probably help with a straw palace," he added.

Just then the Earl sat up and looked straight at Caroline.

"I want you to call the manager," he said. "This bed is ridiculously hard. I've had better night's sleep on Boogie Street."

"And he," she said in a voice that only Shepherd could hear. "Is just one more thing to worry about."

Chapter 31

Silvery dawn was touching the sky as they sat around the camp fire with enamel mugs of tea laced with marrow brandy.

"It certainly does the trick," Lady Caroline said pulling her bathrobe more tightly around her.

Grendo leaned forward to poke the fire with a spear.

"Nothing like a shot of marrow brandy," he said. "Janey makes it every year."

The fire fighters had spent three hours shooting water at the flames until finally they had died down leaving the garden room of Ambrell Priory a black, smouldering mess. Afterwards they had walked over the black cinders in their heavy boots, making sure, absolutely sure, that there were no sparks left which could re-ignite.

No one had needed the ambulance that arrived and parked on the lawn with its blue light flashing but one of the crew had spotted the Earl and spent some time talking to him before deciding he ought to go to the hospital to be checked over.

The Earl seemed quite happy about it, convinced he was returning to his ship and went along willingly. Sowcroft accompanied him, climbing into the back of the ambulance and accompanying him to the hospital.

"I feel so guilty," Caroline said as they watched the ambulance drive away. "Not because of what's happened but because I feel so relieved that he's going. Is that wrong?"

Shepherd didn't know what to say. Family dynamics were alien to him. He'd never had a father and so he didn't know how to answer her question.

"If he's not well then it's probably the right thing," he said.

"Oh he's well enough in the body," she said. "It's his mind that's the problem."

And so the Earl and Sowcroft had gone off to Halifax and here they all were, sitting around the fire in the travellers' field. Grendo passed round a spliff and when it reached Lady Caroline, Shepherd raised his head and looked at her.

"Have you had it before?" he said. "Weed?"

"No," she said, turning the spliff and staring at the burning end. "My brother was the one for this. He grew it in the flower beds, right outside the dining room window, in plain sight, amongst the roses. My mother never knew. It's still there, I think."

"Well don't smoke it if you don't want to," Shepherd said.

"But I'd like to," she said. "It's supposed to make you feel relaxed isn't it?"

"It is," Grendo said. "But if you're not used to it, it's best to take it slowly. Thai grass is strong stuff."

Lady Caroline sucked at the end in such an affected, clumsy way that Shepherd took the joint out of her fingers, placed it between his lips and showed her how to do it.

"Like this," he said, exhaling a curl of smoke. "Like this."

She copied him and then started to cough.

"Always happens the first time," Janey said, holding out a mug of water. "Drink this. It will take the burn off."

Caroline drank from the mug. Beside her, Munro wagged his tail, watching all that was going on.

"Thank you," she said.

The group sat silently for a moment thinking their own thoughts. They were exhausted after their night of fire fighting but they were used to greeting the dawn. Shepherd had done it many times, sleeping by camp fires and waking up to the magical light of early morning.

Lady Caroline took another puff of the joint and passed it to Shepherd. She still coughed but this time she didn't choke and suddenly, she started to laugh.

"You know suddenly I feel quite quite giddy," she said. "Who would like some breakfast? I, for one, am starving."

Chapter 32

"Are you sure we should go back inside?" Janey said as the group stood on the lawn looking up at the smouldering ruins at the back of the house. "Isn't it dangerous?"

"Nonsense," Lady Caroline said, tossing her long blonde hair behind her shoulders. "This house withstood an onslaught by the Roundheads and didn't flinch one bit when those Germans decided to drop a bomb on the Orangery in the Second World War. This house is solid, solid, hundreds of years of solid."

The group exchanged glances but followed her through the door at the side of the house. She was right: the main structure of the house was untouched although the smell of smoke hung heavy in the air. It was only the back section that appeared to be damaged.

"I told Daddy we shouldn't build the garden room out of wood," she said, as they entered the kitchen. "But did he listen? Oh no. Daddy isn't the sort to listen. Now," she said, pulling open the cupboards. "I haven't got a clue where anything is. This is Sowcroft's domain."

A frying pan fell out of a cupboard narrowly missing her foot and making a terrible clanging noise as it bounced on the stone floor. Janey rolled her eyes at Grendo and stepped forward.

"Here your ladyship, let me," she said, crouching down and retrieving the pan from the floor.

"Oh dear," Caroline said, sinking down into a chair at the table. "I'm afraid I'm not much good at domestic things and yet I've invited you all for breakfast! Not a terribly good hostess am I?"

"I'll sort it out Lady Caroline," Janey said as she and two other women in the group started opening cupboards and looking inside.

"Oh please!" Caroline said. "Please call me Caroline. I mean look at me. Dressed in a bathrobe, a little high on weed. I'm hardly worthy of a noble title this morning am I?"

Shepherd smiled. She was funny, he'd give her that.

Within ten minutes, Janey and the other women had found eggs and bread and bacon and the kitchen was full of delicious smells. With a little effort, Caroline managed to open a tin of Chum and tipped it a little haphazardly, into Munro's bowl.

"Oh dear," she said. "I do feel a little stoned."

It was such an old fashioned word to use that some of the party laughed and then Caroline laughed and they all laughed as they sat down at the huge trestle table and tucked in to marmalade and toast and bacon and eggs.

"Now this," she said, waving her fork in the air, "This is what I call breakfast."

The others smiled and raised their mugs of tea in a toast.

"To unusual circumstances," Grendo proposed, raising his mug high in the air. "May they always end in breakfast."

Chapter 33

After breakfast they slept. On ancient rugs, flat on the floor, on French couches and old soft beds. Anywhere and everywhere the members of the Convoy could find to sleep, they slept. Shepherd lay down on the floor in the library. Rose used to say he could sleep on a clothes line and it was true. It was because of all those houses and strange beds he had slept in as a child. Tiny rooms and drafty rooms, bunkbeds and couches: you name it, he'd slept on them. One stood out in his memory: a little room stacked with sacks of potatoes, an ironing board and an empty bird cage. He had been terrified of that bird cage because the other little boy who lived in the house had told him it was the home of a giant raven with sharp claws. Perhaps that was why he remembered it.

"May I?"

Caroline came in sat down beside him, wrapping her arms around her knees.

Shepherd grunted and turned on his side with his back towards her. Caroline touched his shoulder.

"Thank you," she said. "For all that you've done."

Shepherd's voice was thick with sleep.

"S'nothing," he said.

Caroline moved closer. He could feel her warm breath on the back of his neck.

Shepherd grunted and moved further away.

The last thing he needed was a woman coming on to him even if she had been born with a silver spoon in her mouth.

Chapter 34

Shepherd picked up the framed photograph lying on the floor of Idlewild and looked around him. The glass in the frame was cracked and the van was a mess. He didn't have many photographs and this one, this one of him and Rose last year at the Green Moon Festival, was special. Someone had had a camera and caught them laughing by the camp fire not long after they'd found the precious stones. Rose had got it framed and given it to him last Christmas.

Shepherd stepped across the mess on the floor and walked down to the Love Bus where Grendo was standing on the steps with the door wide open.

"You too?" Shepherd said.

Grendo scratched his woolly head.

"Aye," he said. "Looks like the pigs to me."

Shepherd looked inside. All Grendo's precious books were scattered across the floor amongst upturned plant pots with their earth strewn across the carpet. Janey was on her hands and knees with a dustpan and brush.

"How did they know?" Grendo said. "I mean it wasn't like we planned that fire, it wasn't like we knew we was going to stay away from the camp overnight. Even the geese were chased away. Travis has gone out looking for them."

Shepherd leaned on the railing at the top of the steps and gazed out across the camp. The police – for they were sure it was them - had kicked logs out of fires, pulled down lines of washing, upended cooking pots and smashed windows in some of the trucks. Men and women were standing outside their vans and wandering around surveying the damage.

"They even took my fire spear," Grendo said. "Bastards."

"Why do they hate us so much?" Shepherd said.

"The pigs?" Grendo said. "Who knows. Who knows."

And his shook his head and went back inside.

Chapter 35

Later that afternoon, after they'd swept up broken glass, cleaned out their trucks and lorries and vans, found the geese and calmed the goats, Shepherd went back to the boat house to collect his guitar.

A sense of relief washed over him as he opened the door and saw it lying where he'd left it on the wooden bench. If he'd left it at the camp, whoever had trashed the place might have trashed that too. The glass in the photograph frame could be replaced but damage to his guitar, well, that would have been a different story altogether.

Shepherd picked up the guitar and ran his hands over the smooth wood. He sat down for a moment and played a few chords feeling the calm it always brought him when he held it in his hands. Learning to play the guitar in a garden shed was the best thing he'd got from foster care.

"Learn to play it and music will always be yours," Terry had told him. "Something no one can ever take away from you."

He wondered what had happened to Terry and Trixie. They were much younger than some of the foster parents he'd been dumped with and they laughed a lot more. On Friday nights, Terry put Elvis Presley records on the stereo and jived around the front room, throwing Trixie around his waist and over his shoulder. At weekends they took him swimming or to the fun fair or the zoo and he had just about decided he quite liked living with them when he was moved on again. This time the social worker placed him with a vicar and his wife in the middle of nowhere. At night, Shepherd slept with his guitar next to him listening to the night time sounds in that that creepy, creaky old vicarage.

No one ever told him he was moving, no one ever asked if he wanted to go. They just came, packed up his things and put him in the back of a car.

"Penny for them."

Shepherd looked up. He hadn't heard her come in. Caroline was standing in the doorway wearing jeans and a white cotton shirt. He could smell perfume and freshly washed hair. He loved those scents on a woman.

"You were miles away," she said, folding her arms across her chest and smiling as she looked down at him.

"I was," Shepherd said, quietening the strings and looking up. "I just came to get my guitar," he said. "I left it here last night."

"About that…" she said. "I'm sorry about coming on to you in the library. Remind me not to try grass again."

Shepherd shrugged.

"Happens all the time," he said. "It's my irresistible charm."

Caroline laughed.

"I've been meaning to ask you," she said. "Do you have anyone in the Convoy called Tim? About 25 years old with shoulder length fair hair?"

Shepherd thought for a moment.

"Tim? No. Can't say I know anyone by that name. Mind you none of us go by our real names and there's loads of people in the Convoy."

"Oh," she said, sitting down on the bench beside him. "I was hoping I might find him. Hoping he might be part of the Convoy. A little far fetched perhaps but we live in hope don't we?"

"Who is he?" Shepherd said, picking out a light tune on the strings of his guitar. "Your ex?"

"No," she said, shaking her head and releasing fresh waves of shampoo into the air. "Tim's my brother. He left home years ago. I think he joined a travellers group."

"Lots of 'em around," Shepherd said, looking down at his fingers as they plucked gently at the strings of the guitar. "No one can afford to live in houses any more. Grendo told me that the number of travellers on the road has been doubling every year since 1979. Grendo reads a lot," he added.

"Grendo is a wise man," Caroline said. "I can't thank you enough for what you did last night."

"Is there much damage?" Shepherd said. "To the house?"

Caroline sighed.

"Quite a bit," she said. "But it will have to stay as it is for now. No insurance," she smiled ruefully. "Daddy doesn't believe in insurance. Or paying for it."

Shepherd picked out gentle chords and soft music filled the boat house.

"That's nice," she said. "What is it?"

"English Rose," he said. "It's a Paul Weller song."

Caroline nodded.

"It's beautiful,"

They sat listening to the music for a moment and then Caroline stood up.

"I suppose I'd better go," she sighed. "I've got a palace to build."

Shepherd looked up at her. The sun slanted through the glass in the boathouse doors and caught in her blonde hair. For a moment, standing there, she almost took his breath away.

"Need a hand?" he said, standing up. "I've always wanted to build a palace."

One Week Before

Chapter 36

Ursula Bridges looked out of the window as the old van bumped along the farm track. Another festival, another field, another weekend on the road. This one was in the grounds of an old priory. Charlie had been raving about it all the way up the motorway, shouting above the roar of the old engine, telling stories about priests hiding in holes behind the fireplace and papal treasures hidden under the floorboards.

Ursula loved his stories and in a way, she was one of them. After all, he had created her like a character in a book to walk across her own pages and fill them with life.

She had known, from an early age, that her name meant "she-bear" and she couldn't be more proud of it. When other girls teased her for having an unusual name, she'd pull back her lips and growl. It didn't make her many friends but what did it matter when she was never at one school long enough to make any? This is what she lived for, for life on the road, for the music. Charlie and Louise gave her all the education she needed.

Charlie had a thing about bears. He'd named their rock and blues band, *Artaois* after the Celtic bear god. Bears were strong, bears were wild and all of her childhood heroes had been bears: Winnie the Pooh, Paddington Bear, Rupert the Bear. They were her captive audience when she got her first drumkit at the age of five years old and now she was as good as Cozy Powell, or so Ravi said. She loved playing the drums, loved the way the rhythm got into your mind and soul. Sometimes, playing the drums was like galloping through a forest on a winged white horse, sometimes it was like sailing a boat on a wind tossed sea. She had never done either but that didn't matter: drums conjured up a hundred worlds she could live in, one at a time or all at once, depending on her mood.

"So," Charlie said as they pulled up in a front of a huge stage and jerked on the handbrake. "This is Ambrell. And this, my little she bear, is where you are going to make your glorious, unforgettable debut. Are you ready?"

Outside the window, men were climbing and crawling around the stage, shouting at each other, hanging from scaffolding and shifting speakers and boxes and trails of electrical wire.

"I'm ready," she grinned back at her father. "I'm ready."

Chapter 37

Why Lady Caroline hadn't opted for a marquee or built the palace out of wood, Shepherd would never know. All he knew was that he itched. The straw and dust had got into every gap in his shirt, down the back of his neck and up his nostrils. Even the palms of his hands itched.

"Why didn't you put it in the main field?" Grendo asked her as they stopped for something to eat. None of the travellers were particularly fussed about observing a traditional lunch hour. They ate as and when and lunch could be a meal in the middle of the night as far as they were concerned. But Lady Caroline had insisted they stop. The sun was hot, the work was tiring and she was, Shepherd acknowledged, acutely aware of how hard they were working.

"Drainage," she said. "Marshland. Apparently."

Just after midday, Sowcroft, wearing his butler's uniform despite the heat of the day and Robert, who had been supervising operations, appeared, pushing a wheelbarrow over the bumpy ground laden with a wicker hamper and an ice box of cold beer. The hamper contained things he had never tasted before: soft cheeses she identified as *brie* and *camembert* and long sticks of bread that looked like weapons. There were red apples and ripe tomatoes and slices of a cheese and egg sort of pie which she called *keesh*. Shepherd had never tasted anything like it.

They took shelter from the blazing sun under the leafy canopy of a copper beech tree at the side of the field. Caroline billowed a large white tablecloth over the grass and they sat down and tucked in.

Through the trees, Shepherd could see the vans arriving for the festival in the adjoining field. Some festival goers had arrived early and were putting up tents and filling up water bottles. Men crawled up and down the scaffolding erected around the stage like worker ants and the sound of hammer blows and sound tests floated out to them on the breeze.

"So we just need to sort out the lighting and that's it," Lady Caroline said, sipping a glass of wine. She'd even brought out the crystal glasses, Shepherd noted, as the sun glinted off the glass. If this was what she did for a picnic, what did she do for the dinner parties she must surely throw for her rich and titled friends?

"That won't take long," Robert said, his big working hands tearing at a piece of French bread. "It looks good don't it?"

They turned their heads to look at the straw palace. It did look good. It was mad, it was crazy because it had no purpose whatsoever except to amaze those who walked inside it.

"And the music Robert," Lady Caroline reminded him, leaning back on her elbows and tilting her face to the sun. "Don't forget the music."

"Ah yes," Robert said thoughtfully. "The music."

Shepherd got the feeling that Robert was used to her challenges. The damage left by the fire though was a different matter: that was out of his league and for now, the garden room at the back of the house would have to stay as it was: charred and burned and ruined.

Through the trees Shepherd saw a young girl with spiky black hair jump down from a van and join an older man at the back doors. The site was beginning to take on that before the party feeling and he liked it. In just over a week the party would be starting and he wasn't quite sure how he had got roped into putting lights and music into a straw palace instead of lying in the sun with a spliff and his guitar.

Chapter 38

"So what did your men find when they executed the Warrant, Appleby?"

Commander Taylor stared at the neat, grey haired man sitting opposite him in the tea room. It wasn't the most ideal of places to meet but Appleby had said there was some sort of open day going on at the station and it would be better to meet in Strongs. Open day? What on earth was going on up here?

Taylor glanced around at the other occupants of the tea room. All of them were women and none of them a day under sixty. Not one bit of decent skirt to be seen.

"Nothing at all Sir," Appleby said, picking up his teaspoon and stirring the cup of tea in front of him. "Nothing at all."

Taylor stared at him.

"What?" he said in a louder voice than he'd intended, causing some of the women to look over at them.

"What do you mean nothing at all?" he said, lowering his voice. "What about the drugs? The weapons? The hoards of cash?"

"We didn't find any," Appleby said, laying his teaspoon carefully and quietly down on the saucer by his cup. Taylor hated the way he did that. The man was so *precise.*

"But there must have been something!" Taylor hissed, leaning further across the table. "We had intelligence! Reliable intelligence!"

"I'm sorry sir," Appleby said, raising the rim of his tea cup to his lips and maintaining solid, staring eye contact with Taylor as he did so. "We didn't find anything."

"Did they search the vans? The lorries?"

"Yes sir," Appleby said. "All of them, just like you suggested."

Taylor stared at him.

"We know they've got drugs. We know."

"There was no one on the site when the men searched," Appleby said. "Perhaps they took the drugs with them."

Taylor stared at him. Sometimes he got the feeling that the West Yorkshire Constabulary weren't taking this as seriously as they ought to.

"No weapons?"

"No, sir, no. Just a spear. Used for poking a fire I believe."

"No evidence of illicit or subversive material?"

"No," Taylor said. "There was nothing Sir."

Taylor shook his head slowly in disbelief. He should have known better than to let Appleby's local constabulary carry out the raid. He'd wanted a team from London but his request had been refused despite presenting them with the intelligence Jim had provided. Jim could not have got it wrong, not when he was living undercover as part of the Convoy. The trouble was, Appleby didn't know about Jim. Telling him could jeopardise the whole operation.

"I want you to carry out another search," Taylor said.

Appleby shifted his chair slightly and cleared his throat.

"I'm afraid we can't do that sir," he said. "We don't have the manpower. It was difficult enough to organise the search as it was."

"For Chrissake man!" Taylor said, his frustrations bubbling up to the surface. "Find some!"

"But we didn't find anything," Appleby said, his tone steady and even. "So why would we find anything if we went back?"

Taylor stared at him. He didn't like being stymied. He didn't like it when his plans didn't go the way he wanted them to go.

"Because," he said, exasperated. "Because I'm telling you to find something. Take them by surprise, arrive in the middle of the night, storm in at the crack of dawn. Those hippies are clever. They probably got rid of everything when they saw you coming. What about the weapons? The prostitutes?"

Taylor resisted the urge to grab the sergeant by the throat and shake him. No wonder the country was in the state it was in with this sort of policing going on. Where on earth were this man's priorities? Didn't he realise he had a bunch of subversives camping on his doorstep?

"I don't think we'd get another Warrant Sir," Appleby said. "Those magistrates are a tough lot."

Taylor sighed.

"Haven't you heard of PACE?" he said. "The new Police and Criminal Evidence Act? That's what we're using in London. You don't need a warrant under PACE. All you need is reasonable suspicion. Stuff the warrants."

Appleby stirred his tea and swallowed.

"We still adhere to the Judge's Rules up here Sir," he said. "Until we're told otherwise. And there's still the manpower issue."

Taylor picked up his hat and jammed it on to his head.

"I came up here to help out," he said. "But all I get wherever I go is brick walls and old fashioned policing. I'm not happy sergeant. I'm not happy at all."

"No," Appleby sighed, as Taylor stood up. "I don't suppose you are."

The bell on the door jangled harshly as Taylor left the tea shop. After he had gone, the noise level in the café rose slightly as the women who had been observing the exchange between the two men leaned across the tables and discussed what they had seen.

Appleby smiled at a couple of them and ordered more tea and a piece of apple cake. He knew most of the women in here by name and he also knew their children and grand children. It was all part of the policing he did. Know the community. Listen to them. Be interested. He didn't approve of Taylor's way of policing. It seemed so brutal, so disconnected. He had always thought the police were of the people, not against the people, and as long as he was in charge of his area, policing by consent was the way it was going to stay. He would not be conducting another search of the travellers' field, no matter how much Commander Taylor ranted and raved.

Appleby smiled to himself as Molly set down a fresh pot of tea in front of him. There was no hurry to get back. He might even have another piece of apple cake.

Chapter 39

Johnson Jones's office at *The Yorkshire Herald* was the typical lair of a provincial journalist. A teleprinter raced in the corner and piles of newspapers and notebooks towered precariously on every available surface. As he took Taylor into his office, Johnson Jones swept a pile of papers from a wooden backed chair and gestured to him to sit down.

"So," he said, dumping the papers on top of some other papers. "What brings you to the famed and notorious offices of *The Yorkshire Herald* inspector?"

Johnson was wearing a tweed hacking jacket and jeans with a gold coloured tie. He looked like one of those hippy sorts, Taylor thought with disapproval. He rarely trusted a man who wore his tie at half mast.

"Commander," Taylor said. "It's Commander. Not inspector."

Johnson swallowed and flushed red.

"Sorry," he said. "Tea?"

Taylor was full of tea. He'd already drunk three cups of the stuff at that infernal tea room with Appleby and it was only eleven o'clock in the morning.

"No," Taylor said. "No tea. Thank you. I'll get straight to the point Mr Johnson. I want you to write an article about the festival."

"I'm already on the case," Johnson beamed, crossing his arms across his chest and leaning his backside against his desk. "We couldn't ignore that happening on our doorstep could we? I mean Steppenwolf and Van Morrison and Steeleye Span? Those bands are *epic*. Epic. I mean we're just a sleepy little Yorkshire village aren't we and here we are, blessed by the golden presence of some of the greatest bands that ever lived. Do you like rock music Commander?"

Taylor bristled. He didn't like the familiar attitude of this man and he certainly didn't like *rock music*.

Taylor took off his hat and laid it on top of a pile of newspapers as if to assert his rank and authority.

"I'm not talking about the music Mr Johnson. I'm talking about the locals. They must be worried, upset, scared?"

Johnson stared at him.

"Scared?" he repeated. "Of rock music?"

"No not of rock music," Taylor said irritably. "Of the people who follow in their wake. The hangers on. The people who will be attending this, this *festival.* The Peace Convoy for example."

Johnson scratched his shaggy beard and looked up at the nicotine stained ceiling.

"I haven't heard anything about that," he said. "From what I've heard people are looking forward to it. Good business," he added. "In these dark and difficult times."

"Well I've heard that people are worried," Taylor persisted. "And not just worried. Scared. You do know what the Peace Convoy is don't you?"

"I've heard bits and pieces," Johnson said. "Didn't they spend some time down at Greenham Common with those peace women?"

"And you're a journalist?" Taylor said, shaking his head. "Oh dear oh dear."

Johnson looked troubled. He loved his job. He took it seriously. Ok so it wasn't *The News of the World* or *The Times* but the *Yorkshire Herald* was his stepping stone to greater things, he was sure of it.

Johnson swallowed.

"So what's the issue?" he said.

"The issue," Taylor said, pausing for a moment. "*The issue*, is that your paper has a duty to report what is going on in the area. And I for one would feel very let down, as a reader, if your paper didn't make me aware of what was going on on my doorstep. I probably shouldn't tell you this but on Monday we carried out a search of the travellers field at Ambrell, the festival site. We found things that made my blood turn cold."

Johnson's ears pricked up. This was what he'd been looking for. A scoop. A scoop that would propel him to greater things, get him the editor's attention, maybe even the attention of the big London papers. Not so long ago that had happened to a journalist in Cumbria and look where he was now. Working for *The Daily Telegraph* in London.

"Tell me more," he said, reaching for a packet of Benson & Hedges and offering them to Taylor. Taylor shook his head and Johnson took a cigarette from the packet and held it to his mouth, lighting it with a brass zippo.

"The Peace Convoy," Taylor continued. "Is a bunch of subversive anarchists who will stop at nothing to achieve their aim of overturning the forces of law and order in this country. They travel around England in old trucks and vans, taking drugs, spreading propaganda, terrifying women and children and doing just as they please. They have no respect for what the great British public holds dear. No respect at all."

Johnson lifted his chin and blew smoke up at the ceiling.

"I didn't know about this," he said. "Can you give me more details? Are they at the site, this Peace Convoy? I thought the festival wasn't starting until next week."

"Oh they're there alright," Taylor said. "Been given their own field although why only God knows. Like I said, we've got our eye on them."

Johnson stubbed out his cigarette in an overflowing ashtray and looked at Taylor.

"So what did you find when you carried out your search?" Johnson said. "Just out of interest, you know."

Taylor sighed. This was more like it. Someone who was interested. Someone who was listening.

"Axes, pickaxe handles, spears, chainsaws, cocaine, heroin, dope. You name it, we found it. We also believe there is active prostitution on site."

Johnson's eyes widened.

"Prostitution?" he repeated. "In Yorkshire?"

Taylor nodded slowly. Johnson was drinking in every word, just as he'd intended.

"So you see," he said. "It's important to bring this to the attention of the locals through the medium of your newspaper. They ought to know what's going on right under their noses. They may not be safe in their beds."

Johnson nodded slowly, absorbing the enormity of what this man in police uniform was telling him.

"I see, I see," he said. "This is interesting. Very interesting."

He reached for a Silvine notebook and flicked back the top page. He lit another cigarette and with his eyes squinting against the smoke, reached for a pencil and started to jot down some notes.

"Can you give me the exact details?" he said. "Of what you found during the search?"

Taylor sat back in his chair and relaxed. Sometimes this job was as easy as giving candy to a baby.

Chapter 40

Lady Caroline was sitting in the library trying to make sense of the accounts. She could hear some sort of machinery outside and it was cutting through her concentration and making it hard to focus on the figures before her. Munro dozed underneath the writing table, resting his big head on her feet and his ears pricked up and he raised his big wolfhound head as Sowcroft came into the room.

"What is that infernal racket Sowcroft?" she asked irritably. "Is it one of the contractors for the festival because if it is I want you to speak to them and tell them to stop."

Sowcroft walked to the window and pulled back the curtain.

"It's Mr Rex m'lady," he said. "That's what I came to tell you. Mr Rex is here."

Caroline stared at him.

"Mr Rex?" she said, rising from the table. "I thought he was in the South of France."

"He appears to have returned m'lady," Sowcroft said.

Caroline hurried over to the window and held the curtain back as she looked out.

"What's on earth is he doing?" she said, looking down at a yellow digger traversing the back lawn.

"I believe he's clearing some of the debris away from the fire." Sowcroft said. "Or at least that's what he told Robert."

"What?" she said. "He's got no right… no right."

Caroline hurried down the stairs with Munro galloping down ahead of her. Sowcroft hurried along behind them.

"Rex!" she called over the noise of the machine's engine as they reached the back lawn. "Rex!"

A man wearing a tweed deerstalker smiled through the glass of the driver's cab.

"Hello darling," he said, yanking on the handbrake and poking his head out of the open window. "I came as soon as I could. Only got off the boat last night."

Caroline stared at him.

"Don't you hello darling me," she said. "What on *earth* do you think you're doing?"

Rex turned the key in the ignition and the grinding noise of the digger ceased, leaving a loud silence in its wake. He jumped down from the cab and planted a kiss on her cheek.

"I'm just trying to help," he said. "I heard there'd been a fire. A little too much of the old vino eh?"

Rex made a gesture with his hand imitating someone knocking back a glass of wine.

Caroline felt her heart pounding. Rex always had the ability to wind her up.

"Shut up Rex," she said. "And get this, this *thing* off my land."

Rex made a soothing noise.

"Is that any way to greet me *cherie?"* he said. "You should have come to France and had some of those rough edges rubbed off you. Glorious place. Glorious. Sun sea and *enchantement."*

"I think m'lady is asking you to move the digger," Sowcroft said, stepping into the arena.

"When I need you to translate," Rex said, his smile slipping away. "I'll ask you. Now can a man get a drink around here or is he doomed to die of thirst?"

Caroline glared at him.

"Go away Rex," she said. "And take that thing with you."

"But darling," he protested, opening his arms and feigning a look of hurt surprise.

"Haven't you missed me? I thought you'd be hungry for my wit and repartee after our little *separation."*

Caroline glared at him. First he had disappeared to France, sending her a postcard from Cannes raving on about the fabulous time he was having partying on yachts and swimming naked in the sea and now he had the cheek to turn up with a digger spouting stupid French words all over the place.

"I don't remember it as a separation," Caroline said coldly. "What I remember is finding you in the guest bedroom at Veronica's Spring ball with Letitia Herbert. And you weren't helping her on with her coat."

Rex shrugged.

"So a man makes a little mistake from time to time," he shrugged. "You know how it is. I am a mere mortal, prodded by temptation. Letitia Herbert was just a little fun, just a little tickle. Don't be angry darling," he said, catching her wrist and pulling her towards him. "You know you love your little Rexy really."

Caroline shook him off and gave him the coldest stare she could muster.

"Please leave Rex," she said. "I've got hundreds of people arriving for a festival next week and I could do without you and your clowning around."

Rex lit a cigarette and blew the smoke up at the sky.

"Still catering to the down and outs are we?," he said. "Still hoi polloi-ing with the underclass?"

Caroline had forgotten how he made her feel. In the early days it had been heady, joyful, captivating, to have the attention of a man like Rex who owned a vast number of tenanted properties in London and would inherit a mansion and millions of pounds when his cantankerous old mother finally bit the dust. Now she remembered how the gloss had worn off. Now she remembered how often he had irritated her or made her feel silly and foolish and she wasn't having it.

"For your information," she said. "They are not the underclass. They are people who come to listen to music and enjoy themselves. Not that you'd understand," she added. "Your idea of enjoyment seems to involve a much higher degree of subversity."

Rex let out a little high pitched laugh.

"Ouch," he said, exhaling cigarette smoke through his nostrils. "How I've missed you darling. Do you know how beautiful you are when you're cross?"

Sowcroft cleared his throat.

"Will Mr Rex be joining us for dinner?"

"No he bloody well will not be joining us for dinner," Caroline said, glaring at Rex. "Mr Rex is leaving. Aren't you *cheri?"*

Rex shrugged.

"Ouch," he said, clutching dramatically at his heart with both hands. "Ah the slings and arrows, the slings and arrows. All in the course of true love my darling," he called after her as she turned and stomped up the lawn. "All in the course of true love."

Chapter 41

"What do you mean he's just left it there?"

"He said," Sowcroft said, clearing his throat. "He said he'd leave it there because if he knows you, you'll come round in a couple of days. He also said, if you'll excuse me for saying this m'lady, that you don't always know what's best for you."

Caroline snorted. It was typical of Rex. During the two years they'd been together, he'd often treated her as if she was a silly empty headed little girl. Officially they were still engaged but she'd taken off the ruby and diamond ring months ago. You couldn't remain engaged to someone who did what Rex had done. For two years she had turned a blind eye to his arrogant assumptions and his infidelities. He had always seemed so sorry afterwards and she accepted excuse after excuse. But when she had found him lying on top of the coats with Letitia Herbert at Veronica Mansfield's summer ball in May, it was the last straw. Shortly afterwards, he had slunk away to his mother's summer residence in the South of France. And now he was back acting like nothing had happened, presuming she needed his help, trying to take the reins just like he had always done. Daddy had been right. He was a fly by night and a terminal cad. She just hadn't seen it at the time.

"He's got a bloody cheek," Caroline said, looking past Sowcroft out of the window. "I mean who turns up at someone else's house *with a digger?"*

"Mr Rex apparently," Sowcroft said, following her gaze across the lawns.

"Well what are we to do?" she said. "That digger is an eyesore and quite honestly it irritates me."

Sowcroft cleared his throat.

"I could move it m'lady."

Caroline turned to look at him.

"Move it?" she said. "You? Since when have you been able to drive a digger?"

"Since I was in the Army on National Service," he said proudly. "We used them all the time in Khartoum."

"Well Sowcroft," she said. "You are a dark horse."

"Dark horses ride at night," he said mysteriously. "I can drive tanks too."

"Well," she said. "I don't think we need that skill just at the moment. But yes, perhaps you could move it. Maybe over to the trees until I can get someone to take it away. I wish Rex had stayed in bloody France," she sighed. "I could do without him complicating my life."

Sowcroft turned from the window.

"Wait," Caroline said. "I want you to do something else for me please."

Sowcroft turned.

"When you've moved the digger, can you return this to Mr Rex?"

Caroline crossed to the desk and took the engagement ring out of the onyx jewellery box. She'd taken it out of her bedroom after Rex's visit and sat for a moment looking at the ring. It was a beautiful thing and she missed wearing it but what she had to remember was what it meant, what was behind its beauty. Did she really want that?

"I want you to return this to Mr Rex with my compliments," she said.

Sowcroft's eyes widened as she placed the large ruby and diamond ring on the palm of his hand.

"Might you be a little hasty m'lady?"

"No," she shook her head firmly. "Rex and I are finished Sowcroft. There's no going back. This should drive the message home."

"I don't mean hasty in breaking off the engagement," he said. "I mean hasty in returning the ring to him. This is quite valuable m'lady."

Caroline searched his face.

"What are you saying Sowcroft?"

"I merely suggest that if you no longer have any use for it, you might wish to consider selling it."

"Selling it?" she said. "For money?"

"That's usually the idea," Sowcroft said, his face expressionless.

"Is that possible?" she said. "I mean it's an heirloom isn't it? An antique?"

"So I believe m'lady," Sowcroft said. "So I believe. And likely to fetch a good price."

"Hmm…" Caroline said. "How do you know about such things?"

Sowcroft shrugged.

"I have learned a lot from my years in service m'lady."

Caroline gazed out across the sunlit lawns.

"But if I don't return the ring to him he won't know I wish to end the engagement."

"May I suggest you leave that to me m'lady," Sowcroft said. "There are other ways of communicating intentions."

Caroline turned and looked at him.

"How much do you think it's worth? The ring?"

Sowcroft drew in his breath.

"I wouldn't like to say m'lady but I should imagine it might be a thousand pounds or so."

"A thousand pounds?" she repeated. "That would pay for the repairs to the house."

"Quite m'lady," Sowcroft nodded. "That was my line of thinking."

Caroline stared at him.

"It seems a terrible thing to do with a family heirloom. He's going to be awfully cross when he finds out."

"Yes m'lady," Sowcroft acknowledged. "Undoubtedly. But sometimes revenge is a dish best served cold. That is what the Earl always says anyway."

Lady Caroline looked at him.

"Do it Sowcroft," she said. "Do it with my blessing."

Chapter 42

They had two tents: an old brown one for Charlie and Louise and an orange one for her.

"Don't be lighting any candles in there," Charlies said, securing the last guy rope and squinting against the smoke rising from the cigarette stuck to his lower lip. "I know what you're like."

Ursula smiled at her father. He knew she would. He also knew she'd hang ribbons and crystals from the centre pole and persuade Louise to part with some of her soft velvet scatter cushions. And when she had created her inner sanctuary, she would lie on her back watching the way the crystals caught the candle light, smelling the fresh grass outside, listening to the sounds of invisible life going on around her.

Charlie had pitched their tents at the end of the field, under the trees. Fred and Ravi had pitched their tents next to them. *Artaois* was a grass roots band. Other, more famous acts, would arrive at the festival in helicopters or big American tour buses and spent the next few days in a blur of champagne and cocaine. *Artaois* wasn't like that and she was glad. She'd heard the stories. She'd seen the consequences.

As Ursula hung up her crystals and arranged the cushions inside her tent, Ravi appeared in the doorway.

"Ready to do some practise?" he said.

Ursula squinted against the sun. She had known Ravi for ever and he had taught her everything she knew about playing the drums.

"Where?" she said.

"In the barn," Ravi said, pointing across the field. "I've set up the drums."

Ursula grinned at him.

"In a barn?" she said.

Ravi shrugged.

"Why not?" he said.

The barn was a big wrought iron structure with open sides and bales of hay stacked in the corner. Ursula breathed in the scent of hay and earth and stared at the drums set up in the middle. They looked strange and quirky against the pastoral setting. Ravi handed her a pair of drumsticks.

"I got these for you," he said. "They're made from maple. It's lighter than hickory."

Ursula looked at the drumsticks and up at Ravi.

"Thank you," she said, running her finger along the smooth wood. "Thank you."

"They'll bring you luck," he said. "Not that you need it."

Ursula felt her stomach constrict. She was excited about playing on stage but also nervous. What if she messed it up? What if she froze with stage fright?

"Come on," Ravi said, reading her mind. "You'll feel better when you do some drumming."

Ravi adjusted the stool to her height and Ursula slipped on to the leather seat. She was always grateful that he trusted her to play his drums and treat them with respect. He wasn't like some of the drummers she had seen thrashing the hell out of the bass and beating the snare to within an inch of its life. He seemed to get them to speak just the way he wanted them to speak without resorting to all that hair tossing and cymbal spinning she'd seen other drummers do.

Ursula placed the sticks cross wise against the drums, closed her eyes and began to play.

"There's rhythm in everything if you listen," he'd once told her. "In the wind, in the rain, in the sea, in the river… drummers are always the ones at the back, the invisible ones. We listen to the world and play it back through the drums."

One afternoon, Ravi had taken her to a squat in North London where she'd met June Miles-Kingston, the drummer with the Mo-dettes. Their type of music was different from the stuff *Artaois* played and although Ursula didn't get the ska music or the two tone thing, she was in awe of June and wanted to be just like her. Female drummers were a rare species in the rock world.

After they had finished practising, Ursula wandered back to the festival field. Dominating it was the stage, with its black cloth backdrop and massive stage. It gave her a thrill to think that on Sunday night, she would be up there performing. She had dreamed of it for so long.

In readiness for the festival, the canvas tents of the traders and crafts people were already set up. Windchimes tinkled in the light breeze and coloured tie dyed scarves fluttered from tent poles. There were caravans with boards outside promising falafel and lentil burgers and tents where boards outside invited you to have your hair braided, your fortune told or spend an hour in mystic medication with honey and mead. There were chickens running around a stall selling fresh barn eggs and sleepy dogs lying outside tents in the sun; there was colour and noise and magic and mystery everywhere she looked.

Ursula stopped outside a tent where a board offered henna tattoos. She lifted the flap and entered the cool dark interior. The warm scents of orange and cinnamon greeted her, lanterns positioned on the floor gave out a soft glow and ethereal music filled the air. She felt like she had entered a magical cave.

Her mother Louise was lying on a steamer chair smoking a joint, her long black hair hanging loose over her bare shoulders.

"Hello baby," she said. "Where've you been?"

"Practising," Ursula said, bending down to kiss her forehead. "Look what Ravi got me."

Ursula held out the drumsticks. She was enchanted by them. She had had drumsticks before but these were special, magical.

Louise smiled and ran her finger along the wood.

"He spoils you," she said, sitting up and swinging her legs over the side of the chair. "And I love him for it."

Ursula smiled and closed her eyes as Louise hugged her. She might have just played a heavy number on the drums which caused her muscles to ache and the sweat to break on her brow but here, in her mother's domain, she was fifteen years old and cocooned. She was content in both worlds.

Chapter 43

"And I now pronounce the Palace of Versailles officially open!"

Shepherd watched as Lady Caroline smashed a bottle of champagne against the straw as if she was launching a thousand ships. The champagne bottle remained intact and Grendo stepped forward, took it from her and smashed it hard against the metal poles which supported the palace.

The glass shattered and the champagne shot into the air as the crowd clapped and cheered. Grendo dropped the bottle on the ground, wiped his hands on his combat shorts and re-joined the group from the Convoy which had gathered round to watch the grand opening of the straw palace. Some were curious, some critical, some weren't that interested.

Shepherd noticed a girl with short dark hair standing behind them. She wasn't part of the Convoy, at least he had never seen her before. Shepherd moved slightly to the side so she could see the palace.

"What is it?" she asked him, looking up at it.

"It's a palace," he said. "A French palace."

"Oh," she said. "I've never seen a palace before."

Lady Caroline raised a megaphone to her mouth and started to speak, her voice echoing across the fields.

"I'd like to thank all of you who have helped with this project," she said looking out at some of the men and women from the Peace Convoy. "Some expressed doubt as to whether a palace could be built out of straw but we did it, we did it! Please help yourselves to champagne and raise your glasses to this extraordinary and wonderful achievement!"

The crowd murmured and moved forward as she dropped the megaphone and stood aside. Behind her was a long trestle table covered in a white cloth. Sowcroft was positioned behind it, a kitchen apron tied over his butler suit, handing out flutes of champagne.

"Is she a princess?" the girl whispered to Shepherd.

"Probably," he grinned. "Probably."

Chapter 44

After the crowd of people had drifted away and the woman with the blonde hair and the posh voice had disappeared, Ursula remained staring up at the palace.

"You can go in if you want," a man said. "That's what it's for."

Ursula looked up at the palace. A palace? In the middle of a festival? She had seen snake charmers, dancing dogs and stilt walkers at festivals but never a palace made out of straw.

Ursula moved towards the archway which formed an entrance into a narrow corridor. Inside, fairy lights lit up the straw with a soft glow and French love songs floated out on to the air. It was enchanting, intriguing.

"Go on," the man said. "Go in. Have a look around. "

Ursula didn't need any more encouragement. She might have had ambition to be the greatest female drummer in the British Isles, but part of her was still a child attracted to shiny baubles and make believe. She walked in looking up and around her. The corridor curved to the right and exited into a square room with bales of hay stacked on the floor to act as seats. A metal ladder was propped up against the wall leading to a balcony above. Ursula put one foot on the ladder and started to climb. At the top she stopped and looked out on the most magical room she had ever seen. A large four poster bed made out of straw dominated the room which was softened with rugs and cushions. A string of coloured lightbulbs hung across the ceiling giving out a soft glow of blue and pink and orange. Ursula stepped off the ladder and crossed the room. She touched the bed and sat down on the side feeling the hard straw beneath her. The bed was covered with a plum coloured throw and piles of soft pink pillows were piled on top of it. She could sleep here, she thought. She could sleep here and dream magical, other worldly dreams in her very own palace of straw.

An open archway at the side of the room lead out on to a balcony that ran around the upper storey of the palace. Ursula stepped outside. The summer breeze was cool on her face and she looked down on the people below her. Someone waved and she waved back. In the distance she could see the gently rolling hills of Yorkshire, the river criss-crossing the fields, a big red brick house over to her right and vans and cars queuing in the lanes. Below her were the brightly coloured tents of the festival field, girls with sun in their hair, children rolling a coloured hoop, men lying on their backs on the grass. The air was warm and suffused with the smell of hot dogs, bird song, rock music and freshly mown grass.

The moment was broken by voices floating up from downstairs. Ursula took a final look around her and gave the newcomers a quick smile as she came back into the bedroom and climbed down the ladder.

"There you are," Ravi said as she stepped outside into the sunshine. "I've been looking for you everywhere. We're going to have a practise run on stage. Ready?"

Ursula nodded. The enchanted dreams inspired by the straw palace would have to wait.

Chapter 45

"I mean who the fuck writes this stuff?"

Grendo pulled the corner of the newspaper towards him and read the headlines.

SPEAKEASY AT AMBRELL

Local police find evidence of drugs and weapons

By Johnson Jones

A four day music festival will be held in the grounds of Ambrell Priory, the stately home on the outskirts of Beddington, during the August Bank Holiday weekend. Already, hundreds of travellers have descended on the site including members of the Peace Convoy, a group of drug taking drop outs who travel from festival to festival in old buses and lorries.

"We don't feel safe," 74 year old local resident Edna Loughton told us. "People are too frightened to go out. I had a pint of gold top stolen from my doorstep last Thursday and just this morning, there was a naked man sleeping in my neighbour's garden. They say there's drugs and machine guns and everything in that field. Why the Council allow it I'll never know. This is a decent neighbourhood and we don't want their sort here."

With local concerns running high, Sergeant Appleby of the local police force is keen to reassure local residents.

"We have 12 police officers assigned to the 22 acre site," he told us. "We would like to reassure the public that we are here to serve them and will be keeping a close eye on proceedings."

Hundreds of people are already camping in the grounds in anticipation of the festival, which is due to start next weekend. If there are any concerns, local residents should dial 999.

Grendo threw the paper back across the table.

"It never stops does it?" he said as Janey placed a bacon sandwich in front of him. "And as for that wanker Nicholas Winterton, he won't be satisfied until every member of the Convoy has been hung drawn and quartered. I heard him on the radio this morning. Apparently the Peace Convoy is a threat to the very fabric of British Society."

Grendo mimicked a precise, received British accent and Janey turned from the cooker and smiled at him.

"What do you expect from a Tory MP?" Shepherd said, leaning forward and lifting his sandwich in both hands. "Until we all start singing Land of Hope and Glory and living where they want us to live, Margaret Thatcher will be chasing us up and down the country until the day we die."

"Aye well she can piss off n'all," Grendo said. "She'd do better remembering there's two million unemployed in this country and give them some of her attention rather than persecuting travellers."

Janey joined them at the table but no sooner had she sat down than a woman with long fair hair wearing sparkly purple harem pants burst through the open door of the Love Bus.

"There's a woman having a baby in the barn!" she said, breathing heavily.

All three of them dropped their sandwiches on their plates and ran out of the door.

Chapter 46

"She needs to go to hospital," Janey said, sitting back on her heels and pulling her hair off her shoulders. "That baby's isn't coming out any time soon."

Grendo looked at Janey. She had delivered quite a few babies during their time in the Convoy and she wasn't one for dramatics. If Janey said they needed medical assistance, they needed medical assistance.

"I'll run over to the house," Shepherd said. "They've got a phone there." Grendo nodded and placed a hand on his arm as he stood up and the woman lying on the floor groaned.

"Better hurry up," he said in a low voice.

Shepherd nodded, got to his feet and ran down the lane towards the house. Sowcroft met him at the door and let him in.

"A woman's having a baby in the barn," he said. "Can I use the phone?"

"Lady Caroline is in the bath," Sowcroft said solemnly as he if were announcing an event of major importance. "I am quite sure she wouldn't object to you using the telephone."

"Thanks," Shepherd said, heading towards the table in the hall.

As he relayed the information to the ambulance operator, Caroline came down the stairs in a pair of Levi jeans and a white shirt rubbing at her hair which was wrapped in a fluffy white towel.

"I heard what you said," she said. "Is the woman alright?"

Shepherd looked up at her and shrugged.

"No idea," he said, cupping his hand over the receiver. "I don't know anything about babies."

"I do," she said. "I'm a midwife."

Shepherd stared at her and his mouth dropped open.

"You?" he said.

Caroline smiled.

"Oh don't look so surprised," she said. "I'm not the empty headed aristocrat bathing in champagne that you might think I am."

"I never said you were," Shepherd said as she took the receiver from him and placed it back on the cradle.

"They won't be here for ages," Caroline said. "And babies don't wait. Sowcroft," she said turning and looking at her butler who was hovering in the doorway. "Get some towels from the airing cupboard and some jugs of hot water and follow us out to the barn. We have a baby on the way."

Sowcroft's eyes widened.

"Yes m'lady," he said.

"Come on," Caroline said, turning back to Shepherd. "Let's go and see what we can do. I do love a baby being born. It is one of life's most wonderful mysteries don't you think?"

They hurried back across the field where the woman lay with her head on her husband's jeaned legs. A film of sweat coated her brow and above her, her husband's bearded face was pale and anxious.

"It's our first baby," he said. "Will she be alright?"

"Hang on in there mate," Shepherd said. "I've found a midwife."

Janey looked up and smiled at Caroline.

"You?" she said gently.

Caroline nodded and returned her smile.

"I know I probably don't look much like a midwife but it's probably the only worthwhile thing I did in an otherwise much squandered and wasted youth. I did all my training and then ran off to pick oranges on a kibbutz in Israel."

Caroline rolled up her sleeves and knelt down beside the woman's legs.

"I think it's a breach," Janey told her. "It doesn't seem to want to come out."

"Can you kneel?" Caroline spoke to the woman lying on the floor.

She raised her head and nodded and her husband and Grendo helped her sit up and get on all fours.

"That's better," Caroline said. "That might just shift things along a bit. Now push."

"I can't," the woman wailed. "I can't."

"Oh yes you can," Caroline said firmly but gently. "What's your name?"

"Astrid," she said over her shoulder. "Astrid."

"Well Astrid I know you can do this. Come on. One big push. Deep breaths, that's it, count with me one two, one two. Good girl. Good girl."

Shepherd sat back on his heels. This was woman's domain and until now, the whole giving birth thing had remained a mystery to him and something he didn't want to think about too much. Out of the corner of his eye he registered that there was a drum kit in the barn and what a strange thing it was to have a drumkit in a barn but his thoughts were pierced with the woman's cries and it was hard to think about anything else.

"Shall we go for a walk?" he asked Grendo.

"Aye," Grendo said. "Let's leave it to the women. We'll go and wait on the road for the ambulance. If it wasn't for the queues out there, I'd put her in the van and take her to hospital myself."

"No you wouldn't," Caroline said. "The last thing this poor girl needs is to be carried back to the field, dumped in an old lorry and stuck in a traffic jam. Go and keep an eye out for the ambulance. We'll keep things under control here."

Shepherd looked at Caroline. Her face was set with concentration as she tended to Astrid. He hadn't seen this side of her before: Caroline steeped in determination, on her knees in jeans in straw. It was a completely new side to her.

She looked up for a moment, feeling his eyes on her and smiled at him.

"Haven't you seen a baby being born before?"

"No," Shepherd said, swallowing. "No I haven't."

Shepherd and Grendo hurried down the lane and across the travellers' field, past the straw palace and the painted sign at the entrance which said ***Brenda and John present… the time of your life!*** and on through the main festival field towards the entrance.

A stream of stationary cars and vans snaked down the road into the distance. Heat rising from bonnets created a mirage like effect in the air. Dogs with their tongues hanging out poked their heads through open car windows and music from car radios floated on the breeze. Children were being helped to pee in the ditches, men wandered around with their shirts off and one woman, with a garland of daisies crowning her fair hair, sat cross legged on the bonnet of a grey Morris Minor knitting with green wool. It was a hot summer afternoon and the world had come to a standstill.

"That ambulance will never get through that," Grendo said, shading his eyes from the sun as he looked at the line of vehicles. "That queue goes back miles."

Shepherd followed his gaze. What a day to give birth, he thought. What a day.

Chapter 47

It was one of the perks of being away from home, Commander Taylor reflected, as he lay back on the bed and the woman worked on his penis with her mouth. Carol would never do anything like this. In the twenty five years of their marriage she had never once given him a blow job. She had said it was unclean and unnatural and even washing himself three times in a frenzied lather of *Imperial Leather* on their wedding night couldn't change her mind.

He closed his eyes and surrendered to the feeling as he climaxed, pushing the girls head down and closing his eyes.

There was a knock at the door. Taylor's erection instantly shrivelled and he pushed the girl away.

"Get behind the curtain," he told her in a gruff whisper.

"Money," she said, holding out her hand.

"I'll pay you later," he whispered gruffly. "Just get behind the curtain will you?"

The girl rolled her eyes and slipped behind one of the long curtains framing the French windows. Taylor hurriedly pulled on his trousers and grabbed the Bible from the bedside table.

"Come in!" he called, opening the Bible.

A young fresh faced constable came into the room. He didn't look old enough to ride a bike let alone wear a police uniform.

"What is it?" he barked, trying to get his breathing back to normal.

"Sorry to bother you Sir," the downy faced young constable stuttered, holding his helmet flat against his chest. "Sergeant Peters asked me to drop this off. He said you wanted to see the paper as soon as it was published."

The constable stepped forward and held out the local newspaper.

Taylor dropped the Bible and snatched the paper, looking at the young constable over the top of the pages. The boy was smirking.

"Something amusing you constable?" he said. "Or has no one told you you shouldn't go around smirking at your superiors?"

The police constable flushed red and looked awkward.

"I'm sorry Sir," he said. "It's just that your flies are undone. Sir."

After the constable had left, the girl came out from behind the curtain.

"Take this and bugger off," Taylor said abruptly, holding out a handful of one pound notes. "And make sure no one sees you leave. And if anyone asks, you didn't come here to see me understand?"

"Charming," she said, chewing gum as she counted the money. "There's only three quid here. It's five for a blow job."

"Oh for fuck's sake…" Taylor said, glancing at the door. "Here you are," he said, thrusting two more pound notes at her. "Take it and piss off."

She stared at him with her head cocked to one side and then shrugged and left.

After she had gone, Taylor read the article on the front page of the paper. That should do it, he thought, when he had finished reading Johnson Jones's piece. That should make the locals aware of the subversive elements in their midst. And, he smiled to himself, resting the paper on his legs and gazing up at the ceiling, it should also provide enough background to justify what was coming next.

Chapter 48

By the time Grendo and Shepherd got back to the barn, it was all over. The baby, a little girl, had been impatient to get into the world and lay in her mother's arms wrapped up in the blue headscarf Astrid had, until very recently, worn tied around her hair.

"We've called her Bonnie," Astrid smiled as Grendo and Shepherd came into the barn. "Haven't we Peter?"

Astrid looked up at her husband and he smiled.

"We have," he said. "After my grandmother. She taught me everything I know."

Caroline sat back on her knees and looked up at Shepherd. Her blue eyes sparkled and her face was flushed rose pink.

"Looks like we won't need that ambulance after all," she said.

"Good job," Grendo said. "Because it ain't getting here any time soon. The queue for the festival goes back miles."

Astrid was lying on a bed of straw and she shifted a little as Janey rolled up towels and placed them under the small of her back to make her more comfortable.

"Why don't you come back to Ambrell and have a hot bath?" Caroline said.

Astrid's face lit up.

"A bath?" she said. "I haven't had a bath for years."

Janey took the baby as Peter helped Astrid to her feet.

"That's settled then," she said. "Can you walk?"

Astrid held on to Peter's arm and winced.

"Wait there," Caroline said. "I've got an idea."

Shepherd watched as Caroline hurried back towards the house. Music floated from the festival field and hammer blows rang out as the stage was given its finishing touches. He thought about Rose, wondering where she was and if, at that very moment, she might be on her way back, realising she'd acted in haste, realising she missed him, missed it all. She would have loved this festival. The lead up to it was almost as exciting as the festival itself and there was always something happening: like a baby being born in a barn for example. That was life on the road: it was never predictable.

He turned as a noise brought him back to the present and saw Sowcroft pushing a wheelbarrow with Caroline running along behind him.

"It's all we've got," she shouted as they got closer. "But it will get you to the house."

Astrid looked up at Peter who smiled reassurance down at her. They were an odd couple, Shepherd thought, he towering up there around six foot four, she somewhere below at around five foot four. He wondered whether the baby would meet them somewhere in the middle when she was all grown up.

Carefully they helped Astrid into the wheelbarrow where she sat with her knees drawn up to her chest. She probably weighed no more than eight stone, Shepherd thought. As light as a feather. Caroline held the baby.

"It might be a bit bumpy," she said. "But we'll be right beside you."

Sowcroft picked up the handles of the wheelbarrow and titled it forward. It wobbled a little and Astrid held on to the sides. And in that way, the unlikely birthing party left the barn and headed down the lane towards the house.

Chapter 49

How many dinner parties, kings and queens or rich and noble lords had sat around this table? Shepherd reflected as he looked around the room. It was the middle of the afternoon, a strange time for spaghetti Bolognese but in their world, you could have ice cream for breakfast and you didn't have to answer to anyone.

It was a big heavy table, probably made out of some endangered species of hardwood like mahogany or rosewood and it was, he guessed, at least two hundred years old with all the marks and scars of its life etched upon it.

Sowcroft had surprised them all by producing a huge dish of spaghetti Bolognese when they got back to the house with the baby and now they were all sitting back from the table, their bellies full with Grendo was telling the story of how the goats had eaten the tents at the Blue Moon festival.

Across the table, Caroline caught Shepherd's eye and smiled. Shepherd felt something turn over inside him and then felt a pang of guilt for Rose. The moment dissolved as Astrid came into the room with Bonnie in her arms. Astrid was dressed in a white shirt loaned to her by Caroline which fell to her knees and dwarfed her tiny figure.

"We're heading back to camp," she said. "That bath was heavenly. I can't remember when I last had a bath."

"Probably around 1978," Peter said, looping his arm around her shoulders. "It was before we got the van anyway."

"What van have you got?" Grendo said, half turning from the table, holding a piece of French bread in mid air.

"A 1973 converted ambulance," Peter said, the pride evident in his voice. "I did it up myself."

"We painted it bright orange didn't we?" Astrid said, turning her head and smiling up at her husband. "It's the most unambulance like colour we could think of."

"Aye I've seen it," Grendo said, nodding. "You did a good job on that."

"Thank you," Peter said, looking down at Astrid and smiling into her eyes.

Shepherd's heart turned. They way they were together was so simple, so gentle, he envied it and his thoughts turned once again to Rose. Had they ever been like that? So, so, so *together?* So *as one?* Would an outsider looking in have used those descriptions? He wasn't sure. He had, it seemed, spent a lot of time reassuring Rose about everything and whilst there had been quite a few laughs along the way, she was always so anxious, so *scared* of life. He pushed the thoughts away.

"That's the thing with the Convoy isn't it?" Grendo was saying. "Suddenly something happens and you meet people you've probably travelled with for years without even knowing it."

"Best thing we ever did wasn't it?" Truck looked at Astrid again. "Joining the Convoy."

She nodded enthusiastically.

"Yes," she said. "Yes it was. I love the life on the road. And she," she said, bowing her head to kiss Bonnie's warm flushed cheek. "She's going to love it too."

"We'll come back with you," Grendo said, pushing his chair back from the table and standing up. "Wood to chop, water to gather, that sort of thing."

Caroline had sat quietly throughout the exchange and now she stood up.

"Sowcroft can take you back if you need the wheelbarrow," she said. "Make sure you rest. No all night partying."

"Thank you," Astrid said. "Thank you so much for all you've done. We'll never forget it."

Caroline pushed her words away.

"Don't mention it," she said. "I quite enjoyed it actually. Made me realise what I might be missing."

She smiled and Shepherd watched her, unsure of the meaning in her words.

"In fact," she said. "I could do with a walk myself after all that spaghetti. I'll come back with you to the field."

Peter helped Astrid down the stairs and guided her by the elbow as she slowly walked out into the sunlight. Shepherd couldn't imagine what giving birth must do to the anatomy. It was something he didn't think want to think about too much.

Outside, Peter lifted her into the wheelbarrow as if she were nothing more than a feather pillow. Once more Shepherd's heart constricted at the care and attention they gave to each other. He was getting soft, he told himself abruptly. What was wrong with him this afternoon?

"All ready for the festival then?" Grendo asked Caroline as they walked towards the field with Sowcroft pushing the wheelbarrow out in front and Peter walking beside it.

"As ready as we'll ever be," Caroline said, snapping off a young sycamore branch and swishing it through the grass. "I can't believe it's only three days until Friday but everything seems to be ok. Once the structure's in place it tends to run itself. Or that's what the promoter says. Not that Bo's been around much lately. Still the main things are all ready and I'm thrilled with the palace."

Shepherd hung back a little, lost in the thoughts that had dogged him most of the afternoon. He was annoyed with himself that he had got so caught up in them instead of living for the moment and letting himself enjoy the strange turn of events that had unfolded just after breakfast. Instead it seemed his mind had been shrouded in mists and fog all day.

"You're quiet," Caroline said, dropping back to walk beside him as Grendo and Janey walked on in front.

"Am I?" Shepherd said, avoiding her gaze and looking straight ahead.

"What's her name?"

Shepherd turned to look at her.

"What's whose name?"

"The woman," Caroline said. "The woman who's been on your mind all afternoon."

"What makes you think it's a woman?"

Caroline shrugged and looked straight ahead.

"That look usually says it's a woman to me," she said. "People are strange aren't they?" she sighed, swishing her stick as they walked. "You think you know them and then they show a whole new side you didn't even know was there."

Shepherd didn't want to discuss Rose. It was too sensitive, too precious but nevertheless what Caroline had said was surprisingly intuitive. If someone had told him three, six, eight months ago that Rose would up and leave like she had, he would never have believed it.

"That's life I suppose," he said. "People come. People go. Easy come. Easy go."

Caroline darted a glance at him.

"And you?" she said. "Are you like that too?"

Shepherd stopped walking and turned to look at her.

"I don't mean to be rude or anything," he said. "But…"

"Ok," Caroline said, "I get it. I get it. Sorry. I didn't mean to pry."

Just then, their attention was drawn to blue lights flashing in the lane adjacent to the field. An ambulance was trying to get through the cars queuing on the lane.

"I'd better go and speak to them," Caroline said, smiling at him and walking on. "Explain what's happened."

And she walked away, trailing a cloud of perfume behind her, the sun shining in her blonde hair, leaving Shepherd with a whole colourful mix of feelings he didn't understand.

Chapter 50

Thursday 23rd August 1984

Lady Caroline took a last look around the field. It was only half past seven in the evening and the sun was sinking into the distant hills. The festival was officially open from tomorrow but that hadn't stopped the party goers arriving here for the past week. No one knew who she was and in her jeans and t-shirt, she could easily pass for one of them. A clown walked past her on stilts, two gigging naked girls ran into the trees and on the empty stage, a woman in a pink dress danced with her eyes closed to the recorded music playing through the speaker.

Sowcroft had declined to accompany her this evening but Munro, ever faithful, trotted along at her heels. It was fascinating to see how the other half lived, particularly across the border in the travellers' field where Grendo and Shepherd were camped out. Everywhere she walked she kept her eye out for her brother Tim. Would she recognise him now? Would he be that different after five years?

Caroline wandered through the travellers' field and out towards the lane. She would take the river path and walk back to Ambrell that way. All seemed in order and ready for the official opening tomorrow. She had no idea who *The Black Angels* were, one of the headline acts who were playing, but she was familiar with *The Damned.*

Caroline smiled at the painted board at the entrance to the travellers' field.

BRENDA AND JOHN PRESENT
THE TIME OF YOUR LIFE!

In front of it, two white poodles stood on their hind legs balancing balls on their noses.

"Is this Brenda and John?" she asked the girl sitting on the ground encouraging them with a stick held high in the air.

The girl smiled up at her.

"No," she said. "These are my dogs, Snow White and Grumpy.

Brenda and John are goats. White goats. They travel with us everywhere."

"In the vans and lorries?" Caroline asked, fascinated that goats would take to the road like that.

"They don't seem to mind," the girl said. "They've got their very own trailer."

Caroline watched the white poodles for a moment and then moved on. She walked past the tents with their chalked menus offering grass, hash cakes and mushroom tea. A man lay on his back, a straw hat covering his face and his ankles crossed. Children ran around chasing a gaggle of geese from one side of the field to the other and outside the trucks and benders and tents, groups gathered around camp fires which scented the air with woodsmoke.

Caroline felt like she was intruding but the Convoy fascinated her, this colourful troupe of people who had opted for life on the road and who seemed to be able to get right under the skin of their prime minister. Perhaps, she thought if Margaret Thatcher came to see them for herself, like this, on a late summer's evening, she might not be so against their way of life.

Caroline left the field and walked down the lane. In winter it was muddy and sometimes impassable but today, after the dry summer, the lane was dry and the first signs of autumn tinged the hedgerows. Twisting brambles heavy with black and red blackberries, drooping black elderberries, red hips and haws and hawthorn berries slowly turning from green to almost red.

Caroline turned left at the end of the lane and headed along the river bank. At first she thought the man was fishing but she could only see the back of his head. As she got closer she saw that he had heavy earphones clamped to his ears and was speaking into some sort of radio held on his lap. When he saw her, he gave an involuntary start, scrabbled to his feet and hurried away in the opposite direction. Odd she thought. Why would anyone be sitting down by the river when it was almost dark, talking on what appeared to be one of those Citizen Band radios?

Munro suddenly bolted and ran after something he had spotted further up the path. Caroline was distracted and hurried after him. Munro had a habit of jumping in the water and swimming to the other side and then refusing to come back. The last thing she wanted was for that to happen tonight. She planned to get an early night, maybe get a nice cold bottle of

Chablis up from Daddy's cellar and drink a few glasses before she turned in for the night.

Caroline hurried along the path, the man she had seen a few moments early all but forgotten.

Chapter 51

Friday August 24th 1984

Ravi held her hand as they pushed their way to the front of the crowd. When you were fifteen and only five feet tall, it wasn't an easy move to negotiate but Ravi, with his height and his way of smiling at everyone and politely excusing them as they got nearer the front, managed to execute it perfectly.

Ursula felt the crowd pushing behind her and held tightly to Ravi's hand as she looked up at the stage towering above her. Her stomach somersaulted at the electric anticipation that crackled through the air.

Suddenly there was a great surge forward and searchlights raked across the crowd as a mighty crash from the drums and cymbals announced the arrival of *The Damned.*

Ravi looked down at her and grinned as the first strains of *Love Song* reached her ears. Ursula felt the drum beat in her chest, as if it had hijacked her heart and invaded her soul. She had never heard anything like it.

Chapter 52

The public bar of The Anchor and Hope was crowded on a Friday night. A group of men in the public bar were playing darts and a fug of cigarette smoke hung in the air as they cheered at victories and shook their heads when the darts went off target.

The men stopped playing when Commander Taylor and Sergeant Appleby walked into the saloon bar.

"What will you have?" Taylor turned to Appleby, ignoring the quiet chill that had settled over the place.

"A pineapple juice please," Appleby said. "I'm a Methodist. I don't drink."

Taylor sighed. The last thing he wanted to do was have a drink with this namby pamby sergeant but he was trying to be civil to the local force. *Trying.* What sort of man drank *pineapple juice?*

A guffaw of laughter broke out in the public bar.

"Better put a cherry in that Roy," one of the darts players said, nodding at Appleby.

Taylor glared at the man.

"A pint of Watneys and a pineapple juice please landlord," he said firmly to the man behind the bar, ignoring the jibe.

"Watneys is off," the landlord said, his meaty hand resting on the silver beer pump.

"Oh," Taylor said. "What else do you have?"

"Nowt," the landlord said. "All the beer's off."

Taylor stared at the pints of lager sitting on the bar opposite him.

"It doesn't seem to be off in the public bar," he said.

"That's lager," the landlord said. "And that's off too. Nowt I can do about it."

"Do you have any bottled beer?"

"No," the landlord said. "The delivery didn't come."

Taylor felt the sweat breaking out under his armpits and soaking into his shirt. It was obvious they weren't welcome here and it irked him. All the police tried to do was protect the public, keep them safe, and they got treated like this.

"Come on Rosco," Appleby tried. "I got your boy's pushbike back for you last month didn't I?"

"That's different," the landlord said. "It don't mean we have to serve police."

Suddenly the door of the public bar opened and a gaggle of men in dark donkey jackets with yellow stickers bearing the legend COAL NOT DOLE stuck to their lapels, walked in. They were greeted with shouts and back slaps by the men in the public bar and coins started rattling into the collection tins they carried.

"Keep it up lads," one of them said. "We're right behind you."

The men nodded and exited the bar and then came into the saloon bar. They stopped and stared when they saw Taylor and Appleby.

"Ah," one of them said. "I doubt the boys in blue will contribute to our fund. Too busy trying to stop us getting out of Yorkshire. What's your favourite road block Robin?"

The man next to him placed his forefinger on his chin, assuming an air of deep concentration as he looked up at the ceiling.

"Let me think," he said. "It's got to the be t'one down by Flowers Roundabout. Got me nose broken down there. Or mebbe, mebbe it's t'one on main road. Kicked in the back there I were."

Taylor clenched his fists by his side. Miners. Dirty filthy miners. The sort who thought they could hold the country to ransom with their pay demands and picketing.

"We don't want any trouble boys," Appleby said. "We're just here for a drink."

"Aye a pineapple juice!" someone shouted from the public bar.

Taylor turned and glared at the man who had spoken. The man lifted his pint to his lips and drank slowly, his eyes locked with Taylor's.

"Come on," Taylor said. "It's obvious we're not welcome in here."

He picked up his raincoat from the bar stool and headed towards the door. As Appleby followed him, a hail of beer mats hit the wall.

"Bastards," Taylor said when they got outside. "How bloody dare they. All I wanted was a pint."

"Welcome to Yorkshire," Appleby sighed. "I'm afraid we're not the most popular people at the moment."

"It's not a question of being popular," Taylor said. "It's a question of respect. That's what they need to learn Appleby. That's what they need to learn."

Appleby shrugged.

"We can't stop people expressing themselves," he said. "It's a free country."

Taylor muttered under his breath and strode on. Miners. The Convoy. What was happening to the green and pleasant land of the England he loved so much?

They walked on to a children's playground. When the children saw them coming, they tore off up the road and when they had reached a safe distance, they stopped, turned around and shouted swear words at the police officers. Taylor walked across the asphalt and sat down on one of the swings.

"So," he said, as Appleby remained standing. "Have your men found anything?"

"They searched the site again today, as you requested Sir," Appleby said. "There's been no trouble. Nothing untoward. The atmosphere was friendly and our officers were treated politely."

"It's only the first day of the festival," Taylor said. "It's bound to kick off sooner or later. My intention was to head things off before they get critical Sergeant. You disappoint me."

Appleby swallowed.

"As far as the reports of weapons and prostitution are concerned," he said. "We didn't find any evidence."

"Did you search their vans?"

"No, no, we didn't. We had no reason to. No authority. My officers were there to observe and they kept a low profile. Sometimes a police presence can aggravate a situation, as you well know. I thought it the best approach."

"Did you not listen to anything I've been telling you? Are you prepared to give the green light to these, these *anarchists,* these *drug pushers?"*

Appleby stared at him.

"As I said Sir," he said. "We didn't see anything to cause concern or trigger the need for further action."

Taylor stared up at him. The scene in the pub had only reinforced his view of what was going on in Yorkshire. Inefficient, inadequate policing. No wonder they struggled to control the flying pickets, no wonder people were able to get away with murder at a festival. The provincial approach to policing irritated him. If you got a unit up here from London, one of his specialist units for example, they would have quashed the miners within the first few weeks. And now look at the mess it was in. They'd been on strike for five months, holding the country to ransom and stopping decent, honest men having a drink in the pub.

"My wife wondered whether you might like to come for dinner tomorrow night," Appleby said. "We're having a few other people from the force over. She does a very nice Beef Wellington."

Taylor stared down his nose at him.

"No thank you Appleby," he said. "I already have plans for tomorrow evening."

Chapter 53

Saturday August 25th 1984

Katie took one last look at herself in the mirror. She was wearing her Levi's 501s and the Van Morrison t-shirt Juliet had given her for Christmas because she wasn't sure what to wear to a festival. She had never been to one before.

Katie picked up her canvas rucksack and headed downstairs.

"All ready then love?" her dad called out as she came into the hall, his eyes glued to the Saturday afternoon horse racing on the television.

Katie came into the room and stopped next to the arm of his chair.

"You'll be alright won't you dad?"

"Alright?" he said. "Course I'll be alright love. Stop fussing. You're only going away for a few days. It'll be nice for you to spent the Bank Holiday with Juliet. I always liked Butlins. Aye. Me and your mum, we always liked Butlins."

He brought the can of Carling Black Label to his lips and drank, never taking his eyes from the television.

"There's Findus pancakes in the freezer compartment," Katie said. "And beans in the cupboard."

"Aye," he said. "I'll be alright love. Don't worry so much. I can look after meself perfectly well for a few nights although your mother never thought I could. And besides, you never know, she might be here when you get back."

He looked up at her and she could see hope shining in his eyes.

Katie smiled at him but her heart felt heavy.

"That would be nice wouldn't it?" she said, touching his arm.

Her dad grunted.

"Aye well. If she knows what's good for her she'll be back. T'grass isn't always greener you know."

Katie smiled at him. She felt like crying because since her mum had left, all he had done was drink beer and watch the horse racing and now she was about to deceive him by going to a festival. She wouldn't go, she told herself. She'd go back upstairs, put her rucksack down and go and meet Juliet by the river. Keep things normal. And then she thought of the festival. She'd been looking forward to it for weeks. And Van Morrison! She so wanted to see Van Morrison!

"Some of them boys from that posh school come up picket line yesterday," her dad said, his words breaking into her thoughts. "Chucking stuff at us and the like. Stew grabbed one of them by his tie and pushed him over hedge. I don't know who them kids think they are. Just because they pay for their education they think they're better than us. I tell you what love, there's many a thing you could do and I'd forgive you for it but bring one of them St. Clair's boys home and I'll send you packing faster than one of them horses could reach the finish line."

He gave a snort of laughter and raised his beer can to his lips.

Katie swallowed and hitched her bag over her shoulder.

"Best be off then," she said, leaning over to kiss his forehead. "See you on Monday."

"Aye pet. Go and have a good time. And no posh boys eh?"

Katie went into the kitchen and opened the cupboard. Inside were three cans of baked beans and a tin of mandarin oranges. Since the Miners' Strike had started in March, they were used to living on nothing or nothing and strange combinations, grateful for anything the food parcels provided. That was probably one of the reasons her mum had left six weeks ago, Katie thought. To find a place where there was food in the cupboards and men weren't on strike. Katie closed the cupboard and headed to the front door. She hesitated for a moment and then opened it and stepped out into the warm air of summer.

She was going to a festival. She was going to a festival!

Chapter 54

The Dog and Duck was empty on a Friday night. It was one of those dark old fashioned pubs from the 1950s with ceilings and walls stained yellow by years of cigarette smoking. His landlady at the guest house had recommended it.

"Quiet place," she had said. "No one goes in there much these days."

The landlady was probably the only friendly person around here, Taylor reflected. Even the shopkeepers in the village were surly and cold. He couldn't wait to get out of Yorkshire and get back to civilisation but first he had a job to do.

A woman in her sixties wearing a green housecoat sat behind the bar smoking a cigarette and doing a crossword.

"Two pints of Watney's please," he said, placing his raincoat on a bar stool.

She looked up at him but didn't move.

"You're not from round here," she said.

"No," Taylor said. "No I'm not. I'm a Betterwear salesman. Brushes and mops are my speciality."

She stared at him.

"You look more like a copper to me," she said.

"Well I'm not," he sighed. "One glass with a handle please. Can't stand those straight ones."

She slipped off her stool and reached up to the shelf above the bar and removed a dimpled glass with a handle.

"What's it like round here then?" he said, leaning his elbow on the bar and adopting a friendly manner.

She shrugged as she stuck the glass under the pump and pulled the handle.

"What d'you think it's like? Trouble and strife and all men out of work. You won't get many of yer brushes sold round 'ere. No one's got any money. Everyone's on strike."

"Doesn't seem to stop them going to the pub," he said.

"Well they don't come in here," she said, placing a full pint on the *Carling Black Label* beer towel placed on the bar. "My son in law's a miner but he won't strike. They bus him and a few others in to pit every morning. Get all sorts of trouble we do. Windows broken, car windscreen smashed. It's like a civil war it is. We had "scab" sprayed on the front door last week."

"Why do you put up with it?"

She put the second glass under the pump and shrugged.

"Nowt else we can do is there? Mind you if this carries on we won't be here much longer. No one drinks in here no more. And you know why? Because my son in law goes to work down pit."

She shook her head as she placed the second pint of beer on the mat. Taylor picked up the glass with the handle and sucked at the froth on the top. A pint of beer in a pub. At last.

"One pound forty four please love," she said.

Taylor put two pound notes down on the bar.

"Keep the change," he said.

Taylor carried the two pints of beer over to the corner and sat down at a round table covered in dog eared Babycham beer mats. To his right, a cloudy mirror hung on the wall in a heavy gilt frame and in the centre of the room was a cut glass chandelier that needed a good clean. Above his head was a framed photograph of the Queen on her silver wedding anniversary in 1977. The whole place was shabby and stuck in the past.

The door opened and an old man with a walking stick shuffled in. He glanced across at Taylor and continued to the end of the bar. The landlady took down a pewter tankard from the shelf and placed it under the Watney's pump.

"Alright then Alf?" she said as the old man eased himself on to a stool.

Taylor didn't pay him any more attention. He was an old man drowning his sorrows on a Friday night and had probably been propping up the bar for years.

Moments later, the door opened again and the man who came in this time looked straight at Taylor, caught his eye and walked across to join him.

"Thought you could do with a pint," Taylor said as he sat down opposite him. "It can't be much fun living in the middle of a hippy colony."

The man picked up his pint and drank, leaving a white moustache on his upper lip.

"Thanks," he said, when he had finished. "I needed that."

"So are we all set?" Taylor said, dispensing with the small talk.

The man took a packet of Rothmans from the pocket of his leather bomber jacket and offered them to Taylor. Taylor took one and leaned forward to catch the flame from the Zippo the man held out towards him.

"All ready," the other man said, placing a cigarette in his mouth. "All units on standby all the way up the M6. Operation Raymond is ready and waiting. Those hippy bastards won't know what's hit them."

Chapter 55

Rex wasn't sure what to wear to a festival. Music festivals weren't his sort of thing really but if Caroline was going to send her old butler to discharge a gun through the study window, he was going to have it out with her. He felt enormously hurt by her actions and the fact she'd sent that old man along to do her dirty work for her. Of course he knew why she'd done it. If she'd come in person to tell him their engagement was off, she wouldn't have been able to keep her nerve. She had never been able to resist him. All he had to do was run a finger along her spine or push his hand through her hair and she melted. He knew all the moves women loved. They didn't call him Homo Erexus in his London Club for nothing.

Rex knotted his cravat at his throat and winked at himself in the mirror.

"Oh," his mother said as he walked into the sitting room. "Are you going out? I had hoped we might play Bridge this evening. The Davises are coming over."

Rex smiled down at her. All women needed charming, even his mother.

"Not tonight mummy," he said. "I've got some important business to attend to. I'm afraid you'll have to entertain the Davises without me."

"I hope it doesn't concern Caroline," she said. "Nothing but trouble that one. You'd do well to leave her alone."

Rex rolled his eyes. It irritated him that she could read his thoughts so well and it irritated him that she knew his mission this evening concerned Caroline.

"Well," he sighed. "She's being a bit of a silly girl at the moment."

"What was all that noise I heard earlier?" his mother persisted. "I was trying to have a nap but it woke me up. Has someone been shooting in the field? I know it's open season for grouse but even so. It's a bit rich shooting so close to the house. The window in the study will need to be replaced."

"Nothing to worry about mummy darling," Rex said, dropping a kiss on the top of her head. "Just some local tomfoolery."

"I should say," she said, knitting furiously. "Have you upset someone Rex? I mean people don't usually fire guns through windows."

Rex sighed. Nothing escaped the old bird, not even when she was supposed to be upstairs having an afternoon nap.

"I'll deal with it mummy," he said, trying to keep the irritability out of his voice. "It's nothing to worry about."

"Is it the miners?" she said. "I've heard they're a rum lot."

"No," he said. "No it's not the miners and anyway, why would they fire a gun through the study window?"

"You tell me Rex," she said looking at him with her clear bird like eyes. "Lady Morgan caught two of them poaching deer on her land last week. We can't have that sort of behaviour around here Rex. If your father was alive he wouldn't stand for it. He had men flogged for less."

Rex bridled at the comparison to his dear departed father.

"Mummy Papa didn't have people flogged," he said. "You've got mixed up with your book again."

"No I haven't," she said. "I saw it with my own eyes."

Rex sighed. He didn't have time for her one of her rambling conversations this evening. They were always longwinded, challenging and exhausting. He felt sorry for her in a way because he knew she was lonely, rattling around this big old pile of a house and he had been away in France longer than she'd expected. But even so. He was thirty years old with his own life to lead and that didn't include babysitting his widowed mother.

"Will you be late?" she said. "I could leave out some tomato soup."

"I might not be back," he sighed. "It depends."

"On what mood the Lady Caroline's in, I suppose," she said, nodding at her knitting. "She always was a difficult girl. I remember when she was in that pony show and I didn't give her a blue rosette. She walked right up to me and demanded to know why."

"Oh mummy," Rex sighed. "She was only ten. And you should have given her the blue rosette, you know you should. She rode better than anyone else."

"Even so," his mother said. "I didn't want her to think that just because she was the daughter of an Earl she could just romp through life taking everything as if it was rightfully hers. Someone needed to make that clear to her. She was spoilt rotten, that's what she was. Spoilt rotten."

Rex sighed again.

"Look," he said. "I'd better be off. Don't wait up ok?"

"Do you want me to leave you a cheese sandwich?"

"No!" he said and then realised he'd more or less shouted at her. "I mean no," he said, in a more reasonable tone. "Thank you. I have no idea what time I'll be home."

Honestly Rex thought. Sometimes she treated him like he was still a teenager. It had been a source of great embarrassment to him that she'd insisted on waiting up for him when he was younger, particularly when he'd tried to bring girls home. And she was still doing it.

"Did you clean your teeth?" she asked.

Rex rolled his eyes at the portraits on the wall and strode out of the room into the hall.

"Drive carefully!" she called after him.

Rex got into his car and started up the engine. The sooner he got back into the real world the better. But for now, his dire financial situation forced him to be here and for the time being, he had little other option.

Chapter 56

Caroline leaned back on her elbows, enjoying the warmth of the sun on her face. She felt invisible lying in the festival field and she liked it. Here she wasn't Lady Caroline or the occupier of Ambrell Priory. Here she was just like any other festival goer: anonymous, lying on the grass in the sun on a Saturday evening letting the world float by.

Caroline had never heard of any of the bands who were lined up to play this evening but the one playing as she lay there with her eyes closed was perfect for the laid back, early evening atmosphere that floated over the fields. People wandered around without a care in the world, girls in floppy straw sunhats, boys in patched up jeans. A group of Tibetan monks in dark red robes walked past, ringing bells and chanting, blending with the hippies and the punks and the mix that Ambrell had drawn to its fields. This, she thought, was a real study of life and she had made it all happen. Caroline opened her eyes as a shadow blocked the setting sun.

Sowcroft was standing in front of her holding a gin and tonic on a silver tray.

"I thought you might be glad of some refreshment your ladyship," he said, lowering the tray.

Caroline smiled up him. Good old Sowcroft still in his butler's uniform despite the heat of the day. The festival goers probably thought he was in fancy dress. She'd seen all sorts today: a pink panther, a man dressed up as a yellow chicken, John Wayne, Elvis Presley. Anything seemed to go here.

"Thank you Sowcroft," she said, sitting up and lifting the drink from the tray. "Tell me, did you get that little business with Mr Rex sorted out?"

"I did m'lady," he nodded sombrely. "I called upon him this morning. I think we can safely say you'll have no more trouble in that department."

Caroline looked up at him.

"I hope you didn't' commit murder Sowcroft," she teased.

"Only attempted m'lady," he said. "Only attempted."

Caroline raised an eyebrow. She never knew whether Sowcroft was joking or not.

"And the ring?" she said.

"All taken care of m'lady. I think you'll find the household accounts a little healthier as a result."

"Will you stay?" she asked him. "I mean it doesn't seem fair that you're still working when I'm lying out in the sun and there's a festival going on."

Sowcroft looked around him as she gestured across the field with her hand.

"I'd rather stick pins in my eyes," he said. "If your ladyship will pardon the expression."

Caroline smiled at him.

"Please," she said, sipping at her drink. "Please don't do that."

"I have no intention of doing so," Sowcroft said. "It is just an expression. Will that be all m'lady?"

"Yes Sowcroft," Caroline smiled at him. "That will be all. And thank you. Thank you."

Sowcroft gave a little bow, turned and walked back across the field.

Caroline watched him go and then turned her eyes back to the stage to watch the lead singer. She had always liked wild unruly looking men, particularly when they were wearing tight leather trousers.

Chapter 57

Katie stood looking at the field in front of them. It was full of parked vans and lorries and men with long hair wandering around with fat cigarettes stuck to their lips. Bob Marley music blasted out from invisible speakers and she could smell fried onions and a sweet, heavy scent she didn't recognise.

"Cannabis," Hugo said. "Don't breathe in."

Hugo grabbed her hand and hurried her through the field past the trucks and camper vans and lorries and buses and tents and wigwams that had boards outside like menus. Her eyes widened as she read what was on offer. Surely these people weren't selling *drugs?*

"This is like the Bronx," Hugo muttered, as he pulled her along. "Trust Stevens to drop us off in the wrong field."

Katie wasn't sure what the Bronx was and tried to tear her eyes away from the sights all around her. They had to stop suddenly as two white geese came flying across their path cackling and flapping and two little children who weren't wearing any clothes, laughed and chased them. People wandered around in jeans or long floaty dresses and smoke rose from the tin chimneys perched on top of the vans and she stared in amazement at a huge structure hung with fairy lights which appeared to be made out of straw.

"Do people live in those vans?" she asked incredulously.

"How should I know?" Hugo said gruffly, struggling with their bags and a rolled up tent. "They're just dirty hippies, all of them."

Katie hurried along behind him. This wasn't how she'd imagined it. She didn't know what she had expected but it wasn't this. In fact none of the afternoon so far had been what she'd expected. She thought they'd arrive at the festival in the early afternoon but Hugo's friends, who had picked them up in the car, had different ideas and didn't seem in any hurry to take them to the festival. First of all they had stopped in a house where they all sat round the front room smoking a joint. Katie hadn't known what to do because she didn't take drugs and so she had perched awkwardly on the edge of an armchair and tried to make polite conversation with a boy who was convinced the world would end in precisely two weeks and thirteen days' time. She got lost in his long drawn out theory and tried to catch Hugo's eye but he was laughing and joking at the other end of the room and seemed unaware of her predicament.

After they'd left that house, they'd stopped at another one on the way only this time Katie had stayed in the back of the hot car, winding down the window to get some air and then as they finally got on the motorway, Hugo had fallen asleep, his head lolling heavily on her shoulder.

And now it was five o'clock and the day was nearly over. As they left the field, she glanced at the board propped up at the entrance.

"Brenda and John present… the time of your life!"

"Do you think they're the organisers?" she asked Hugo, running a little to catch up with him.

"Oh for God's sake," Hugo said irritably. "Stop asking questions will you?"

They entered the adjoining field and Katie saw the black pyramid stage for the first time. This was it! This was the festival! The field was scattered with tents and stalls and people sitting around on the grass listening to the music.

"Not much room to pitch our tent," Hugo grumbled as they picked their way through the bodies lying and sitting on the ground. A man on stilts wearing a clown costume stalked past them and placed a glittery bowler hat on Hugo's head. Katie laughed but Hugo snatched it off and threw it on the ground. He was pink in the face from the sun and Katie could sense he wasn't in the best of moods.

The only space they could find was at the far end of the field where Hugo slid the bags he was carrying from his shoulders and threw the tent on the ground where the metal tent pegs made a jangling sound inside their canvas bag. Katie stared at it.

"Come on," he said. "Let's get this up."

Katie had never put up a tent before. Years ago they had gone camping in Cleethorpes but she'd had nothing to do with the tent. Her dad had put it up while her mum got the camping gas out and made a cup of tea.

"Haven't you put up a tent before?" Hugo asked.

"No," she said. "Never."

Hugo crouched down and unrolled the tent.

"Where's the other one?" she said. "Perhaps I could start on that."

"There isn't another one," he snapped.

Katie swallowed.

"But you said…"

"Never mind what I said," Hugo said. "There's one tent ok?"

"But I thought…"

Hugo straightened and stared at her.

"Are you going to moan all evening?" he said. "Or are you going to help me?"

Katie slid her rucksack off her shoulder and crouched down. She didn't have a clue where to start but she thought that maybe if they laid it flat on the ground to start with they could see what they were faced with.

"Not like that!" Hugo snapped. "We need to get it upright!"

Katie decided it was best not to say anymore and let Hugo take the lead. After all it was his tent. How were two of them going to sleep in one tent? He'd promised there'd be two, promised they would sleep separately and she was a bit worried about that.

"You can always go home if you don't like it," Hugo said.

"No…" Katie said. "No it's fine. I'll help. Here."

It took them an hour to get the tent up and during that time, amused festival goers walked past and smiled at them. A couple of the men asked if they needed a hand but Hugo gruffly refused their offers of assistance although privately, Katie thought they might have got it done in half the time if he'd accepted.

Katie's stomach growled. She was starving.

"Shall I get us some food?" she said, hoping it might help to put him in a better mood. "I saw a van back there selling hot dogs."

"I'd rather have a beer," Hugo said, wiping his nose with the back of his hand and looking thoughtfully at a long metal pole.

"Ok," Katie said. "Shall I see what I can find?"

Hugo shrugged.

"Do what you want," he said.

Katie left him with the tent and meandered back through the festival field. Girls walked by with flowers in their hair and children rode on their fathers' shoulders. Babies slept in shaded prams and dogs ran around sniffing at the ground and lying in the sun. Katie took her place in the queue for the beer van and turned her head to look at the stage as she waited. Two men were standing at the front tuning up their guitars and suddenly there was a mighty roar from the crowd as the lead singer ran on stage wearing a silver spangled top. He had long hair and jeans and cowboy boots and as he grabbed the microphone the crowd went wild.

"Hello Ambrell!" he called in a rough wild voice. "Let's get this party rockin!"

Katie smiled. Despite the afternoon she had had, they were here now. She'd take Hugo his beer and then they could come here, sit on the grass in front of the stage and enjoy the evening. He was bound to be hot and tired after their journey but when he'd had a beer and some food, he would be in a much better mood, she was sure of it. The bass guitar and the drumbeat filled the air and she could feel it in the ground under her feet. This was going to be the best adventure ever. And tomorrow night, Van Morrison would be standing up there on stage. She could hardly wait.

Chapter 58

The sun sets earlier on late August evenings and lying on his back on the grass, Shepherd watched as it sank into the distant Yorkshire hills. If you lived in a house you wouldn't be so in tune with nature, he thought, you wouldn't notice when the sun went down or how it set a little earlier each day. Just that morning he had felt the chill of autumn in the air with its promise of the mists and frost to come.

Shepherd turned at a noise behind him and saw a man coming out of the trees and bushes which formed a border with the traveller's field. It was the miner who'd pointed the gun at him in the woods a few weeks back and who'd shared food with them by the fire.

"Hello John," he said as he came closer. "What brings you here?"

John stopped in front of him and scratched his head.

"You found Ambrell then," he said.

"Yes," Shepherd grinned. "Thanks to you. Your directions were spot on."

John narrowed his eyes and looked at the distant horizon.

"Grendo about is he?"

Shepherd got to his feet.

"He was chopping wood earlier," he said. "But he's probably back by now. Everything alright?"

John sighed.

"Something he ought to know about, that's all," he said.

Shepherd got to his feet, hearing the serious note in his voice.

I'll come with you," he said.

When they reached the Love Bus. Janey was sitting on the steps peeling potatoes with a washing up bowl clamped between her knees. She looked up and smiled when she saw them.

"Hello John," she said. "Come to see Steppenwolf have you?"

"Who or what is Steppenwolf?" John said.

Janey laughed.

"Only one of the biggest rock bands of all time," she said. "They're on stage tonight. Sit down, sit down," she said, gesturing to the chairs arranged around the fire. "We're going to eat when Grendo gets back. You're welcome to join us if you like. It's not much, just rabbit pie and potatoes."

"If I eat any more rabbit," John said. "I'll be hopping to the picket line. But that's kind, that's kind. Thank you."

John sat down by the fire and Shepherd went inside the Love Bus and came out with an opened bottle of beer which he handed to John.

"Ah cheers, ta," John said, taking the bottle.

"So," Janey said, coming to sit by the fire. "How are you getting on? With the strike? We don't hear much out here, just what comes through on the Citizens Band radio and there isn't much on there about the strike."

"Well," John said, sitting back in his chair and resting his beer on the arm as Shepherd sat down beside him. "We're still out. Still fighting. Still no sign of a national ballot."

Grendo arrived, a pile of wood balanced on his shoulder. He dropped it at the side of the Love Bus and nodded at John.

"Hello John," he said. "Good to see you again. We'd still be driving around looking for this place if it weren't for you."

John nodded.

"Pleased to hear it," he said. "Mind you I didn't know it were this big. You can hear the music from the main road."

"That's festivals for you," Grendo said, taking the beer Janey held out to him and sinking into a vacant chair by the fire. "Staying for some grub are you?"

"Aye," John said. "And very kind of you n'all. I didn't drop in to sponge off you mind. I've got some news."

"Oh?"

Grendo looked at him and slowly sipped his beer.

"It's the police," John said. "They're planning a raid."

Grendo lowered his bottle and stared at him.

"A raid?"

"Aye," John nodded. "There's this old boy called Alf. Drinks in t'pub in village. No one drinks there no more because the son in law's a Scab. Alf's alright though, decent sort of bloke. Injured in a mining accident in '78 he were so we just turn a blind eye to where he drinks. He were in pub last night and heard two coppers talking about a raid."

Grendo exchanged a look with Janey.

"I thought they'd been a bit quiet," he said.

"There's been a few of them walking around the site," Shepherd said. "Seemed alright to me."

"Ah but it en't the local coppers you got to watch is it," John said, tapping the side of his nose. "Same with us. The local coppers weren't involved with Orgreave oh no. They sent the big guns in, the riot police, their so called specialist units. That's why there weren't no shoulder numbers. That's why all their statements were made up. They didn't know the area so someone told them what to write. Funny how all their statements were the same. It'll all come out one day, it'll all come out one day."

"Riot police?" Janey said. "They sent in riot police? To Orgreave?"

"Aye and the rest," John said. "Reckon there was army boys there too. It's the same on t'picket lines. You can hear it in their voices. Ain't no Yorkshire in 'em."

Grendo was quiet for a moment.

"Did he hear any more? This Alf bloke?"

John shook his head.

"No," he said. "But we thought we ought to warn you. They're planning something you mark my words."

"It doesn't surprise me," Grendo said. "They've been following the Convoy for months."

"Aye well," John sighed. "Anyone who dares to stick their heads above the parapet gets shot down by this government. It's that Thatcher woman, that's what it is. She's behind it all she is. All of it."

Chapter 59

Katie felt light hearted as she meandered back through the crowd of festival goers balancing a pint of beer in one hand and an orange juice in the other. It had taken quite a long time to get to the front of the queue at the refreshments van and she'd been gone for about forty minutes.

Katie reached the tent. It was up and tethered by guy ropes but there was no sign of Hugo.

"Hugo?" she called, ducking down under the trees to look behind it. "Hugo?"

When he didn't appear, she sat down on the grass in front of the tent. He had probably just gone to the loo. She'd seen the queues. He would have to wait quite some time.

Katie placed the pint glass on the grass and sipped at her orange juice. So this was a festival! She could hardly believe she was here and a part of it all. She couldn't wait to tell Juliet all about it.

Time ticked on. She could hear the music from the stage but she couldn't see the band that was playing. She was itching to get up and go nearer but was reluctant to go on her own.

Katie's eyes scanned the people who walked past as she waited for Hugo to come back. She began to feel a little panicky at being on her own and a little frustrated that she was at a festival but not taking part in it. She also needed a pee but didn't want to leave their things unattended.

She would wait. He'd be back soon.

Chapter 60

It was like being let loose in a sweet shop, Rex thought, downing his third pint of cider under the setting sun. All these pretty half dressed girls! His eyes had nearly popped out of his head when one of them had walked past him topless and there were more wearing next to nothing. He didn't know where to look there was so much eye candy.

He hadn't found Caroline yet but there was no rush. He was enjoying himself meandering from one cider stall to the next, trying Somerset's Finest, Dog Chuck Black (infused with honey) and Old Lame Fox and chatting amicably to random festival goers. Everyone seemed very friendly and whilst rock music wasn't really his thing, he had to admit that he quite liked what went with it.

Rex spotted Sowcroft hurrying across the field in his black butler's uniform. He almost laughed. It was a warm summer evening and there was the old fool shuffling along with a silver tray like he was at Henley Regatta. Didn't he ever take that thing off? Didn't he ever lounge around in jeans and a t-shirt?

Rex hurried over to him and blocked his path.

"I suppose you think your little display yesterday was funny?"

Sowcroft stopped. Rex hated the way he looked at him, like he was some sort of dog muck on the sole of his shoe. It irritated him no end and he should give him, as a Right Honourable, far more respect. After all, he was only a common or garden butler.

"On the contrary," Sowcroft said looking him straight in the eye. "I rarely find things amusing."

"You can't just go round firing shotguns through people's windows!" Rex said, keeping his voice down but nonetheless conveying his annoyance through it. "Mummy was terrified!"

Sowcroft's expression remained unchanged.

"I was merely discharging my lady's orders."

"With a gun?" Rex said. "Oh come on man. This is 1984 not 1894.

You'll be challenging me to a duel next. Not that you could of course, with your status."

Sowcroft continued to hold his nose – and the tray – in the air.

"Will that be all Mr Rex?" he said.

"For now," Rex said. "Where is she anyway? Caroline?"

"Where I last left her I imagine," Sowcroft said non committally. "I didn't realise she'd invited you."

"She didn't," he said. "I came of my own volition. Anyone can come to a festival Sowcroft. You don't need to be invited. Show me where she is will you?"

For the first time Sowcroft's expression changed and his eyes flashed.

"I don't believe m'lady wishes to see you," he said. "I thought I'd conveyed her wishes quite clearly yesterday."

"By firing a shot gun through the window of my study? Oh come on man!"

"And you Mr Rex, if I remember rightly, told me I was an 18th century relic and should go forth and multiply, to paraphrase."

"There was no need to fire a gun!"

"And there was no need to close the front door in my face," Sowcroft said. "Now if you'll excuse me…"

Rex grabbed hold of his elbow.

"Where is she?" he said, his fingers biting into Sowcroft's bony arm.

Sowcroft raised his elbow and shook him off.

"She doesn't want to see you," he said. "Please don't make a scene."

Rex let go of his arm.

"Very well," he said. "I'll find her myself."

Sowcroft stared at him.

"You may regret that," he said.

Rex watched as Sowcroft hurried across the field with his silver tray. Cantankerous old bugger, he thought. How dare he speak to him like that! How dare he come round and tell him that the engagement was off! How dare he fire a shotgun through the study window! Why couldn't she have told him herself? Why did she have to send her butler? They could have talked it through but oh no. She sent her butler instead. She was a coward, that's what she was, a coward who couldn't be trusted. And he had got engaged to her! She wasn't the sort of woman he should care about, let alone the sort he should marry. He'd had a lucky escape, that's what mummy said anyway. Yes, a lucky escape! On the other hand he did love her. Yes he loved her!

Rex swayed a little on his feet as his thoughts ran one way and then another, torn between a feeling of anger at the way she'd treated him and sorrow that she had, in effect, dumped him. Rex felt wronged and rejected, angry and released, all at the same time.

He stumbled towards another cider tent. He would have another drink and then he'd have it out with her. Yes, that's what he'd do. He'd have it out with her once and for all.

Chapter 61

In the festival field, flaming torches blazed against the night, lanterns glowed outside tents making silhouettes of those inside, large spotlights shone down from the stage on to the dancing, singing crowd who waved their arms in the air and surrendered to the rock music. Katie wished she was in the crowd with them. She was at a festival and she hadn't even danced yet! She'd been sitting outside the tent for two hours waiting for Hugo to appear. The sun had gone down and still there was no sign of him. Worse, her bladder felt like it was about to burst.

Katie got to her feet. She would have to use the loo. She would also see if she could find Hugo and then she could relax and start to enjoy herself.

Katie walked towards the stage.

"Do you know where the toilets are?" she asked a woman with a baby strapped to her chest.

The woman pointed over to the corner.

"There's portaloos over there," she said. "Bit of a mess though," she said, making a face.

Katie thanked her and retraced her steps to the darker corner of the field. She could smell the toilets before she reached them but there was nothing for it. Her bladder was ruling her brain right and she had never felt so uncomfortable in her life.

"Hold your nose and go for it!" a woman said, coming out of one of the doors. "And try not to stand on the floor. It's covered in piss."

Katie went in and shut her eyes. The woman was right: it stunk.

"Is there a basin?" she asked a girl as she left the cubicle. "To wash your hands?"

"Basin?" the girl laughed. "Where do you think you are love? The Ritz?"

Katie flushed red in the darkness.

"No… I… sorry…" she said. "I just thought…"

Just then, she felt a hand on her shoulder and she turned around.

Hugo was standing there, swaying slightly on his feet.

"There you are darling," he said, his eyes glazed, his breath drenched in alcohol. "I've been looking for you everywhere."

Katie felt a great wave of relief wash through her.

"Sorry," she said. "I just came to use the toilet."

Hugo slung his arm around her shoulders. His hand was so low it rested on her breast. Katie wondered whether she ought to say something but decided against it. She felt so relieved at having found him, at not being alone anymore.

"Shall we go and dance?" she said.

Hugo stopped and turned towards her.

"Dance?" he said, pushing his hands up under her t-shirt and cupping both her breasts in his hands. "Who wants to dance when I've got tits to play with?"

He leaned forward and started kissing her neck. Katie stood frozen to the spot not sure what to do. This wasn't what a boy should do on a first date. There were rules.

"Hugo…" she said, as his breathing got heavier. "Hugo I'm not sure you should be doing that."

"Relax darling," he said, his breath warm against her neck as he started to nibble her ear. "This is what you wanted isn't it? You've been giving me the come on all day."

"Have I?" Katie said, feeling a little alarmed. "I didn't mean to. No Hugo… Hugo…"

She pushed him away and he stood back and stared at her in surprise. His eyes were glazed and a cold expression crossed his face.

"You little prick tease," he said, staggering backwards. "You little bitch."

And then he turned and stomped away towards the stage.

Katie hurried after him.

"No wait..." she said pulling at his arm. "Please. Hugo."

He shook her off but she kept following him and Katie felt panic rising up inside her.

"I'm sorry," she said, catching his hand. "Let's go back to the tent. You can do it there if you want..."

Hugo stopped and turned, a slow smile spreading across his face.

"That's better," he said, grabbing her wrist and pulling her roughly into him. "That's better."

Chapter 62

Wretched people lying around all over the place! Rex thought as he staggered through the field and tripped over another body. Why couldn't they stand up like normal people?

"Oy watch where you're going mate!" someone called after him.

Rex muttered under his breath and hurried on without apology. His legs seemed to have a momentum all of their own and he wondered if this was why people came to festivals because their legs took over their minds. The thought struck him as hilariously funny, the insight startling, and he laughed to himself, didn't see the guy rope, tripped and fell head first on to the ground.

Rex wasn't sure how long he'd been lying there but he quite liked it, really he did with the sky spinning up above his head and the stars… oh the stars… they were moving like they'd never moved before. Perhaps he was witnessing something momentous, some great meeting of the planets or maybe even the end of the world. Rex got to his feet again except he wasn't able to fully stand and adopted a sort of half crouched gait as he bounced from one tent to another and from one object to another. And then he came up against an object that was warm and soft and didn't yield.

"Rex," a vaguely familiar woman's voice said. "You're drunk."

He narrowed his eyes and looked up trying to focus on who was speaking to him. He knew the voice but he couldn't place it. Her name was on the tip of his tongue but it kept evading him. And then he remembered.

"Caroline," he slurred. "Darling."

"Go home Rex," she said. "You've had far too much to drink and you're making a spectacle of yourself."

Rex swayed on his feet.

"Who are you telling me to go home," he slurred. "Lady Muck. Yes that's what you are," he said, pointing a finger at her double vision. "Lady Muck."

"Rex," she said. "Please. You're making a fool of yourself. You've already trashed two tents and people aren't very happy with you."

"Oh piss off," Rex said. "Who do you think you're talking to? I'm a rye hon… rye honrable you know… you ought to… well. Yes. You should."

Caroline caught his arm to stop him falling over. People were staring at them and shaking their heads. Rex had just come through a gauntlet of tents crashing into them and trashing their possessions. They didn't look particularly happy. Where was Sowcroft when she needed him?

Rex swayed on his feet, his eyes half closed.

"I'm at a feshival," he said. "And I'm enjoying myself. What are you going to do about it? Get your butler to shoot me?"

Caroline sighed. She couldn't handle Rex when he was like this.

"I'd push him in the river if I was you," a man said walking past hand in hand with his girlfriend.

"Disgusting," the girl said, making a disapproving face as she looked at Rex. "Disgusting."

Chapter 63

After John had left, Shepherd wandered over to the festival field. So they were planning a raid of the camp. Didn't the pigs have enough to deal with round here without looking for trouble that didn't exist?

"Don't you believe it," Grendo had said. "Don't you remember that helicopter that followed us for two miles when we left Birmingham? We'll post some lookouts tonight to keep an eye on things. Those bastards don't play fair. Best to remain vigilant."

Shepherd volunteered to be part of the Watch Party and Grendo slid the machete they used on long grass out from under his bed.

"Just in case like," Grendo said. "No one's going to come near you if you've got a machete at your feet."

Shepherd wandered towards the festival field. It was ironic, he thought, that just one field away, people tried on the life of living under the stars, emulating the life the Convoy lived and yet when you lived it for real, the forces of law and order tried to stop you.

Shepherd stopped in his tracks and stilled his thoughts. He could see a man and a woman arguing. She was trying to push him away and he was swaying on his feet and pointing his finger in her face in an aggressive manner. He thought it looked a little like Caroline but in the dark it was hard to tell. Shepherd moved forward to take a better look and at that moment the man lost his balance and fell forward taking the woman down with him.

Shepherd hurried over. He could see it was Caroline now although he had no idea who the drunk man was. She was lying underneath him and thumping him on the back and shouting at him to get off while he had both of his hands pinned to the ground on either side of her shoulders. Shepherd stepped forward and hauled the man up by the back of his leather jacket.

"What the fuck's going on man?" he said.

The man hung there panting like a dog in a harness as Caroline sat up and shuffled backwards and out from under him.

"Thank you," she said. "I thought I was going to suffocate from alcoholic fumes."

"Are you ok?" he said.

She nodded, lifting up her hair and letting it drop back on her shoulders.

"I'll live," she said.

"She's trouble…" the man slurred as Shepherd held him by the jacket. "I tell you… I tell you you don't want to go near her… she's a viper… yes… a viper…"

"Want me to get rid of him?"

Caroline looked up at Shepherd. In the light from the lanterns and torches, her eyes were wide and liquid.

"He's very drunk," she said. "My ex," she added by way of explanation.

Just then, two of the Hells Angels who were unofficially employed as security guards came forward.

"Come on mate," one of them said, lifting one of Rex's arms up and hooking it around his shoulder as the one on the other side did the same thing. "Party's over."

Shepherd watched as they walked away with Rex between them, dragging his toes across the ground.

"Thank you," Caroline said. "I'm afraid he's a bit of a nightmare when he starts drinking."

Caroline tried to get to her feet but her legs buckled and she crumpled back down on the ground.

"What is it?" Shepherd said, looking down at her with concern in his eyes.

Caroline made a face.

"I'm not sure," she said. "My ankle doesn't feel quite right."

Shepherd crouched down beside her and felt her right ankle with his hands.

"Might have a break there," he said.

Caroline bent her knee and gazed at her ankle.

"He did land on it with a bit of a thump," she said. "I hadn't appreciated how heavy drunk men are."

"What are you doing with a man like that?" Shepherd said.

"I'm not with him anymore," she said. "That's why he's so drunk. I broke off our engagement and he's not happy about it. I'm not sure what he expected when he's spent most of the time in bed with other women."

Shepherd raised her arm and hooked it around his shoulder.

"Best off without him then," he said. "Can you walk?"

"I'll try," she said as Shepherd helped her up. "Oh bother," she added. "I was having such a lovely time."

Shepherd took her weight, holding her arm around his shoulder and Caroline hopped along beside him, her injured leg bent at the knee. People moved out of their way casting sympathetic smiles at her in the light of the blazing torches and on stage, Steppenwolf kicked up a storm.

"Just hold on," Shepherd shouted above the music as they passed in front of the stage.

"This isn't any good," Shepherd shouted after a while. "We won't get to the house until morning at this rate."

He bent down and placing one arm under her legs, bounced her up into his arms. Caroline looked up into his face with surprise.

"You're much stronger than you look," she smiled.

"And you're much heavier," he grinned.

Shepherd carried her out of the field and down the lane, as behind them the music and lights of the festival faded.

"I'm sorry to be such a nuisance," she said. "I'm sure it's nothing to worry about. Just a sprain or something."

"You've got a bloody nose too," he said. "Right mess."

Caroline wiped at her nose and looked at her hand.

"Who would have thought a drunken idiot could cause so much chaos," she said.

As if he had a sixth sense, Sowcroft came hurrying across the back lawn as they came through the gate, his dark figure cutting a silhouette against the backdrop of trees and bushes.

"My lady!" he exclaimed as he got closer. "Are you unwell?"

"She had a little fall," Shepherd said. "Her lump of an ex boyfriend fell on her."

Sowcroft's face darkened.

"Mr Rex?"

"If that's what you call him, yes," Shepherd said. "Personally I'd call him something else."

"He was drunk," Caroline sighed. "You know how he gets."

"Do we need medical assistance?" Sowcroft said, his face a mask of concern as he trotted along beside them. Shepherd smiled. Sowcroft was oh so 19th century.

"Let's get her inside first," Shepherd said. "What's the best way?"

Sowcroft stepped forward raising his arm and pointing ahead.

"This way Mr er…"

"Shepherd," Shepherd said. "No mister."

"This way Mr Shepherd," Sowcroft said, hurrying towards the side door which led to the kitchens. "I'll go on ahead."

Shepherd carried Caroline into the kitchen where just last week, they had all sat round the table eating Sowcroft's surprisingly good spaghetti Bolognese.

Shepherd leaned forward and carefully deposited Caroline onto one of the kitchen chairs and pulled out another one. Carefully he raised her injured ankle and placed it on the edge. Caroline winced and Sowcroft wrung his hands.

"Might a brandy be in order m'lady?"

Caroline looked up at him and smiled.

"What a bloody good idea Sowcroft," she said. "What a bloody good idea."

Chapter 64

Hugo led Katie back to the tent. At the entrance, he tripped over the guy ropes and swore and then pushed her inside ahead of him. Katie thought about trying to run away but in the next moment he pushed her down on to the sleeping bag. Katie screwed her eyes tightly shut and lay very still as she waited for whatever was to come. Hugo fumbled with the zip on her jeans and tugged them, with her brand new pants, down to her thighs. Katie held her breath like she'd done once with Juliet when they'd hid under the bed at her house and didn't want to be found. She tried to move her head away from his slobbering kisses and the fumes from the alcohol he'd drunk. Her whole body tensed as he wrestled with his trousers but she kept her eyes shut because she didn't want to see, she didn't want to see. Katie felt like crying. This wasn't how she'd imagined the weekend at all. She had thought it would be romantic to stay in a tent; romantic to stay away at a festival with Hugo. Katie tensed, bit her lip and prepared herself for the worst.

When nothing happened, Katie opened her eyes and lifted up her head. Hugo's full weight was on top of her and he was snoring. Katie tried to shuffle out from under him. He let out a louder snore and Katie knew with relief that he was fast asleep, fast asleep with his trousers round his ankles and his arms above his head. Katie managed to roll out from under him and held her breath in case he should wake up. Hugo muttered but kept his eyes closed and then turned his face into the pillow. Katie breathed a sigh of relief and scuttled as far over to the side of the tent as she could. She thought about going home but she didn't know the way and it was dark.

Katie pulled up her jeans and curled up into a ball at the side of the tent with her back to him.

She lay awake for the rest of the night.

Chapter 65

"No, I absolutely will not go to the hospital," Caroline repeated. "If you just bandage it up I'm sure it will be fine. There's a festival going on out there, I can't just leave in the middle of it."

The paramedic exchanged a glance with Shepherd over her head.

"I don't think it's broken," he said. "But she should avoid putting weight on it for the next few days."

"No dancing then?" Caroline said with a rueful smile.

"No dancing," he said, packing up his bag.

"There's some crutches in the stable," Sowcroft said. "The Earl had them when he fell down a fox hole. He always meant to return them but somehow he never did. Would you like me to fetch them for you m'lad?."

"If you must," Caroline sighed.

It was the last thing she needed during the festival, being half immobilised with so much to do. "And on your way back Sowcroft fetch another bottle of brandy would you?"

Sowcroft nodded.

"Of course m'lady," he said as he left the room. "Medicinal purposes of course," he added, looking at the paramedic.

The paramedic zipped up his bag.

"Keep your foot up and place some ice on it," he said. "Sprains can take a while to heal."

"Thank you," Caroline said. "I'm sorry to call you all the way out here in the middle of the night."

"It's hardly the middle of the night," he said. "Just gone eleven by my watch."

Shepherd saw him to the door with Munro trotting along behind him.

"Make sure she rests," the paramedic said before he left.

Shepherd nodded.

"I'll try," he said. "I'll try."

Shepherd went back into the kitchen where Caroline's leg was outstretched on the chair in front of her.

"I'd best be getting back," he said. "I'm taking the watch party tonight."

"Watch party?" she repeated.

"We had a visit earlier," he said. "From some locals. They said the police are planning a raid."

"Are they now," Lady Caroline said thoughtfully, reaching for the glass of brandy on the side table. "And why would they be planning a raid on *my* property?"

Shepherd shrugged.

"Because we're the Peace Convoy," he said. "Which makes us public enemy number one. After the miners and Arthur Scargill of course."

"Perhaps I should have invited Mr Scargill," Caroline smiled. "I'm sure that would have gone down a storm. Won't you stay for a brandy?" she said. "Sowcroft won't be long and it's not that late. Surely watch parties come into their own in the early hours, not at eleven o'clock at night."

Shepherd hesitated. He knew he should get back but equally he quite liked the thought of a brandy.

"You must think I court trouble wherever I go," she smiled up at him. "I mean first I walk in on you stark bloody naked, then the house goes on fire and now this."

Shepherd smiled.

"It's certainly been an interesting couple of weeks," he said.

Sowcroft clattered into the room holding a bottle of brandy and a pair of wooden crutches. Shepherd rushed over to help him before he dropped the lot.

"Thank you young man," he said. "Quite a strange combination isn't it? Courvoisier and crutches."

Shepherd took the crutches over to Caroline as Munro sat back on his haunches and watched with his bright, alert eyes.

"Do you want to have a practise?" he said. "Or are you planning to sleep in the kitchen?"

Caroline scraped her chair back on the stone floor. Shepherd handed one of the crutches to her and she put it under her arm.

"I have no idea how to use these bloody things," she said as she put the second one under her other arm. Shepherd went to her side.

"Just take your time," he said. "Concentrate on getting on your feet first and then find your balance."

Caroline pushed forward and raised herself upright bending her knee behind her.

"That's it," Shepherd said, holding her elbow. "Now try walking."

Caroline raised her head.

"You can go Sowcroft if you wish," she said, looking up at the butler. "Don't spend the whole night dancing will you?"

Sowcroft allowed himself a rare smile.

"On the contrary m'lady," he said. "I haven't attempted the foxtrot since 1947. Are you sure that will be all?"

"Yes," Caroline said. "Shepherd is going to stay a while and after that I'll be going to bed. If I can get up the stairs," she added.

"I could make up a bed in the Orangery," Sowcroft suggested.

"Oh I'll just sleep on the couch," Caroline said. "No need to make a fuss."

"As you wish m'lady," Sowcroft said, bowing and leaving the room.

"Does he ever leave the 19th century?" Shepherd asked after he'd left.

Caroline was staring down at her feet and trying to move the crutches forward.

"Only on Sundays," she said. "And not for long."

Shepherd smiled as he watched Caroline trying to get the hang of the crutches. Her long blonde hair fell forward across her face as she stared intently at her feet.

"This is such a nuisance," she said, raising her head and looking at him with her clear blue eyes. "I'll never get the hang of this."

"Yes you will," Shepherd said. "Be patient," he said. "Be patient."

Chapter 66

Shepherd wandered along the first floor landing, opening doors and peering into the bedrooms behind them. A quiet hush hung over the empty old house and he wondered about all the people who had walked these corridors, slept in these rooms; the births, marriages and deaths these walls had witnessed. In every room, the curtains were closed and the furniture was shrouded in dust sheets. It was like wandering through a museum, he thought, except the exhibits were hidden.

It was the bathroom that took his breath away. Rose would have loved it. It had a stand alone bath with claw feet and it was positioned so that the occupant could look out of the window. Shepherd couldn't see much because it was dark but his reflection stared back at him. A tall thin shaggy looking man standing in an opulent bathroom. The contrast was striking.

Shepherd tried to remember the last time he'd had a bath; the last time he'd stretched out in warm water and he couldn't. Soaking in baths was part of the world he'd left behind and the only washes he had these days were make shift showers under carrier bags filled with water or in rivers and streams. There was no soap, no indulgence, just a wash.

A noise in the doorway startled him and he turned.

"Are you casing the joint?"

Caroline stood there smiling, leaning on her crutches.

"I thought I'd have a trial run," she said. "The stairs aren't that difficult if you go up backwards on your bum."

Shepherd felt himself flush red for being in her bathroom, for being in a place he had no right to be.

"I was trying to think when I last had a bath," he said as if to explain himself.

Caroline tilted her head and watched him from the doorway.

"Oh?" she said. "And when was that do you think?"

"I can't remember," he said, turning away. "I can't remember."

Caroline hopped into the room.

"This was my favourite room when I was a child," she said looking around her. "I used to sit in that bath with bubbles up to my chin. It was my sanctuary, the place I came to to escape the madness."

"Madness?" Shepherd said. "What possible madness could you have known living in a place like this?"

"Oh," Caroline said airily. "There's madness everywhere if you look closely enough. Even in houses like this. It might look all grand and splendid from the outside but there's always undercurrents. Always."

Shepherd turned and saw something in her eyes he couldn't read.

"Anyway," she said more lightly, shrugging it away. "How long is it? Since you had a bath?"

"Probably five years," he said.

Caroline stared at him.

"*Five years?*" she repeated. "Was that when you joined the Convoy?"

"No," Shepherd said. "That was three years ago. Before that we lived in a flat, me and Rose… on the seafront… in Hartlepool. Rose… my girlfriend… we had a bath in the flat but the heater never worked so we used it for storage."

Caroline stared at him.

"And where's Rose now?" she said.

Shepherd turned his head and looked out of the window.

"She left," he said. "She didn't want this life anymore."

Caroline moved forward and placed a gentle hand on his forearm.

"Would you like one?" she said. "A bath?"

Shepherd turned. She was so close to him, so close he could smell that exotic perfume she always wore. He didn't know its name but it made him think of far away places; places with lemon trees and sparkling blue seas; places he had never seen.

"I miss her," Shepherd said, his eyes still fixed on the dark world outside the window. "Rose. I miss her."

Caroline nodded.

"I know," she said. "I can see it on your face every day. I knew there was someone, somewhere. I knew there was a shadow."

Shepherd looked at her. He could see the flecks of gold in her irises, the bridge of tiny freckles running across her nose.

"And you?" he said. "Is there a shadow in your life? What about that man who fell on top of you?"

"Oh Rex," Caroline sighed, looking up at the ceiling. "The less said about him the better. He's more of a nemesis than a shadow."

Shepherd got stuck on the word.

"What's a nemesis?"

"Something sinister that stalks you wherever you go," she said. "I was engaged to him for two years. And then I caught him in *flagrante delecto*."

"Oh," Shepherd said. "Is that abroad?"

"No," Caroline said. "Sorry. I should use proper English. It means I caught him with another woman. On top of the coats. In the spare room at a party."

"Wow," Shepherd said. "That must have been tough."

They stood there for a moment in the dim light, looking at each other.

"Come on," Caroline said, breaking the spell as she turned away and hobbled off on her crutches. "I'll get you a towel and you can have a bath. Baths are good for soaking away shadows. I've got some Badedas bubble bath somewhere. It makes magical things happen or so the advert says."

"It won't make me smell like a pansy will it?" Shepherd said looking concerned for a moment.

"Probably," she grinned, turning back to smile at him. "Probably."

Chapter 67

It was after midnight when Shepherd returned to the camp. He knew it was ridiculous but he felt lighter after the bath, as if it had washed away some demons as well as cleaning his physical body. He smelt fresh and light too although he didn't particularly want anyone at the camp to realise he'd been soaking in scented bubble bath for the last half an hour.

He found Grendo sitting in his chair by the fire, stoking it up with a new spear. The twigs crackled and hissed and the flames shot up into the dark sky.

"You smell like a pansy," Grendo said as he came close. "Got something to tell us?"

Shepherd grinned.

"I had a bath," he said. "At the big house."

Grendo raised an enquiring eyebrow.

"On my own," Shepherd added hastily. "Perfectly legit."

Grendo smiled.

"What you do is your business," he said. "I can't remember when I last had a bath."

"Nor could I," Shepherd said. "That's why I had one."

He could still feel the warm silky lap of the water, the smell of Caroline's exotic bubble bath, the steam rising up to the ceiling, the bubbles of foam crackling and popping around him.

"We've got four look outs posted on each corner of the camp," Grendo said, bringing him back to the present. "I've asked Butcher to take the Watch with you. Any sign of the pigs and you blow on this ok?"

He handed him a silver whistle on a cord which he hung around Shepherd's neck.

"And if you hear the whistle from the other look outs, blow on this one twice."

Shepherd nodded, looking down at the whistle hanging against his chest.

"I'll take over at four," Grendo said. "So you can get some sleep. Are you going back to your van or is it a four poster tonight?"

Shepherd flushed red in the dark at the implication in his words.

"It was innocent Grend," he said. "Honest."

Grendo stood up and pushed his fist gently against his upper arm.

"Aye course it was," he said, a big grin splitting his face. "Course it was."

Shepherd held his hands out to the fire and the warmth seeped into them. It made a halo of light around him against the dark backdrop of the camp and the fields and trees beyond. People were still partying in the festival field on the other side of the trees and someone was singing *hi ho silver lining*.

Grendo strode off towards the Love Bus leaving Shepherd alone with his thoughts. For the first time in days, weeks, his mind was calm rather than a washing machine on spin cycle. It was amazing what a long soak in a bath could do. He reached in his pocket for his dope pipe to have a quiet smoke and reflect on the day but his pocket was empty. He must have left the pipe in the bathroom when he got undressed.

A twig snapped and Shepherd instinctively felt for the whistle Grendo had hung around his neck.

"No need to do that," Butcher said, appearing out of the shadows. "It's only me."

Butcher eased himself into the chair Grendo had vacated.

"I should have brought some beer," he said, leaning forward, his hands dangling between his outstretched knees.

"Best not," Shepherd said. "Not if we're on Watch."

Butcher looked across at him, the flames of the fire licking at the darkness between them.

"You really think they'll come?" he said. "The police?"

Shepherd shrugged.

"Who knows," he said. "If they do, we're ready for them."

Butcher nodded at the machete lying on the ground by Shepherd's feet.

"Use that would you?" he asked. "If the police came?"

Shepherd looked at him.

"That depends," he said. "On what they do."

"But would you?" Butcher pushed. "Use a weapon against a police officer?"

Shepherd looked at him. It seemed a strange question to ask and his choice of words was odd too. No one in the camp called the pigs the police or referred to them as police officers. They were pigs through and through and that was that.

"Would *you*?" he said, turning the tables.

"Course," Butcher said, looking away at the darkened landscape surrounding them. "If they threatened my family I would."

"I didn't think you had a family," Shepherd said.

"I don't," he said. "It's just hypothetical like."

Shepherd poked at the fire with the spear.

"Where you from?" he said, hearing a tone in Butcher's voice he couldn't quite place. "That accent? Where's it from?"

"Oh," Butcher breezed. "Here and there, there and here. A little Lancashire, a little Brum. Lived all over the place I have."

"Been in the Convoy long?" Shepherd asked.

"Two year," he said. "Joined in Shropshire. Had enough of trying to get a job, paying the rent, just trying to exist you know?"

Shepherd nodded but all the while he was thinking. He had joined the Convoy three years ago and as far as he could remember, they hadn't travelled anywhere near Shropshire.

"Aye it's not an easy life is it?" he said.

The two men were silent for a moment as they stared into the bewitching flames of the fire.

"Where do you think the Convoy will go next?" Butcher said, breaking the silence.

Shepherd wished he'd be quiet. All this talking was preventing him from listening out for sounds, any sounds that could give the slightest indication that the pigs were circling. They shouldn't be just sitting by the fire either. One of them should be walking around the boundaries, going up to the hedges by the road, checking things out.

"Who knows?" he said. "It depends on what the Committee decides."

"And does the Committee decide on everything?" Butcher asked.

"You know they do," Shepherd said, shooting him a look. "Haven't you been to the meetings?"

"Not for a while, no," Butcher said. "That's why I'd like to know where we're going next. I've got a daughter," he added. "Back home. Haven't seen her for three years. She'll be eight by now."

Shepherd nodded.

"Oh aye," he said.

"Do you think we'll head south?" Butcher persisted. "To Stonehenge? Greenham?"

Shepherd lit a roll up and blew the smoke up at the sky. This man was irritating him.

"I don't know man, I don't know," he said. "I'm going to take a walk around and see what's what. You ok staying here?"

Butcher looked up as Shepherd got to his feet.

"I'll go if you like," he said.

"No you're alright," Shepherd said, keen to get away. "If you see anything you better make a loud noise or something. I'll take the whistle."

"I'll do my owl hoot," Butcher grinned. "Twice in a row."

Shepherd didn't return his smile. An owl hoot? What did he think he was, a boy scout? He was reluctant to criticise anyone in the Convoy. They were supposed to be tolerant, living as one big family, but this bloke was a bit of a nob and getting on his nerves.

Shepherd wandered away from the fire. He felt the chill of the autumn night as he left its warmth and light and moved into the darkness. To his right was the festival field where lanterns and flaming torches flickered through the gaps in the trees. Shepherd allowed his shoulders to relax as he listened to the sounds of the night. If the pigs came tonight, they'd have one hell of a surprise waiting for them.

Chapter 68

Sunday 26th August 1984

Shepherd woke to a chilly dawn. In the east, the sky was becoming lighter revealing the mist hovering over the distant fields. For a moment he wondered where he was and why he wasn't inside Idlewild and then he remembered the Watch.

The fire had gone out and there was an air of peace and calm settled over the camp. Even the festival goers in the next field were quiet; sleeping off the excesses of the night before. The chair opposite him was empty: Butcher had probably got cold and skulked off to his van.

Shepherd yawned and stretched out his legs and arms. This was such a perfect time of day before the world woke up, a time to savour the peace and quiet of his surroundings. All he needed now was a cup of tea.

Shepherd stood up and rolled his shoulders to ease their stiffness. He wasn't surprised the pigs hadn't made an appearance: he didn't think for one moment that they would. They had better things to do round here than bother with the Convoy: like policing the miners and pickets for example.

Shepherd stepped across the dew damp grass and opened the door of Idlewild. There was time for a little sleep before the day began.

Chapter 69

Ursula woke early. Today was the day! The day she'd play drums on stage with *Artaois!* She felt an enormous surge of excitement as she pushed back her sleeping bag and stuck her head out of the tent flap. Around her was a canvas sea of tents including the brown one that belonged to Charlie and Louise who were sleeping opposite. Their tent was old army issue but Charlie loved it and as it aged he had patched it up again and again despite Louise's protests that it leaked and smelled.

Ursula sat cross legged in the door of the tent looking out at the world around her. To her right she could see the stage where she'd play later that night. She could hardly believe she'd be playing the drums up there; on the same stage where *Steppenwolf* had cooked up such a storm last night sending the crowd into a rock 'n' roll frenzy.

A girl was walking towards her: a girl with long red hair wearing an ankle length blue nightie and carrying what looked like a wash bag. Ursula stared at her: she looked so out of place. Whoever wore nighties and carried their washbag around at a festival?

"Do you know where the bathrooms are?" the girl said, stopping next to Ursula's tent.

Ursula heard Yorkshire in her voice and estimated the girl was about the same age as she was.

"There aren't any," she said. "There's portaloos and that's it."

"Oh," the girl said sounding disappointed. "Where are we supposed to wash then?"

Ursula shrugged. The thought had never occurred to her. They washed before they left and when they got home and in between they just did what they could with baby wipes.

"I don't know," she said. "We use baby wipes."

The girl stared at her.

"Oh," she said. "I was looking forward to a bath."

Ursula gave a little laugh.

"A bath?" she said. "At a festival? Haven't you been to one before?"

"No," the girl said. "This is my first one."

"What's your name?" Ursula said.

"Katie," the girl said. "Is it your first one too?"

Ursula shook her head.

"No," she said. "I've been to loads of them. Don't worry about washing. Anything goes at a festival."

Katie didn't look so sure.

"You could go to the river," Ursula suggested, waving her arm behind her. "You can't use soap or anything but you could have a dip."

Katie stared at her.

"In a river?"

Ursula smiled. This girl was fresh out of suburbia.

"Yes," she said. "In a river."

Katie turned and Ursula watched her go. She looked so out of place, she thought, like she'd just landed in a foreign country and didn't have a clue.

The zip whined on the brown tent and moments later Charlie's shaggy head poked out. His face looked heavy and creased with sleep.

"Morning baby," he said as he looked around him. "Chatting up the locals are we?"

"That girl wanted to know where the bathrooms are," she said, nodding at Katie as she meandered through the sea of tents and away from them.

Charlie followed her gaze.

"Blimey," Charlie said. "She'll be asking what time breakfast is being served next."

Chapter 70

Katie made her way back to the tent. She hadn't managed to find anywhere to have a wash and the suggestion of having a dip in the river was not something she was brave enough to do. She often wished she was braver but, she told herself, coming to a festival was brave and she was going to forget all about what had happened with Hugo last night. The sun was rising over the hills beyond and mist lay across the fields. All around her people were stirring, crawling out of their tents and lighting fires and wandering around with blankets around their shoulders. Today was a new day and tonight she would see Van Morrison, live on stage!

Katie swallowed a lump of toothpaste to make her breath taste fresher and walked back to the tent as the church bells rang out across the fields. Inside, the tent was warm and fuggy and Katie wrinkled her nose at the sour odour. Hugo lay on his stomach, his face turned sideways and squashed up against his kitbag which formed a makeshift pillow.

Katie crouched down and wrapped the long skirt of her nightie round her legs.

"Shall I get us some tea?" she whispered. "There's a man selling it from a caravan by the stage."

Hugo grunted, flung his arm out and turned over without opening his eyes.

Katie leaned forward and touched his arm.

"Tea?" she repeated hopefully.

Hugo muttered foggily into his makeshift pillow.

"Stop talking will you?" he said. "It's the middle of the bloody night."

Katie recoiled as if she had been stung and sat for a moment staring at the back of Hugo's head, not sure what to do.

"Well," she said brightly. "I'll go and get some anyway. My dad always says a cup of tea first thing makes everything look brighter."

Hugo didn't respond and Katie reached for her jeans and t-shirt and sat down to put them on. It was difficult getting dressed in a tent particularly when you couldn't stand up and Hugo was taking up most of the room.

When she was dressed, Katie crawled out of the tent and breathed in lungfuls of fresh air as she stood upright in the fresh bright morning. She could feel the chill of autumn in the air: the time for going back to school, the time for making a fresh start. In two weeks' time she'd be starting her last year at St. Edith's Comprehensive but she wasn't going to think about that now. She was at a festival, *a festival!* And school and the rest of the world could wait.

Chapter 71

Caroline was woken by the church bells. They always rang on a Sunday morning from the Norman church down the road. They reminded sinners like her that it was far too late to be in bed.

Caroline pushed off the covers and Munro, who had been sleeping on the floor by her side, raised his head and wagged his tail.

Caroline hopped out of bed and reached for her crutches. She had slept particularly well last night thanks to the brandy she had consumed. It was a bloody nuisance to be reliant on crutches but she would have to make the best of it.

"Well Munro," she said, placing the crutches under her armpits and shifting her weight to their wooden support. "Let's get on with the day shall we?"

Sowcroft met her on the landing.

"Will your ladyship require assistance navigating the stairway?" he asked. Caroline thought back to last night when Shepherd had carried her effortlessly up the stairs and deposited her in the bedroom. Something in her had hoped he would stay, that he wouldn't turn and leave. It was ridiculous. Ridiculous. Shepherd was a traveller and she, she wasn't and really, she must be mad to entertain such a notion. Even so, she thought wistfully, even so.

"No thank you Sowcroft," she said brusquely. "I believe I'll manage if I sit down and take it slowly."

"As you wish m'lady, as you wish. Will m'lady be requiring breakfast?"

Caroline smiled at him.

"What I'd really like," she said. "Is smoked haddock kedgeree followed by toast and marmalade and Lapsong Souchong tea. Is that possible Sowcroft?"

"No m'lady," he said. Not today. But after you've been to town and visited the bank, you may be in a position to purchase some smoked haddock."

Caroline raised her eyebrows.

"Has our money situation improved Sowcroft? Because the last time I looked, smoked haddock was very low down on our list of priorities."

"It is vulgar to discuss financial issues on the landing," he said, his nose tilting upwards to the ceiling as if there was a bad smell beneath it. "Let's just say the sum of a thousand pounds may well be very welcome."

"A thousand pounds?" Caroline said. "For that old ruby ring?"

"Yes m'lady," Sowcroft said, nodded soberly. "Apparently it was quite rare."

"Well the old bugger!" Caroline said. "I had Rex down as a bit of a cheapskate. Fancy him giving me a ring like that."

"Oh I don't believe he purchased it," Sowcroft said. "More of an inheritance I should say."

"Oh dear," Caroline said. "Have we sold the family silver?"

"Yes m'lady I believe we have," Sowcroft said without a flicker of emotion. "But I wouldn't lose any sleep over it. Mr Rex is hardly poor."

"Lady Adelaide won't be impressed," Caroline said.

"Lady Adelaide is rarely impressed," Sowcroft said.

Caroline sat down at the top of the stairs preparing to make the descent on her backside as Munro bounded down ahead of her.

"If you'll allow me to pass m'lady," Sowcroft said from behind her, "I think we could possibly stretch to some Frank Cooper's vintage marmalade on our toast this morning."

"That would be wonderful Sowcroft," she smiled up at him. "You know how partial I am to vintage marmalade. And as soon as I get to the bank, you will be rewarded handsomely for your efforts."

Sowcroft bowed.

"That won't be necessary m'lady," he said. "Although I would quite like to partake of the smoked haddock kedgeree if at all possible."

Caroline smiled.

"You'll have it in spades Sowcroft," she promised, throwing the crutches down the stairs ahead of her. "In spades."

Chapter 72

Rex wished his mother wouldn't enter his bedroom without knocking. Honestly, sometimes she treated him like he was still five years old! And now she was standing at the foot of his bed firing questions at him. His head was throbbing and the room was spinning and he felt like a caravan of camels had slept in his mouth.

"Well?" Lady Adelaide barked, yanking open the curtains. "What have you got to say for yourself?"

Rex winced as daylight streamed into the room.

"I don't know Mummy," he said. "I don't."

"Well!" she said. "I'd like to know! I'd like to know why my grandmother's ruby ring has turned up in Oliver's Jewellers in town! It can't have got there by itself!"

"Caroline broke off the engagement," Rex muttered.

There. It was out and make of it what she would. He was too tired to clash swords with her this morning.

"Breaking off an engagement is one thing Rex," Lady Adelaide insisted. "But selling your grandmother's ruby ring is another thing entirely. Do you have any idea how much that ring is worth? I knew that woman couldn't be trusted. I knew it! She might be the daughter of an Earl but I never trusted that one. Never!"

Rex sighed.

"I didn't know," he said. "All I know is that she broke off the engagement the other day, or rather Sowcroft did. And then he fired that gun through the study window."

"I knew it," Lady Adelaide said. "All that poppycock nonsense about miners and poachers. We can't have people firing guns all over the place. We should call the police!"

Rex raised his head and pushed his elbows up behind him. It was an effort and he sank down again against the pillows.

"Don't do that mummy," he sighed. "Please don't do that. Couldn't you speak to Mr Oliver? Isn't he a friend of yours?"

"Friend or not," Lady Adelaide blustered. "He's not going to give me the ring back is he? Not unless I pay him and why should I pay him for what's rightly mine? Money doesn't grow on trees you know. It's about time you realised that."

Rex sighed. It was too much to think about on a Sunday morning. He closed his eyes, turned his head against the pillow and willed her to go away.

"You can't just go back to sleep!" Lady Adelaide said, grabbing at the eiderdown and pulling it off him. "If your father was alive he'd march over to Ambrell and demand an explanation!"

"I can't march anywhere at the moment," Rex said. "I am not feeling too well this morning."

"That's because you've been up half the night," Lady Adelaide continued. "It must have been three or four o'clock in the morning when I heard you crashing into the furniture. You're getting far too old for that sort of caper Rex. You need to start taking some sort of responsibility."

Rex wanted to sink through the bed and vanish into a distant realm, one where he didn't have a crashing hangover and one where his mother wasn't haranguing him from the end of his bed.

"Let me sleep for an hour," he said. "And then I'll see what I can do."

Lady Adelaide grunted.

"I'm going to church," she said. "And I expect to see you up and dressed when I get back."

She flounced out of the room leaving Rex, finally, in peace, only he knew there was not going to be any peace. Not until she got the answers she wanted.

Chapter 73

Rex tugged on the bell pull again and stood back, looking up at the upstairs windows for a sign of life. He didn't want to be here but if he didn't try to sort this out, his mother would make the rest of the day and possibly the rest of his life, even more hellish than it was already.

Suddenly the first floor window flew upwards and Sowcroft stuck his head out.

"Mr Rex," he said. "Is there some sort of emergency? Only the way you've been banging on the door makes me think the end of the world may be nigh."

"Open this door!" Rex shouted up at him. "I need to speak to lady Caroline!"

"Lady Caroline is not at home," Sowcroft said. "And so may I suggest you leave quietly?"

"Leave quietly?" Rex said. "How dare you! What do you think I'm going to do? Cause a riot?"

"Quite possibly Mr Rex judging by your behaviour last night. As a result, Lady Caroline has a badly sprained ankle. It is doubtful she would welcome your presence today."

"What?" Rex barked. "What are you talking about?"

"You," Sowcroft said. "You were blind drunk last night and you fell on her."

Rex's face darkened with anger. He already had a headache throbbing at his temples and he didn't need this upstart of a butler making it worse.

"Don't talk rot Sowcroft," he said. "And don't pretend she isn't in either because if she *has* got a sprained ankle as you have suggested, why isn't she at home resting?"

"I have no reason to lie to you," Sowcroft said. "Lady Caroline is quite a formidable lady as you know all too well. She isn't going to put a little obstacle like a sprained ankle in the way of life."

Rex stared at him. He knew Caroline was home. Where else would she be? At that wretched festival next door, wandering around a field in a long floating white dress? He didn't think so.

"I need to speak to her about my grandmother's ring," Rex said. "So I either do it today or I come back another day. I would like to know why it's turned up in the jeweller's shop in the village."

Sowcroft raised his eyebrows.

"Oh her ladyship won't know anything about that," he said.

"What do you mean?" Rex said crossly. "Of course she knows! I gave her the bloody thing!"

Sowcroft sighed.

"Yes you did," he said. "But I was the one who sold it. On her instructions of course. Good day to you Mr Rex. Please don't bother us again."

And he pulled down the window and slammed it shut.

Rex stared up at the window. How dare he! How dare he speak to him like that! He was a right honourable and he… he he was a… a nothing. A cheapskate tuppence butler who had airs and graces far above his station in life.

"Come down here at once!" he called up at the window. "Sowcroft! Sowcroft!"

The window remained shut and Rex pulled at the knot of his tie in hot frustration.

From across the fields he could hear the sounds of the festival: strains of music floating over the hedges, a man speaking over the MC, a dog barking and here he was, a man alone on a Sunday afternoon shouting up at the window of his ex girlfriend's house like some sort of common layabout.

He was better than that, he told himself as he walked back to his car. Much better. He didn't need to beg. He didn't even want Caroline back, not really. What he wanted was an explanation about the ring. How dare she sell what was rightfully his and had been in his family for generations! How dare she! How dare she!

Chapter 74

Shepherd lay under the blanket Rose had crocheted over the course of several winters. His face was burning and yet he was so cold he was shivering. He had felt like this ever since he'd got up that morning and finally after lunch, he had given in and gone back to bed. Now it was late afternoon and he could hear the music floating over from the festival field: a distant reminder that life was going on without him.

"It sounds like the flu," Janey said as she stood at the door. "I've brought you some Lemsip. Drink some and stay in bed."

"Thank you," he said. "I'll be alright for the Watch tonight."

"Don't worry about that," she said. "Butcher said he's happy to do it on his own. Rest."

After she had gone, Shepherd opened a sachet of lemsip and tipped it into a mug but his hands were shaking so much a large quantity of the white power spilled onto the draining board. Shepherd was too tired to clean it up and so he left it where it was and went back to bed. All he wanted to do was sleep.

Chapter 75

Katie wasn't sure what to do. Hugo had been asleep all day and now it was evening She had taken him cups of tea in polystyrene mugs and a burger in a bun but he had brushed her away and gone back to sleep every time. How could anyone sleep for this long? How could anyone stay in bed all day? They were at a festival and they were missing it all and tonight, Van Morrison was playing and she didn't want to miss that too. Life was passing her by. What if that boy at that house had been right? What if the world *was* going to end in two weeks and thirteen days? She was wasting what precious little time that might be left.

Katie got to her feet.

"Hugo?" she said, poking her head inside the tent. "I'm going over to the stage to watch the bands. Will you be alright?"

Hugo grunted.

"I'll come later," he said.

Katie felt her heart lift.

"You will? You'll come to see Van Morrison?"

Hugo didn't answer and Katie let the flap of the tent fall. When she got home she'd tell Juliet how fabulous it had all been but really it didn't feel fabulous at all. She had thought it would all be very different from how it had turned out to be.

Katie left the tent and headed towards the stage. If she was at a festival she wanted to see at least one band. And no way was she going to miss Van Morrison. No way.

Chapter 76

Ursula looked at herself in the mirror as she painted another star on her face. She was wearing a long black gypsy skirt and a black short sleeved top trimmed with lace. She liked her arms to be free as it got hot up there on stage under the lights when you were drumming your heart out.

Ursula pushed the flaps of the tent aside, crawled outside and stood up. The fairy lights glowed blue and pink and green in the trees and torches blazed and flamed amongst the sea of tents surrounding her.

Ravi was waiting for her.

"Ready?" he said.

Ursula nodded. She felt excited but apprehensive at the same time. There were hundreds of people here and the largest crowd she had ever played to was fifty people in a basement bar.

"Last minute nerves," she told Ravi, lighting a cigarette.

"You shouldn't smoke," he said. "But I'll let you off tonight."

There were no such things as dressing rooms in their world. Those luxuries were for the big bands, the famous bands, not for *Artaois* who were neither. Instead, Charlie had pitched a large tent behind the stage where he and the other band members were lounging around on blow up lilos drinking cider and shooting the breeze. Her mother smiled at her as she walked in with Ravi and Ursula could feel the anticipation and electricity in the air.

"We'll go straight in with *Howling Wolf,"* Charlie was saying. "That will get the crowd buzzing. Then *Bachelor's Waltz*, followed by *Musketeer*. Ursula you'll take over the drums on the beginning of *Musketeer* ok?"

Ursula swallowed and nodded, staring at her father. Suddenly it all felt so real.

"Come on," Charlie grinned, squeezing her arm in encouraging reassurance. "You'll be fierce out there. My fierce little bear."

Ursula smiled at him.

Fierce was a good word and fierce was exactly how she intended to be.

Chapter 77

Caroline leaned her head against the back of the chair in the library and closed her eyes. It was never easy spending a Sunday afternoon at Summerfields and her father had been particularly difficult today.

At her feet, Munro dozed and Caroline let her mind drift away and empty itself of the nursing home. It was a dreadful place, truly it was, with all those old people wandering around in their bri nylon nighties and sheepskin slippers and it was always so bloody hot she was surprised she hadn't sprouted.

The Earl had been in a particularly bad humour today. He had become fixated on the Pope for some reason, convinced he was behind what he believed was his incarceration in an Italian jail. Sometimes it was extremely difficult to stay with him in his fantasy world particularly when he accused Caroline of being in on the plot.

"I want you to write to the Queen," the Earl had said, taking her aside and insisting on speaking to her in the linen cupboard.

"Daddy I'm not sure we should be in here," she'd said. "Isn't it out of bounds?"

"Out of bounds be damned," he had said. "Promise me Caroline. You're my last hope of getting me out of this hell hole."

They had finally been rescued by matron who discovered their hiding place as she searched for fresh towels and ushered the Earl back into the sitting room where a couple of old women were throwing a green cushion backwards and forwards and the staff were excitedly preparing for a beetle drive.

"They treat us like imbeciles in this place," the Earl had complained. "Still," he said, tapping the side of his nose. "I know what they're up to. It's all part of their plan to make us think nothing untoward is going on."

Caroline found it all exhausting but what choice did she have? There was guilt mixed up in it too, but in her heart of hearts she knew sending him to a home had been the right thing to do. She could never manage him here.

"Penny for them m'lady,"

Caroline opened her eyes as Sowcroft came into the room carrying a silver tray.

"Oh I don't think they're worth that much," Caroline sighed, shifting upright and rearranging the cushion at the small of her back. "I was just thinking of the Earl," she said. "It makes me sad Sowcroft, really it does."

Sowcroft lifted a gin and tonic from the tray and placed it on the Edwardian side table beside her chair.

"The Earl is in the right place," Sowcroft said wisely. "No need for sadness."

Caroline sighed and reached for the drink.

"Thank you Sowcroft," she said. "I hope you're right."

"We had another visit from Mr Rex this afternoon m'lady," Sowcroft said. "He wasn't happy that his grandmother's ring has turned up in Oliver's Jewellers."

Caroline allowed herself a little smile.

"I bet he wasn't," she said. "Was he awfully cross?"

"Just a little m'lady, just a little."

"Oh dear," she said. "I'm sorry you had to take the brunt of that. I know what Rex is like when he gets cross. He can be very rude."

Sowcroft remained where he was.

"Will m'lady be visiting the festival this evening?"

Caroline sank back against the cushion.

"I'm not sure," she said. "My ankle is a little sore after all the hopping around I did today. I'd quite like to see Van Morrison but I'm not sure Sowcroft, I'm not sure. I'll see how I feel later on."

"Right you are m'lady," Sowcroft said. "Will that be all? Only I was intending to put my feet up and watch *Upstairs Downstairs* this evening."

"You do that Sowcroft," Caroline said. "If I need anything I'm quite capable of getting it myself. Enjoy Eaton Place."

"That was when life was much simpler m'lady," he said. "Much much simpler."

Chapter 78

Katie had never been in the middle of a crowd like this. The atmosphere was electric. Somehow she had managed to get quite near the front where she had a good view of the stage. She'd already seen a band called *Vertigo* and now the crowd were whistling and calling and waiting for the next band to come on stage.

"They're called *Artaois,"* the man next to her told her. "They're brilliant. Great rock music."

Katie nodded as if she knew everything there was to know about rock music when the truth was she knew nothing at all. She had never been to a rock concert in her life let alone stood in a crowd at a festival amongst strangers like this. She turned her head and Hugo appeared beside her.

"I had to queue for half an hour to get a drink," he grumbled. "And it cost me two quid."

Katie stared at him as he drank half of the pint of lager he was holding in a plastic glass.

"I didn't get you one," he said. "I didn't think you'd be the sort to drink beer."

"Didn't they have anything else?" she asked. It was good to see Hugo up and about but she could have done with a drink. It was very hot out here.

"What?" he said. "I don't know. I didn't ask. Look I can't stay at the front like this. There's too many people. You enjoy yourself. I'll see you later."

He turned to go and Katie touched his arm.

"Where are you going?" she said.

She had hoped that now he was up and about they could enjoy the evening, forget about the last twenty four hours and have a good time.

Hugo stared at her hand until she removed it.

"Are you always like this?" he said.

"Always like what?" she said.

Hugo stared at her.

"Clingy," he said. "Needy."

Katie removed her hand and felt her face burn red.

"Sorry," she said, not quite sure why she was apologising but feeling she needed to anyway. "It's just we came to have fun and we don't seem to have spent much time together."

Hugo stared at her.

"Well that's not my fault is it?" he said. "Standing in a crowd of strangers watching a band might be your idea of fun but it isn't mine."

"Well why did you come then?" she said, the words escaping from her mouth before she could stop them. "Why did you invite me to a festival?"

"God knows," he said, turning on his heel and walking away.

Katie watched him push his way out of the crowd. She felt like crying, really she did. All around her people were having a good time: laughing, dancing and singing and she felt completely removed from it all.

"Affairs of the heart?" a man next to her said, not taking his eyes off the stage. "Don't worry about him love. People like that aren't worth it."

Katie looked at him with tears in her eyes and smiled. She could hardly believe Hugo had spoken to her like that, hardly believe how he'd been since they got here.

"You need to dance," the man said, grinning at her and taking her hand. "Dancing cures everything."

"Does it?" Katie asked.

"Why don't you try it and see?" he said. "You're at a festival aren't you?"

Katie felt a little self conscious trying to dance. She wasn't sure how to do it or what to do with her arms but suddenly he took hold of both of her hands and started twirling her this way and that way and despite the way she'd been feeling just moments earlier Katie couldn't help but laugh.

"See?" he said. "It's easier than you think."

As Katie danced, the lights dimmed and the drums rolled.

"And now," the MC announced through the speakers. "Please welcome ARTAOIS!"

The crowd erupted, surging forwards and cheering loudly as the band ran on stage in the dark. Suddenly the lights came on, white lights raking through the crowd like searchlights and the crowd undulated like a sea.

"Hold on," the man next to her grinned. "You're in for one hell of a ride."

Chapter 79

Ursula waited nervously at the side of the stage. Her mouth was dry and her heart was pounding and she didn't know if it was from the beat of Ravi's drums or from the anticipation she felt at being minutes away from playing on stage. The crowd were going crazy, waving their arms in the air, jumping up and down and dancing and generally having a wild time. What if she dropped a drumstick? What if she broke one? What if she missed a beat?

"When was the last time you did that?" Ravi had said to her when she voiced her concerns to him earlier.

"When I was five," she said, swallowing.

"Well then," he said. "You just answered your own question."

A man wearing a headset came over and gave her the thumbs up. She nodded and followed him to the back of the stage. The band were playing the closing bars of *Bachelor's Waltz* and she knew she had to get up there quickly so that there was a seamless transition from Ravi to her as she took the drums for *Musketeer*. Right in the middle there was a minute's solo where you could play your heart out, a solo that made her think of African drums and wild horses galloping across the American plains.

Ravi grinned as he slipped out from behind the drums, sweat running down his face.

"Play like a demon," he told her. "Show 'em what you're got."

Ursula had brought her new drumsticks and she held them in one hand as she slid onto the stool. It was warm from where Ravi had sat on it and she instantly tuned in to what the other members of the band were doing, anticipating where they were going next. *Musketeer* started with a steady drum beat after which Fred, on bass guitar, would join in and then when the music was rising to a crescendo, Charlie would come in on lead guitar and vocals and they'd ride towards the middle together.

Charlie turned and winked and nodded at her. It was the sign, her signal. Ursula looked out at the crowd dancing in the dark and felt the heat of the spotlights on her. She raised her drumsticks in the air and felt the adrenalin course through her body. It was time to raise a storm.

Chapter 80

Katie had never felt so wild, so free, so *like this*. She loved the feel of the breeze in her hair as she danced and she loved the infectious atmosphere of the crowd around her. It was like one big happy family. The man next to her, whose name was Simon, had fought his way out of the crowd to get her a drink and she had rebelliously asked for a pint of lager. He had nodded and if he was surprised at her choice, he hadn't said so. And then he had somehow managed to weave his way back through the crowd, holding the drink high above his head.

Katie wasn't sure about the taste of lager but she wanted to fit in, she didn't want to feel like the outsider and that's how she had been feeling ever since they'd arrived at the festival. Now it was different. Now it felt like she belonged. Now it felt like everyone around her was her friend and she forgot all about Hugo. Simon grinned at her. When you looked at him closely, she thought, he wasn't bad looking with his blue eyes and red gold hair catching the lights from the stage.

"Viking blood," he had said, when she had expressed her surprise at how he had managed to bring the drink through the crowd without spilling it. "Natural warrior instinct."

And then, out of the blue, he swung her up on to his shoulders. She protested at first and then a girl who was sitting on someone else's shoulders next to them, grinned and reached out her hand. Katie squeezed it and they smiled at each other and let go. Simon had hold of her legs although she wasn't quite sure about her private parts resting against the back of his neck but he didn't seem to notice and no one else seemed to care and so she relaxed. That was what she was learning: here, there were different rules, different ways of being and it was no use trying to live by the rules of the outside world. Simon had told her she needed to let go and go with the flow whatever that meant and sitting up on his shoulders on top of the world with a bird's eye view of the stage, she felt like a princess, like the queen of all she surveyed.

Katie closed her eyes and let her body move to the intoxicating rhythm of the drums. This was living life. This was being at a festival. This was letting go.

Artaois finished playing and the lights on the stage shut off leaving it in darkness. The crowd continued to whistle and call and someone threw a beach ball in the air and fingertips bounced it around for a while. Simon swung Katie back down to earth.

"Enjoy that?" he said.

Katie nodded. She felt alive, exhilarated, she had never felt so free and soon, Van Morrison would be up there, on the stage. She could hardly believe she was going to see him standing just feet away from her.

"I'll go and get us another drink," Simon said. "Stay there. Don't go anywhere."

"I won't," Katie grinned.

Simon pushed his way through the crowd. An air of electric expectancy hung in the air and people started calling Van Morrison's name and chanting. Next they broke into a chorus of *"Oh why are we waiting"* and Katie could see men scuttling around the stage rolling things and moving the mikes. To think that Van Morrison was behind that stage, in the same field, breathing the same air as she was, waiting to perform!

And then there was a drum roll that went on for what seemed like ages. The crowd whistled and cheered and called out to the dark stage and Katie stood on tiptoe craning her neck to see above the people in front of her.

When she felt someone hold her elbow, she turned, expecting to see Simon returning with their drinks. Instead Hugo was standing next to her, an apologetic grin on his face.

"There you are," he said, slinging his arm around her neck. "I've been looking for you everywhere. Look, I'm sorry about earlier. It's been a hard week and I've been exhausted. Why don't we just go back to the tent and spend some quiet time together? We've got to go home tomorrow."

Over his shoulder Katie saw Simon approach. The smile on his face faded as he saw her standing with Hugo's arm around her neck and then he shrugged and turned away and walked back the way he had come. Katie felt something pull at her heart. He had been so kind so her, such fun… whatever did he think of her now?

"Look, Hugo…" Katie started to say as she watched Simon disappear.

Whatever she was about to say was drowned out by an almighty roar from the crowd as the stage lights blazed and a man in a hat walked out with his hand raised in the air in greeting and sat down on the high stool positioned by the microphone. He took the microphone in his hand and waited for the noise to die down. Katie felt her heart pounding. Van Morrison! It was Van Morrison!

Hugo was kissing her neck. Katie wished he wouldn't. She wanted to drink in everything she was seeing on stage, see the man, take in the shape of him, his curly hair, how he sat on the stool with such poise, waiting patiently for the shouting and cheering to die down.

"We could have more fun in the tent," Hugo said, nuzzling her ear. "You don't want to stay out here and watch this do you? Some old Irish crooner?"

Katie tried to move her head away from him but he didn't get the message and under the sea of the crowd, his hand, hidden and covert, was squeezing her backside.

"Come on," Hugo said, pulling at her hand. "Don't tease me."

Katie felt like crying. It was what she had come to see. Hugo had ignored her up until now and right at the moment, right at the moment when she was about to watch her idol on stage, Hugo was pulling her away from it. She didn't want to offend him: after all they had to spend tonight together and she didn't want a repeat of last night where she had lain awake, pushed up against the side of the tent with Hugo grunting and snoring beside her.

Reluctantly she let Hugo drag her out of the crowd. She kept her head turned, watching Van Morrison get smaller and smaller as Hugo pulled her forwards and the crowd moved into the space she had occupied and swallowed the gap.

Katie could hear his voice, that beautiful voice, singing *Brown Eyed Girl* and she wanted to pull her hand away from Hugo's and run back but she didn't dare. She wasn't brave enough. Hugo had brought her here and she couldn't just go off on her own.

Inside the tent, he didn't waste any time, Hurriedly he pulled down his trousers, treading them down to the floor with his feet and then he reached out and tried to pull her down on top of him.

Katie stood where she was and hung her head.

"What's wrong?" Hugo said, holding both of her hands as he sat on his crumpled sleeping bag and looked up at her. Katie couldn't help it. Tears escaped from her closed eyelids and slid down her face as she shook her head, unable to speak.

"Oh for God's sake," Hugo sighed. "What's the matter *now?* I knew I should have asked that other girl to come with me. What's her name? That podgy friend of yours with the short black hair?"

"Juliet," Katie said in a small voice thinking of her friend and wishing more than ever that she was here. She could hear Van Morrison singing his heart out into the night beyond but she couldn't see him and she had never felt so overwhelmingly disappointed and sad in her life.

"Come on," Hugo tried again in a more conciliatory tone of voice. "We can have a quick roll in the hay and then you can go back out there if you like."

Katie raised her head and opened her eyes.

"Come on," Hugo cajoled, pulling at her hands.

Katie shook her head.

"I can't," she said. "I've never done this before."

Hugo threw back his head and laughed up at the canvas roof.

"Oh come on," he said. "I've seen you comp girls. You're always behind those bike sheds copping off with each other. Don't act the vestal virgin with me. I know what girls like you are like. Acting all shy and demure but get you in the sack and it's a whole different ballgame isn't it?"

Katie stared at him.

"No," she said truthfully. "No it isn't."

Hugo's face darkened.

"So why did you come with me to this festival if you didn't want it? Did you think we'd sit around all night playing snakes and ladders and drinking lemonade?"

"No," Katie said, wishing the ground would swallow her up, wishing he wasn't speaking to her like this or expecting her to do things she didn't want to do. She had thought it would be romantic, lying under the stars, holding hands in the tent, whispering in the dark. She never thought it would be so *awkward,* so *difficult.*

Suddenly Hugo let go of her hands and reached for his trousers.

"Well you know what you can do then," he said. "You can fuck right off."

Katie's eyes widened.

"Yes, go on," he said, pushing his feet into the legs of his trousers. "You heard me. This is my tent. Fuck off if you want to act Miss Prim and Proper. You're just a prick tease aren't you? Just a little fucking prick tease."

Katie remained where she was. Van Morrison was singing about it being a wonderful night for a moon dance but it didn't feel like that, it didn't feel like that at all.

"Where am I supposed to go?" she said.

"I don't know," Hugo said, struggling into his trousers and fastening the fly button. "You should have thought about that before you got all Mary Whitehouse on me. I'm going to get a drink. Where you go and what you do is up to you."

Hugo glared at her.

"I'm sorry," Katie said, holding out her hand.

Hugo brushed it away.

"Fuck off," he said, leaving the tent.

Katie went outside and watched him stomp away. Van Morrison was on stage and yet she had never felt so miserable. She could go back and join the crowd but she didn't feel like it now. That bubbly golden feeling she'd had earlier had gone.

Katie sat down heavily on the ground. If she had known it was going to be like this, she would never have come.

Chapter 81

Katie woke with a start as noises outside the tent broke into her sleep. Suddenly, a girl fell in through the flap with Hugo stumbling in behind her. They were in high spirits and clearly drunk. Katie sat up and quickly moved her legs out of their way.

Hugo started pawing at the girl and Katie felt her face flush hot with embarrassment. Didn't they know she was in here? She had to make them realise or she was about to witness something she didn't want to see.

"Um… excuse me… excuse me…"

Hugo, who had fallen on top of the girl and was doing something to her in the darkness that made her giggle, raised his head and squinted in her direction. His eyes were out of focus and with a lurch to her stomach, Katie saw that he was very, very drunk.

"What are you doing in here?" he slurred. "I thought I told you to fuck off?"

The girl lying next to Hugo sat up and re-arranged her top.

"Charming," she said.

"It's not what you think," Hugo said as the girl moved away from him and crawled towards the exit.

"Sorry mate," she said. "I ain't into threesomes."

"No… wait…" Hugo called after her.

The girl slid out of the tent and disappeared into the darkness.

Hugo stared at Katie.

"Oh well done," he said, clapping his hands together slowly. "Well done."

Katie swallowed.

"Sorry," she said. "Sorry."

Hugo glared at her.

"Sorry?" he said. "*Sorry?*"

Katie felt her face burning. This was the worst night of her life. She wished she was home. She wished she was on the other side of the world. She wished she was anywhere but in a tent with Hugo.

Katie grabbed the straps of her rucksack and started to crawl towards the flap of the tent.

"Oh no you don't," he said, grabbing the backs of her ankles.

"You can finish what she started. You're the only fuck I'm going to get tonight."

Katie wriggled and tried to kick her legs free.

"Feisty little thing aren't you?" he chuckled. "Feisty little prick tease."

Katie kicked one last time and felt her foot make contact with something soft.

"You bitch," Hugo said, releasing her ankles and clutching at his nose. "You bitch."

Katie pulled her foot free and turned around just as Hugo vomited all over her and all over the sleeping bags.

Chapter 82

Ursula was on a high. It had been the greatest moment of her life drumming with the band and as they came off stage, hot and dripping with sweat, Charlie had hugged her proudly and Ravi had given her a high five. She wanted to do it all over again and again and again.

Afterwards she joined Charlie and Louise and Fred in the make shift dressing room tent. Louise fired a bottle of Pomagne and poured it into enamel mugs. Ravi had stayed by the stage waiting for Van Morrison but Ursula had too much energy to stand in a crowd and listen to other people's music tonight.

"I think I'll go for a walk," she said as Louise and Charlie snuggled up on one of the lilos and Fred snuck off to find girls and booze.

"Don't get lost," Charlie grinned at her. "We don't want one of the most promising drummers of the new generation vanishing into the unknown."

Ursula smiled at him.

"I'm going to stay in the palace tonight," she said.

"Oh?" Charlie said, raising his eyebrows as he kissed the side of Louise's hair. "The straw palace or Buckingham?"

"Ha ha," Ursula said. "The straw palace of course. It's magical. It's just where I want to be after a night like tonight."

Louise nodded slowly and looked at the tip of the glowing joint she was holding.

"The first night Charlie played," she said "We spent the night in a barn didn't we babe?."

"We did," Charlie grinned. "Remember that farmer finding us in the morning?"

Louise turned and smiled up into his face.

"Yes," she said. "You told him you'd help with the milking."

"And I did didn't I?"

"Yes," she said. "And roped me in too. It wasn't what I expected when I got off with the lead singer."

They laughed at the memory and Ursula watched them. She loved the way they were together. She didn't understand when she heard other girls moaning about their parents. Charlie and Louise were like teenagers, even after all the years they had been together and she, as Charlie often told her, was the product of their love.

Ursula left the tent. Lights beamed down from the stage, music filled the air and torches, candles and lanterns lit up the darkness. People stumbled around with their arms slung around each other's necks laughing as they wove between the tents. Ursula headed towards the path which led to the river. She'd wash the sweat off first and then go and sleep in the palace. It was the perfect way to end the night after playing her first solo on stage.

The tents thinned out at the edge of the field and there weren't so many lights here. Ursula focused on where she was walking so she didn't trip over any guy ropes and God knows what else might be lying on the ground. At the end of the field, under some trees and just before the path started, was a tent all on its own. As Ursula approached it a girl burst out of it and a man followed her shouting and grabbing at her legs. Ursula stopped and remained in the shadows.

"You bitch!" the man shouted as the girl desperately tried to crawl away from him. "You bitch!"

He made a clumsy rugby lunge for her legs and the girl desperately tried to move forward and away from him. Ursula could see she was crying and very upset.

"What are you doing?" Ursula said, her voice cutting through the darkness.

The man raised his head and tried to focus on where the voice was coming from. He was drunk. Very very drunk.

"Are you alright?" Ursula said, crouching down and talking to the girl kneeling on the ground. It was the girl with the long red hair, the girl she'd seen looking for the bathroom.

"Fuck off," the man said. "This is none of your business."

Ursula took hold of the girl's hand and pulled her upright. The man tripped and fell forward on to the ground.

"He's very drunk," the red haired girl said, wiping at her nose with the back of her hand. "He… he brought this girl back and she saw me and she's gone and he's angry and I'm not sure what to do… I'm not sure what to do."

Ursula looked at the man lying on the ground. He was not so much a man, she thought, as some sort of overgrown chubby faced boy. He raised his head and his eyes were completely out of focus.

"I'll sue you for this," he slurred. "My father knows the best lawyers in London."

Ursula looked down at him.

"Well good for you," she said. "My dad is Giant Haystacks. So you better get out of here before I go and find him."

"What?" Hugo slurred. "What's that you say?"

Ursula pulled the girl over towards the trees.

"What's your name?" she said.

"Katie," the girl said. "I'm so sorry… it's all so horrible."

Ursula put her arm around her shoulders.

"Is he your boyfriend?" she said, smelling the acrid aroma of vomit rising from the girl's clothes.

"No… I just came to the festival with him. To see Van Morrison."

"Have you been sick?" she said.

"Sick? Not me, no. Hugo's been sick. On the sleeping bags. I think he had too much to drink."

Ursula looked at the girl.

"I've got some clothes you could wear," she said. "You're probably a lot smaller than me but I'll find something."

Hugo was lying on the ground on his stomach, his arms stretched out in front of him. A soft snored escaped from his mouth.

"We can't just leave him here," Katie said, looking down at him.

"Why not?" Ursula said. "He's drunk and he's not your problem."

Katie searched her face.

"I'm supposed to be sleeping in that tent," she said. "But it's full of sick."

"Don't worry," Ursula said. "There's plenty of other places to sleep."

Ursula guided her gently away by the elbow.

"You've got stars and glitter all over your face," Katie said as they headed towards Ursula's tent.

"Yes," Ursula smiled. "Yes I have."

Chapter 83

If he closed one eye, Rex thought as the car veered sharply to the right, he could just about see in a straight line. Rex righted the car and glanced quickly in the rear-view mirror. It was nearly midnight. No police would be around to notice that little misdemeanour. Even so he needed to concentrate, concentrate, concentrate. The last thing he needed was to get pulled over.

Rex had been drinking all day and was feeling very sorry for himself. It was partly his mother's fault he reflected as he drove towards Ambrell. She whipped him into a frenzy. *Whipped him into a frenzy.*

"Good words Rex," he told himself, nodding his head in satisfaction as headlights came towards him and flashed past. "You should have been a poet."

He could have been many things, he thought. He'd been unfortunate to have a mother who yes *whipped him into a frenzy* and then to fall in love with Caroline Oxley, she of the silver spoon in her mouth variety. And then there was Deirdre. He'd been to see her this afternoon but she, dashed she devil that she was, wasn't up for playing today. He was wronged by women. Wronged. Completely and utterly wronged. Maybe he should take vows and enter a monastery and spend his days in the silent prayer of contemplation wandering around in clouds of incense reciting monotonous incantations.

Rex glanced in the mirror and then glanced again. Blue lights were flashing up behind him.

"Damn it," he said to the empty car. "Haven't the boys in blue got anything better to do on a Sunday night?

Rex pulled over as the police car pulled up alongside him. He wasn't a rebel, he was a good boy. It was other people who had done him wrong. Women in particular.

Rex wound down the window and gave the approaching police officer the most charming smile he could muster. The smile of an Honourable, the smile of a dependable member of the gold plated upper echelons of Society.

"Good evening officer," he said. "How may I assist?"

The officer stopped beside the car and frowned down on him.

"Have we been drinking sir?"

"I haven't," Rex grinned. "Have you?"

"Step out of the car please sir," the officer said, stony faced.

Rex sighed and unclipped his seatbelt.

"Do I have to?" he said.

"I would say it's in your bests interests to do so sir yes."

Rex lifted up the door handle and pushed at the door. As he stepped out he wobbled a little and had to hold on to car roof for support.

"Good party was it sir?" the officer said, his pocket notebook and pen poised in front of him.

"Look," Rex said. "I may have had a drink or two but I'm perfectly capable of driving. Clean record. Not a mark on it. I wonder if there might have been some sort of misunderstanding."

"And what sort of misunderstanding might that be sir?" the officer said.

"Well," Rex said. "Do you know who I am?"

"No sir," the officer said politely. "I can't say that I do."

Rex offered his hand for the officer to shake. The officer looked at it for a moment and then raised his eyes back to Rex's face.

"The Honourable Rex de Beaufort," he said. "My mother went to school with your Chief Constable and until very recently I was engaged to Lady Caroline Oxley of Ambrell Priory That's where I'm going now. Not to the festival of course, that's not my sort of thing. Not with all those drugs. Oh no. I never touch drugs. Dreadful things."

The officer hovered his pen over his notebook and stared at him.

Rex hurried on.

"Look officer," he said. "Let's not be hasty about this. Yes I've had a drink or two but I tell you it's nothing compared to what is going on up the road at Ambrell." Rex searched his mind to remember what had been written in that dreadful local rag his mother insisted on reading.

"Drugs, prostitution, where do I start?" he said. "There's things I could tell you. Oh yes. Lots of things."

The officer glanced behind him at the police car and waved the other occupant over. The blue light on the roof flashed in the darkness.

"This gentleman is the Right Honourable Rex de Beaufort," he said as his colleague joined him. "He says he has information about Ambrell which I think the Chief might be interested in."

The second officer who had stripes on his arm stared at Rex.

"Do you have identification sir?"

"What?" Rex blustered. "Identification? Of course I don't have identification. What do you need identification for? My word should be enough."

"I'm sorry sir," the second officer said. "Only we've got a highly sensitive security operation in progress at the moment the details of which I am not at liberty to say. We just need to check you are not a member of the Peace Convoy."

"I most certainly am not a member of the Peace Convoy," Rex said indignantly. "However could you mistake me for one of the great unwashed?"

"I'm sorry sir," the officer said politely. "They can be… how can I say it… very cunning. I wouldn't put it past them to pass themselves off as a member of the aristocracy."

Rex stared at him.

"Really?" he said. "That's quite outrageous. Let me reassure you officer I am nothing but an upstanding, rightful member of Society and if you don't believe me, you can telephone my mother. Lady Adelaide."

"Lady Adelaide?" the officer said, suddenly looking pale. "Lady Adelaide Carter?"

"That's her," Rex said. "My illustrious mother. Do you need her telephone number officer?"

The second officer steered Rex to the side of the road by the elbow and spoke to him in a low friendly tone.

"I had the good fortune to meet your mother last year," he said. "A charming woman, charming. She presided over our annual awards ceremony and had tea with us afterwards. She was very impressed with my wife's Dundee cake."

Rex nodded thoughtfully.

"Ah," he said. "Was she, was she."

"Between you and me," the officer continued in a low voice. "We've got units lined up all along the roads between here and Ambrell. I can't tell you any more than that but perhaps we could forget all about this little incident and see it as misunderstanding."

Rex nodded and gave his most charming of smiles.

"Very gracious of you officer, I'm sure. If there's anything I can do…?"

"Well yes there is," the officer continued. "Now you come to mention it, perhaps you could tell us more about what is happening at Ambrell? You know the festival? I overheard you say you know Lady Caroline Oxley."

"Yes," Rex said. "Unfortunately I do."

"Unfortunately?"

Rex sighed.

"It's a long story but since *the great unwashed* descended for this festival, relations between us have become somewhat tense and soured."

"Oh?" the officer said. "In what way?"

"Oh you don't want to hear my tales of woe," Rex sighed. "But I do believe those, those *travellers* are a bad influence on her. Caroline would never steal. Caroline would never take drugs. However over the last few weeks, she has done both."

"She has?"

Rex nodded.

"You're a busy man officer," he said. "You've got better things to do than listen to me."

"Go on," the officer said. "I'm all ears."

"Well," Rex sighed. "I have just discovered she has stolen my grandmother's antique ruby ring. We were engaged you see. Engaged. Until recently."

"That's theft Sir," the officer said. "Theft."

"I know I know," Rex sighed again. "I don't know what's come over her. And then there's the drugs."

"Drugs Sir?"

Rex nodded.

"I found a pipe a few days ago. In her bathroom. I shouldn't have been in there, I know, but I was hurt officer, hurt by her selling the ring. So I had a look around when she and that wretched butler of hers were out. That's when I found the pipe. The sort, I believe, used for smoking illicit substances."

The officer looked straight ahead.

"I see, I see," he said. "And this pipe. Is it still in your possession?"

"It's at the house," Rex said. "I wouldn't keep it on me. I was on my way to Ambrell to speak to her about these things when your colleague stopped me. I wanted to stop her going down this dreadful path she seems to have chosen. To make her see this is not the right way for a member of the aristocracy to behave."

The officer gave a slow, satisfied smile.

"We need more citizens like you sir. Perhaps we could talk more in the police car," he said, steering Rex towards the blue flashing light. "It's a little warmer in there."

"I'd be delighted," Rex said, carefully putting one foot in front of the other. "Delighted."

Chapter 84

Katie and Ursula looked up at the straw palace looming large against the night sky.

"Are we really going to sleep in there?" Katie whispered.

"Yes," Ursula said. "Unless you fancy spending the night with that boyfriend of yours. He's going to have a very big headache in the morning."

Katie didn't want to think about the morning. It made her feel panicky inside.

"He's not my boyfriend," she said. "I wanted him to be… but I'm not so sure now."

Ursula looked at her.

"Well you can think about that tomorrow can't you," she said, linking her arm. "Because tonight we are going to sleep in a palace!"

Katie swallowed.

"I've never done anything like this before," she said.

Ursula squeezed her arm.

"Well it's about time you did then isn't it?"

Ursula flicked on the torch she was carrying and the beam lit up the corridor that led inside the straw palace.

"Wow," Katie said. "This is magical. Are there always palaces at festivals?"

"No," Ursula said. "It's the first one I've seen. Apparently it's the palace of Versailles."

"What's that?" Katie said.

Ursula shrugged.

"Charlie… my dad… said it was a famous palace in Paris in the olden days."

"But why's it here?" Katie persisted. "At a festival?"

Ursula shrugged.

"You'd be surprised what happens at festivals," she said. "Come on. Let's go inside."

Katie followed Ursula into the straw palace.

"Wow," she whispered. "It's amazing. I wanted to come in when we got here but Hugo said there'd be rats and mice so we didn't."

"Hmmm..." Ursula said as she led the way inside. "Nice bloke."

"I don't really know him that well," Katie said as her eyes adjusted to the gloom inside. She had never seen anything so magical, so quiet. Fairy lights twinkled lending the straw a soft golden glow. "I only came because I wanted to see Van Morrison. And that didn't work out either."

She followed Ursula into the main chamber.

"There's a bedroom up there," Ursula whispered, pointing to the ladder. "It's beautiful."

"Why are you whispering?" Katie whispered.

"I don't know. Why are you?"

They laughed as Ursula shone the torch on the ladder.

"Will anyone mind us sleeping in here?" Katie asked.

"No one will know," Ursula said. "And I don't think anyone would care anyway. This is a festival. It's all about freedom and peace and sleeping in straw palaces."

Katie followed Ursula up the ladder, a little worried she might fall but she kept her eyes on Ursula's feet and they entered the chamber above. It was as beautiful as Ursula had said it would be with a big straw bed covered in a ruby coloured throw and big pink cushions. She had never seen anything like it.

Ursula climbed up onto the bed and Katie followed.

"This is amazing," Katie said, looking around her. "It really does feel like a palace doesn't it?"

The girls sat on the bed with their backs against the straw bale headboard and pulled the ruby throw up to their waists.

"I brought some iced gems," Ursula said, taking a small packet out of her pocket. "Want some?"

Outside, the festival wound down for the night as tired party goers wandered around looking for their tents and the roadies finished clearing the stage. They could hear faint music and people talking as they walked past the palace.

"Didn't I see you the other morning looking for the bathroom?" Ursula said.

"Yes," Katie said. "You must have thought I was mad. It's just I haven't been to a festival before."

"I didn't think so," Ursula said. "But it doesn't matter. I've been coming to festivals since I was a baby so it's easy for me."

Katie looked up at the ceiling. Even that was made out of straw.

"Is your dad really Giant Haystacks?" she said.

Ursula gave a little laugh.

"No," she said. "My dad's called Charlie and he plays in a band called *Artaois.* I played drums with them tonight."

"Wow," Katie said. "You play drums? With a band?"

"Sometimes," Ursula said, putting iced gems into her mouth.

"My dad's a miner," Katie said. "He's on strike at the moment."

"I saw some miners shaking tins outside the Post Office in Halifax at Christmas," Ursula said. "It was freezing cold and they weren't allowed to go in the shopping centre to get warm. Dad gave them some money. He said he couldn't imagine how it must feel having to fight the government for survival."

"It's not easy," Katie said. "But they're going to win."

"Are they?" Ursula said, turning to look at her.

"I don't know," Katie said. "That's what my dad says. I don't really understand it all."

They finished the iced gems and Ursula crumpled the packet and put it away in her pocket.

Katie yawned.

"Sorry," she said. "I didn't get much sleep last night."

"That's ok," Ursula said. "I'm quite tired too."

The girls snuggled down under the covers, pulling them up to their chins.

"I love this," Katie said feeling warm and safe as she started to drift off to sleep. "Thank you."

Ursula smiled into the dark. In her head, she was playing the drum solo again.

Chapter 85

Monday 27th August 1984

At three o'clock in the morning, the world was peaceful and quiet. A grey pearly light hung over the fields and the festival goers were fast asleep in their tents. A few lanterns and torches burned here and there but the stage was empty, the drum kits and speakers silent in the shadowy dark. A man with his arm slung across the shoulders of a woman, meandered across the festival field as they returned to their tent. They were the only signs of life at that time of the morning.

In the traveller's field, the fires of the night before had burned down to embers and smoke rose from the chimneys of the vans and lorries and coaches. Dogs slept stretched out by the dying fires and the mascot white goats slept under a caravan on a bed of hay. Inside Idlewild, Shepherd slept soundly, his fever taking him into a deep sleep and over the fields and behind the solid red brick walls of Ambrell Priory, Lady Caroline slept on the couch with Munro at her feet, dreaming of red-haired kings of England.

Behind the fields, the dark river ran its silent course towards the sea and in the dark, the trees stood shadowy like sentries. It was the time for nocturnal creatures to roam and from time to time, an owl hooted and a fox took his chance and slunk out of the undergrowth and sniffed around the site to find what the humans had left behind.

Two miles away, a convoy of police vans and vehicles advanced along the A64, heading towards Ambrell.

Chapter 86

It was the nervous braying of the goats and the dogs barking that woke him. At first Shepherd wondered where he was and then he sat up dishevelled and disorientated wondering whether it was night or day. Shepherd pushed off the quilt and swung his legs over the side of the bed and stood up, pushing aside the curtain to look out of the window.

As he did so, the door of the camper van flew open and banged against the wall as three men in riot gear and helmets burst in.

"Stay where you are!" one of them shouted. "Where are they? Where's Brenda and John?"

Shepherd stared at the men holding riot shields and stepped back from the window.

"What the fuck?" he said. "What the fuck are you doing?"

"Brenda and John," the officer repeated. "Tell us where they are or we'll smash the place up. We know they're the organisers."

"They're not," Shepherd said, raising his hands in the air and backing away. "They're not the organisers. They're goats. Goats. Mascots. Goats."

From out of the dark, Butcher appeared and Shepherd felt relief at seeing a familiar face.

"Tell these bastards would you?" he said. "Tell them Brenda and John are goats."

Butcher stared at him.

"You can tell them yourself down the station," he said, grabbing Shepherd's right arm and yanking it up behind his back. "You're under arrest."

"Fuck off," Shepherd said over his shoulder as he winced with pain. "What the fuck are you doing man? Is this a joke?"

"No joke," Butcher said. "You're under arrest on suspicion of possessing offensive weapons, intent to supply Class A drugs and anything else we can think of."

Shepherd turned his head and his eyes blazed at Butcher.

"You bastard," he said. "You're undercover aren't you? I knew there was something about you. I knew."

"Well well what have we got here," one of the police officers said, dipping his finger into the white powder on the draining board and holding its tip in front of his shielded face. "Been having a little snort have we?"

Shepherd turned and looked at him.

"It's Lemsip," he said. "I spilt it. Earlier. I spilt it."

"Did you really," the officer said. "Looks like cocaine to me. Oh dear oh dear."

He turned and nodded at the men in helmets behind him and then stepped to one side as they moved into the van. Before Shepherd could do anything, they raised their batons and brought them down heavily on the crockery stacked up on the draining board. The cup Rose always used for her morning cup of tea shattered and cutlery flew into the air and landed on the floor.

"What the fuck?" Shepherd protested, trying to wrench himself free from Butcher's grip and the handcuffs he was placing on his wrist. "This is my home! You can't just come in here like this! You've got no right to do this! No right!!"

"We'll do what the fuck we like," the police officer said. "So I suggest you keep your mouth shut and leave quietly with this nice officer here. Take him away Sullivan. Get him out of my sight."

Shepherd glared at him, his heart pounding with outrage and defiance.

"You bastard," he said. "You bastard."

The police officer smiled nastily at him.

"Fuck off," he said. "Get him out of here Sullivan. Take him to one of the vans."

Shepherd stared defiantly up at the officer as Butcher dragged him to the front of the caravan. As they passed, Shepherd spat and it landed on his shiny black left boot.

"You'll pay for this," he said. "All of you."

The officer glared at him and raised his baton. Shepherd couldn't raise his arms to defend himself and the next moment the baton cracked down on his shoulder and Shepherd winced with the pain.

"Now fuck off," the officer said. Shepherd looked on helplessly as the officers started opening the cupboards, throwing everything they found on to the floor. He watched helplessly as the fat mirror tumbled from the wall and shattered on the floor.

"This is my home!" he said. "You've got no right to do this! No right!"

Butcher jerked on the handcuffs and a pain shot through his back as he pulled him down the metal steps.

"Shut the fuck up," Butcher said. "Shut the fuck up."

Chapter 87

Outside there was chaos as police dressed in black visored helmets holding batons and riot shields ran with full force into tents and benders swinging their batons and kicking out with their black booted feet not caring if they were occupied or not.

"Make for the palace!" Grendo shouted as he ran around banging on doors and shouting up at windows. "Police raid! Make for the palace!"

As Butcher dragged Shepherd towards a convoy of police vans parked at the end of the field, Shepherd watched in disbelief as the police swarmed over the camp. He'd seen a film once where a battalion of Roman Legionnaires invaded a village. It was just like that. Women were screaming and he watched helplessly as an officer dragged one past him by her hair.

"Leave her alone!" he shouted. "You bastard! Leave her alone!"

In response to his outburst, Butcher tugged his arm higher up his back and Shepherd thought it would come out of its socket. These were his people and he couldn't do anything to help them. Children were running around crying, women were screaming, dogs were barking themselves into a frenzy and men were being dragged to the ground where they fought with the police. Butcher dragged Shepherd to the entrance of the field where a police officer was smashing the window of a bright orange van with his baton.

"There's a young baby in there!" Shepherd shouted as they went past, recognising Ingrid and Peter's converted ambulance. "There's a young baby in there!"

The police ignored him and continued to hit at the doors and windows smashing glass and splintering wood.

"Didn't you hear me?" Shepherd shouted, straining at his handcuffs. "I said there's a woman and baby in there!"

Butcher kicked him hard behind his right knee and Shepherd buckled and fell, hanging in the air by the handcuffs behind his back. He felt excruciating pain shoot up his shoulder blade and he looked up at Butcher who stood above him, his dark eyes glinting with menace.

"I can break your arm," he said. "Or you can shut the fuck up."

Shepherd tasted blood in his mouth.

"You cunt," he said, spitting at the ground. "You cunt."

Chapter 88

Ursula sat bolt upright. She could hear people shouting and screaming outside the palace although she was half asleep and wasn't sure if she was dreaming. She looked down at Katie sleeping beside her and gently shook her by the shoulder.

"Wake up," she said in an urgent whisper. "Katie. Wake up. There's something going on outside."

Katie opened her eyes and looked around her sleepily. An almighty crash from outside made her sit bolt upright, her eyes wide.

"What was that?" she said.

"I don't know," Ursula said, her heart pounding and her eyes wide in the darkness. "I don't know."

The two girls held hands and listened as all around them they heard thuds of wood on metal, men shouting and women screaming.

"Do you think it's a riot?" Katie asked. She'd seen one on the telly earlier this year when gangs of youths ran riot in Wolverhampton and she remembered how, when she was twelve, all the shops in the town centre had pulled down their iron grids and shutters early in the day and her dad made them all sleep downstairs just in case.

Ursula pushed off the covers and listened to the voices floating up from below: panicked voices, raised voices, confused voices.

Katie sat very still staring at the ladder as a man's head suddenly appeared and his eyes widened in surprise as he saw the two girls sitting upright on the straw bed.

"Alright girls?" Grendo said. "There's a bit of trouble going on outside. People are going to come in here to take shelter."

Ursula looked at him as he bent his head and stepped off the ladder.

"What sort of trouble?" she said.

"Nothing to be scared of," Grendo told her. "Just a little misunderstanding with the pigs. I mean the police."

Ursula had a horrible feeling something was very wrong and she suddenly wished Charlie and her mum were here but she didn't want to look like a baby and so she looked back at him like she was completely in control when her legs had turned to jelly and her stomach felt like it was caving in.

"What sort of misunderstanding?" she said.

Katie sat motionless on the bed looking very pale and frightened.

"Nothing for you to worry about," he said. "You just stay up here ok? We'll all be alright if we stay together. Where's your mum and dad?"

Ursula swallowed. She'd been trying to act mature and sophisticated but the mention of Charlie and Louise made her feel like 15 years old again.

"They're in the festival field," she said. "My dad's in a band and my mum does henna tattoos."

"They'll be alright," Grendo said. "The police are only in the travellers' field. Old scores to settle," he said, smiling at the girls to reassure them. "Nothing for you to worry about."

Katie looked up at him.

"Are they killing people?" she said. "Outside? Are they killing people?"

Grendo looked at her.

"Course they ain't," he said. "Like I said it's just a bit of a misunderstanding that's all. Ever heard of the Peace Convoy?"

Ursula nodded. Katie shook her head.

"Well," he said. "It's to do with that. The police don't like us and we don't like the police. It will be alright. It will be alright."

Katie looked up at him.

"Will we be arrested for sleeping in here?" she said.

Grendo looked down at the two girls. They were so young, so innocent.

"Course not," he said, sitting down on the bed beside them. "I'm here aren't I?"

Chapter 89

When Caroline heard the crash downstairs, she thought it was Rex.

"What does that idiot want now?" she said sleepily, reaching down to stroke Munro's head. Munro's ears twitched and he sat up and barked. Caroline opened her eyes. Munro never barked.

"Rex?" she called, swinging her legs off the couch and wincing as she remembered her sprained ankle. "Rex?"

Caroline reached for her crutches and as she did so, she heard heavy footsteps running up the stairs and in the next moment, four police officers were standing in the doorway.

"Stay where you are," the officer at the front shouted. "Stay where you are!"

Caroline wrapped her dressing gown more tightly around her and let the crutches rest against the edge of the couch.

"I have no intention of going anywhere," she said, eyeing the officers with cool disdain. "Because in case you hadn't noticed, this is my home. So would you mind telling me what you are doing bursting into it in the middle of the night?"

"Shut up," the officer said, moving forward. Munro started barking as the officer approached.

"Call that dog off before I put him out of his misery."

Caroline glared at him.

"Did you leave your manners at the station officer?" she asked. "Or is this how you usually speak to those you surprise in the middle of the night?"

"I said call off the dog!"

There was a movement behind the officers and Sowcroft came bustling into the room.

"I tried to stop them m'lady," he said. "I tried."

"It's alright Sowcroft," she said, keeping her eyes fixed on the police. "Take Munro down to the scullery while I finish this conversation with these very charming policemen."

"But m'lady…"

"Take him," she firmly. "Take Munro."

Sowcroft came forward. He was wearing a paisley dressing gown and tufts of grey hair stuck up on his head. Caroline would have found it amusing at any other time had she not felt so outraged by what was happening in front of her. Sowcroft caught Munro by the collar and pulled him away. Munro resisted and snarled and barked at the officers.

"Go Munro there's a good boy," Caroline soothed him. "I'll be down in a minute."

Sowcroft managed to slide Munro across the floor by the collar, keeping his back to the officers as he coaxed him out of the room.

"Lady Caroline Oxley?" the officer said, his self importance and confidence edging his voice now that Munro had left the arena. "I am arresting you for conspiracy to supply Class A drugs. You do not have to say anything if you do not wish to do so but anything you do say may be used against you in a Court of law."

"What?" Caroline half laughed in disbelief. "Is this some sort of joke?"

The officer stepped forward and caught hold of her wrist.

"I rarely joke," he said. "Especially when I'm arresting someone."

He clamped the handcuff around her wrist.

"This is outrageous!" Caroline protested. "You can't just force your way into my home in the middle of the night and arrest me!"

"We can if we have reasonable suspicion to believe you have been involved in a criminal offence. And we have reason to believe you have been involved in the supply of drugs."

"What?" she said in disbelief. "That's ridiculous! Drugs? What on earth…"

Behind him, other police officers started opening doors and cupboards and tipping out the contents on the floor.

"Stop that!" Caroline said. "I want a lawyer. I want to speak to my lawyer."

"You can do that down at the station," the officer said. "Now we can do this the easy way or we can do it the hard way. You upper classes are all the same. You think you can get away with murder but let me tell you you're the same as everyone else when it comes to breaking the law."

Caroline looked up at him.

"I haven't done anything wrong," she said. "You can't just arrest me like this. And in case you haven't noticed officer, I'm in my dressing gown and I'm using crutches."

"I'd say that's your problem," he said. "Not mine."

Caroline glared at him.

"Am I at least allowed to put some clothes on?"

The officer stared at her cleavage showing above the join in her dressing gown.

"No," he said. "There's no time for that."

Chapter 90

The palace was so full of people and more kept crowding in, stepping off the ladder and pushing into the bedroom. There were dogs and babies and women and children and chickens and even two goats. It was hot and noisy and no one seemed to know what was going on.

"Everyone stay calm!" Grendo shouted, raising his hands. "Everyone stay calm! They can't get us in here. We're safe for now."

Ursula didn't understand what was going on. Surely the police couldn't just come along and start smashing up people's vans and lorries? But that is what the people were saying they were doing.

"They smashed all my windows and arrested my husband," a woman holding a very young baby said, her eyes filling with tears. "It took us months to get that van up together. Months. The police hate the Convoy so much they'll do anything to destroy us."

Ursula was trying to process it all but none of it made sense.

"But why?" she asked, puzzled. "Why do they hate you so much?"

The woman shrugged.

"Ask Margaret Thatcher," she said. "She's the only one who knows."

Grendo pushed his way through to the girls.

"We're going to try to get you and the other kids out," he said. "Can you get down the ladder?"

Ursula nodded. Katie looked fearful.

"What do we do at the bottom?" Ursula asked, her eyes wide, her heart pounding. Outside were terrible noises. Men shouting and screaming, crashes and thuds and dreadful sounds that made her feel afraid. Somewhere out there were Charlie and Louise. What if they were hurt?

"You make a run for it," he said. "There's woods over to the east. Turn right when you get out of here and run and keep on running. Don't stop for the police, not even if they tell you to. They'll haul you in just like they'll haul us in. They won't care that you're kids."

Katie looked up at him.

"Can't we stay here?" she asked in a small voice.

Grendo crouched down in front of her and held her forearms as he looked into her face.

"No love," he said. "Best you go. You won't be on your own. There's a whole group of you going. Don't be frightened."

Katie nodded. She had never been more frightened in her life.

"Come on," Ursula said holding Katie by the elbow and sounding braver than she felt. "All we have to do is get down the ladder, get outside and run."

"That's it," Grendo nodded, straightening up. "That's just how you do it."

"Will you be ok?" Ursula asked him. She didn't know this man but he had been so kind to them. She didn't understand why it was all happening but there were things that fifteen years olds like her couldn't understand, not yet, and when they got out of here, Charlie would explain it all, she knew he would.

"Aye," he said. "I've seen worse. Off you go girls. Godspeed."

Ursula took Katie's hand and they moved to the top of the ladder.

"Come on," she said. "Stay close to me. We'll be ok. We will. We'll be ok."

Chapter 91

Chief Inspector Taylor stood on the edge of the field and surveyed the scene in front of him. He always liked to see a battlefield. It gave him an enormous sense of pride, of self fulfilment, of job satisfaction if you wanted to use one of those phrases they bandied about these days. Next to him, Ray Peters, in a thin raincoat, shivered.

"Operation Raymond is going well I see Sir," he said.

"Of course it is," Taylor barked. "Nothing more satisfying than the smell of burning hippy."

In front of them, in the pearly light of dawn, he watched as his men dragged the Peace Convoy out of their caravans and lorries. He watched as his men ran into the benders and tents swiping left and right with their batons and fought with those who resisted. He watched as half naked women were dragged along by the hair. It almost gave him a hard on. Smoke rose from the lorries and vans and children clung to their mothers legs and the air was filled with the sound of shouting and screaming and chaos.

"Did you find the ring leaders?" he asked Peters. "This Brenda and John?"

"Apparently they're goats sir," Peters said looking straight ahead.

"Goats?" Taylor repeated. "What do you mean they're goats?"

"Goats sir," Peters said. "Brenda and John. White goats."

Taylor looked pissed off.

"Think they're so clever don't they," he said. "Not so clever are they now eh Peters?"

Peters swallowed.

"No sir. I think we can safely say we're giving them a lesson they won't forget in a hurry."

A young officer who had lost his helmet ran over and stopped in front of them.

"They're refusing to leave that straw hut," he said, breathing heavily. "There's hundreds of them in there. Hundreds. Some of them are chucking glass bottles and all sorts of shit and stuff from the balcony. "

Taylor set his mouth into a hard line and stared across at the straw structure which towered incongruously at the edge of the field.

"Is that so," he said, his eyes glittering with anger in the half light. "Then you know what you need to do constable. Torch it," he said, without emotion. "Torch it."

Chapter 92

"Is this really necessary?" Caroline asked as the officer dragged her along by the handcuffs attached to her wrists. "I'm having trouble keeping up with you."

Caroline had chosen to leave the crutches in the house but every time she put her right foot down on the ground she felt a twinge of pain shoot up through her calf.

"Shut up," the officer said. "Just shut up."

Caroline stared at the back of his head.

"What's your collar number officer?" she said. "I looked for it earlier only you seem to have it covered up."

He stopped so quickly in the lane that she almost toppled forwards. It was dark and there were no lights and in the field ahead, the festival goers were sleeping off Sunday night's excesses under canvas roofs, oblivious to the drama that was being played out in the travellers' field.

"You might be one of the upper classes," he snarled, fingering the baton at his waist. "But that won't stop me from using this if you continue to resist arrest."

Caroline stared at him. This whole thing was like something out of a nightmare. She almost expected to wake up any moment and feel the relief that came after a particularly bad dream.

Caroline remained silent as they started to walk again. As she limped along behind him, she felt insignificant and at the same time, outraged and appalled that something like this could happen out of the blue.

"Is there a fire in the traveller's field?" she said as she saw plumes of smoke rising above the trees which separated the festival field from the travellers' field.

"You could say that," the officer said smugly. "Or you could say we've paid the Convoy a nice little visit to remind them what law and order is."

Caroline swallowed.

"You do realise that what you're doing is completely illegal," she said. "That even the police aren't above the law?"

He turned and raised his baton.

Caroline saw stars as he brought it down on the side of her head.

Chapter 93

The police van was hot and crowded with bodies and every so often the back door opened and more were shoved, herded and pushed inside. Shepherd could hardly breathe. He had been in the back of more police vans than he cared to remember but not like this. Women and men were shoved in indifferently, some of them were bleeding and had a dazed look in their eyes and looked like they needed to go to hospital rather than the police station. Some had pissed themselves, others had emptied their bowels. The stench was nauseating.

The van rocked as people moved around inside, banging on the sides, shouting and calling the police every name under the sun. Shepherd stood towards the back of the van as the door opened and a woman was roughly pushed inside. Shepherd's eyes widened when he saw who it was and pushed his way to the backdoors.

"What the fuck?" he said as Caroline swayed on her feet. She had blood running down the side of her face and she looked paler than a ghost. Shepherd caught hold of her forearms.

"Are you ok?" he said, concern etched into his face. "What the fuck are you doing in a police van in your dressing gown?"

"I thought you might ask me that," Caroline said, her voice slurred. "I'm afraid the police officer who arrested me wouldn't let me get dressed."

Shepherd felt a flare of anger light up inside him. It was bad enough what the pigs were doing to them without dragging her into this. And she was wearing a dressing gown for fucks sake! He bet the pigs had got a twisted kick out of that.

"Do they know who you are?" he said.

"Of course they know who I am," she said. "They came to my house didn't they? Apparently Rex kindly told them I'm involved in supplying drugs. Oh and that I've stolen an item of jewellery from him. And so I am under arrest."

Caroline swayed again and he caught her before she toppled over and put his arm around her waist.

"Fuck," he said. "Fuck fuck fuck."

A cheer went up as the back doors suddenly sprang open. Some of the captives jumped out of the van and started to make a run for it and in the next moment they were on the ground, the sickening thud of batons on skin and skull and screaming piercing the night. Shepherd turned Caroline's head away into his shoulder as she closed her eyes and winced.

"I've never seen anything like this," she said, her voice muffled against his t-shirt. "I had no idea."

Shepherd caught the fragrance of her hair and leaned his chin on it as he looked out. It was like a war zone out there.

To his right, headlights suddenly shone through the darkness. At first he thought it was a police wagon driving into the field but as it got closer he saw it was a yellow digger.

"Fuckin' hell," he said softly as he watched it. At the tone in his voice, Caroline raised her head and turned round to see Sowcroft driving the digger at a reckless speed towards the field, Munro sitting up in the seat beside him.

Chapter 94

It took far longer than they'd expected to get down the ladder and push their way to the corridor which led out to the field and the woods beyond. Ursula was holding Katie's hand so tightly that her fingernails were digging into her palm but she knew if she let go, she'd lose her. People were pushing and shoving, some pushing into the palace, some trying to get out. Children and babies were crying and there was a dreadful smell in the air where some people had been so afraid they'd evacuated their bowels. Ursula tried not to look at what she was treading in; she didn't care what she was treading in. Every nerve and fibre in her body was screaming at her to get out, get out, get out. She was terrified they'd suffocate with all these bodies towering over them or be knocked to the floor and trampled on. That was why she held on so tightly to Katie, pulling her along behind her as they tried to find a way out.

"Excuse me," she tried, pushing against the backs of bodies blocking the entrance. "Excuse me!"

It was the smoke she smelt first. The smoke which smelt of the fields they burned every August. Ursula had camped in enough fields to know the smell of burning straw.

"They've set it on fire the bastards!" someone shouted. "It's on fire!"

Panic seized the crowd as they surged towards the exit. Some people started clawing at the walls. The fairy lights flashed on and off and stayed off and darkness settled inside. Ursula felt disorientated. She no longer knew which way was out and which way was in. The push of the crowd was hot and urgent and she felt Katie's hand slip from hers as she lost her balance and fell backwards into darkness.

Chapter 95

Commander Taylor would have been knocked down by the digger if Ray Peters hadn't pulled him out of the way.

"What the hell is going on?" Taylor shouted, holding on to his hat as Peters seized his arm and he staggered backwards.

The digger came dangerously close to them and kept on going, ploughing towards the police who were dragging people out of their vans and lorries, making them abandon their quarry and jump out of the way.

Taylor looked up at the cab and felt overwhelmed with anger when he saw Lady Caroline Oxley's butler sitting behind the wheel.

"Arrest that bastard," he shouted. "Arrest him and stop that digger!"

A mob of blue surrounded the digger and swarmed into the cab. The digger juddered and came to a sudden halt.

"What the hell are you doing you fool?" Taylor asked as he looked up at Sowcroft sitting in the driver's cab.

Sowcroft looked straight ahead, his hands resting on the controls.

"Ow bastard!" the officer withdrew his hand and shook it. "That dog bit me!"

Taylor frowned.

"Get him out of here," he said. "And as for that mutt, put a boot up his backside and chase him away. He'll find his own way home if he knows what's good for him."

Munro stayed where he was, barking furiously as Sowcroft was dragged from the cab with his arms pinned behind his back. Sowcroft looked straight at Taylor as he passed him with defiance flashing in his eyes.

"Get him out of my sight," Taylor said. "And keep him away from her Ladyship. Make sure they're separated. Different vans."

"Yes sir," the arresting officer nodded and Taylor turned away and looked at the smoke rising from the burning vans and lorries.

They had done it, he thought triumphantly. They had done it.

Chapter 96

There was something about the telephone ringing in the middle of the night which struck fear into the most hard hearted of men. David Crawford had seen some sights in his time and didn't scare easily but the sound of the phone ringing in the hall could mean only one thing: trouble.

David Crawford stumbled down the stairs in his pyjamas and lifted the receiver from the table in the hall.

"378," he said, reciting the last three digits of his phone number.

"Is that Mr Crawford?" a woman's voice said. "Mr David Crawford?"

"Aye it is," David said, rubbing his eyes with the thumb and forefinger of his free hand. Dear God let nothing have happened to Agnes.

"Mr Crawford it's Sergeant Caterham from Ilkley police station. Do you have a daughter, Katharine Crawford born on the 11th July 1969?"

David swallowed. Katie?

David sat down on the stairs, opened his eyes and stared at the wallpaper.

"Aye, yes, I do," he said. "Is owt wrong?"

"Nothing to worry about," the sergeant said. "Just a matter of precaution. Only in view of her age we are obliged to notify you that she's in police custody."

David opened his mouth and closed it. Police custody?

"Are you still there Mr Crawford?"

David stared at the wallpaper. Pink roses with green leaves. Vertical columns of gold.

"Aye," he said. "Aye I'm still here… Is she alright? Katie?"

"She's fine," the officer continued. "When can you come to collect her?"

David looked up at the clock on the wall. He hadn't changed the batteries since Agnes had left and the hands were stuck at ten o'clock.

"What time is it?" he said.

"It's half past three in the morning sir. What time can we expect you?"

David's mind raced. Ilkley police station was half an hour's drive away and he didn't have a car: that had gone months ago when money got tight. A car was a luxury a striking miner could ill afford.

"I can fetch her in about an hour," he said. "I'll have to knock up me mate. Get a lift like."

"So about half past four then?"

"Aye," David said. "Aye. Can I speak to her like? On the phone?"

"I'm sorry sir," she said in a smooth and practised voice. "That's not possible at the moment. We'll see you later ok?"

"Aye. Aye. See you later. Thank you. Thank you."

The buzzing noise coming out of the receiver told him she had hung up. It was at times like this that he wished Agnes was here. Wished he could turn around and see her in the doorway and share this with her. But Agnes had been gone six weeks now and although he had hope in the beginning, that hope was fading fast.

David hesitated, tapped the bar on the hand set and placed his forefinger in the dial. He hated doing it, hated ringing people in the early hours of the morning but Stewart was his best mate and the only one he could think of with a car. His mind went blank as he tried to remember his phone number. Was it 474801 or 474108? He couldn't think straight. He couldn't imagine why his daughter was at the police station when she was supposed to be staying with Juliet.

David closed his eyes and forced his mind to calm. After three attempts, he dialled the right number.

Chapter 97

Juliet stood in the hall. She was wearing her nightie, the pink one with the *Love Is…* cartoon on the front that Katie had given her last Christmas.

"Well?" her dad said. "Cat got your tongue?"

Juliet shook her head. She could feel tears pricking her eyes. Katie was probably dead and it was all her fault.

"I'm sorry Dad," she said, raising her head. "I'm sorry."

"Never mind sorry," he said. "Katie told Mr Crawford she was staying with us this weekend. Why did she say it if it wasn't true? What do you know about it all?"

Juliet looked up at the men standing in front of her. There was Mr Spencer, who always dressed up as Father Christmas at the Working Men's Club, and Mr Crawford, Katie's dad, who was smoking cigarettes and pacing up and down the hall. Something terrible must have happened for them to be here in the middle of the night.

"Is… Is Katie dead?"

Her dad shook his head and Mr Crawford lit another cigarette.

"No love, no, not dead," her dad said. "But she could be in trouble. She's at the police station and we're not sure what's going on. Do you know anything?"

Juliet bit her lip and looked up at him.

"I told her not to go," she said. "To the festival. But Hugo invited her and she wanted to see Van Morrison."

Above her head, the three men exchanged glances.

"When did she go?" Mr Crawford asked her.

"On Friday I think," Juliet said. "Why is she in the police station?"

"That's something we want to know 'n' all," her dad said.

At that moment, Juliet's mum came into the hall. She was wearing a quilted dressing gown and had a printed scarf tied around her hair.

"I just tried to ring the station again," she said. "No one's answering."

"Well we'll just get along there then," Juliet's dad said. "Come on lads. If we put our foot down we'll be there in half an hour. Go back to bed," he said, turning to Juliet. "I'll deal with you later."

Juliet nodded and turned away. It was the end of the world and she was probably going to go to prison.

Chapter 98

It was pandemonium when they got to the police station. The front hall was crowded with people demanding to know what was going on. Some of them were sitting on the floor, others were squashed up, three deep, at the enquiry desk banging their fists and all talking at once. Behind the desk, a harassed looking police woman was appealing for calm and patience.

The three men surveyed the scene with dismay. It had taken over an hour and a half to get here because they'd been stopped at a police roadblock and the young constable, suspicious of three striking miners out in the early hours of the morning, had insisted on radioing his superiors for clearance and advice.

"Bastards," David said after they were waved on their way. "Even at four o'clock in the morning they still hound us."

"Aye," Juliet's dad Dennis nodded. "With nowt common sense between them. What would pickets be picketing at this time o' morning?"

"Excuse me love!" David called, standing on tiptoe and waving his arm in the air. "We're here to collect a fifteen year old girl called Katie Crawford. I'm her dad. You rang me earlier."

The woman behind the desk looked over at him across the sea of people pushing and shoving against the desk.

"Wait your turn sir please," she said. "It's very busy at the moment."

"Aye and we're busy and all," Dennis called back. "All we want to do is to collect her and we'll be on our way."

The woman pursed her lips and glared at him.

"Take a seat," she said. "I'll be with you as soon as I can."

The men turned their heads and looked behind them. There were no seats.

"I don't want a seat," David said stepping forward. "I just want my daughter."

Stewart placed a calming hand on his forearm.

"Steady lad," he said. "If no one's spoken to us in five minutes I'll go and speak to her again."

A woman in a chiffon headscarf raised her handbag from a seat to vacate it.

"Might as well sit down," she said to David. "It's chaos in here. I've been waiting two hours for news of my Steven."

David stared at her.

"Joy riding again," she sighed, placing her handbag on her knee. "And that police operation up at Ambrell means no one knows anything. He's only sixteen. They've had him here for hours. I mean it's not right is it? Keeping a young lad locked up in a cell. That Peace Convoy has a lot to answer for if you ask me."

David shook his head as Stewart nodded at the empty seat. He didn't want to sit down. The adrenalin was too strong to sit down.

"Aye," the man next to her nodded, joining in. "Arrested 400 of 'em so I've heard. At that festival. Drugs, weapons and the like. Most of 'em have been brought here."

David and Stewart and Dennis felt out of their depth. They didn't trust the police at the best of times not with what they'd seen on the picket lines and the horrors of Orgreave still vivid in their minds and now it seemed they'd have to wait here, in the enemy camp, in the lion's den, for God knows how long and none of them knew or understood what was going on and how Katie might have anything to do with the Peace Convoy or joy riding. None of it made sense.

"If them travellers have hurt her I'll kill them," Martin said.

"Calm yourself lad," Dennis said. "We don't know what's happened yet. We don't know what's happened."

Chapter 99

"I'm going to ask you one more time," the officer said, staring down into Shepherd's face. "What's your name?"

Shepherd looked down at the ground and remained silent. Everyone else standing in the queue for processing was doing the same thing. No one ever gave their name to the police.

"Right you bunch of bastards," the police officer shouted. "Seeing as how none of you will give your names, you've won the consolation prize, a trip to HMP Armley. Maybe after you've spent a night in prison you might change your minds about co-operating. Because until you do," he added. "No one's going anywhere."

No one in the queue moved. Everyone kept their head down and refused to look up at the sergeant who had made the announcement. Filthy pigs, Shepherd thought. Coming into the field and attacking people, burning and looting their vans. Why should he do anything they asked him to?

Shepherd felt an officer grab his arms. They were handcuffed behind his back, everyone's arms were handcuffed behind their backs. That was the way it was. That was how the police got their kicks. That was their power trip.

"I would remind you all," the sergeant continued, determined to have the last word. "You are all under arrest for possession and supply of drugs; possession of offensive weapons, resisting arrest, obstructing arrest and GBH. Now fuck off."

The queue shuffled forwards. Police vans with blue lights flashing waited outside in the yard. Shepherd watched as the officers rough handled men and women into the vans. Children were separated from their mothers and taken away as the women protested and screamed at the officers. Shepherd kept his eyes down. If he saw anything else tonight he may just end up on a charge of murder.

Chapter 100

"It's just a precaution Mr Crawford," the doctor said as he led the men down the pristine white corridor with curtained cubicles on either side. "We brought both girls in for observation. If the man hadn't got them out, we might be looking at something very different."

David was conscious of how shabby and dirty they must look in the clinical bright lights of St. George's Hospital and the nurses looked away as they hurried past. On the other hand, the three of them had been up all night and it wasn't until an hour ago that the police had finally told them that she wasn't at the station at all but in the local hospital.

The doctor stopped and with one arm, swept back a flowery curtain behind which were two beds. Katie was sitting up in one of them and he rushed over to her and took her in his arms.

"I'm sorry dad, I'm sorry," Katie said, her face pressed into his shoulder as the two other men stood awkwardly in the doorway, holding their flat caps in their hands.

"It's alright love it's alright," David whispered into her hair. "It's alright."

He held her away from him by the upper arms and looked into her tear stained face.

"Are you hurt?"

Katie shook her head and her long red hair swung across her face.

"No," she said. "The man rescued us but lots of people were injured," she said.

Over her shoulder David caught sight of another girl with short dark hair sitting up in bed watching them.

"Hello," she said. "I'm Ursula. I'm Katie's friend."

David's face darkened.

"Oh aye," he said. "Was it your idea to go to a festival?"

"No dad," Katie jumped in. "I only met Ursula when I got there. It's nothing to do with her."

David stared at Katie.

"I don't understand love," he said. "Why did you lie to me?"

Katie hung her head.

"I'm sorry," she said. "I'm sorry."

"Well aye," he said. "That's for me and you to discuss later. The doctor said there was a fire."

"There was a lot more than that," Ursula said, hugging her knees. "The police raided and lots of people got hurt. The police set the straw palace on fire. If it hadn't been for Grendo we wouldn't be here."

David swallowed. There was so much he didn't know, so much that didn't make sense but the main thing was, Katie was safe. There would be plenty of time to piece it all together later, when they got home.

"Where's your mum and dad love?"

Ursula shrugged.

"I don't know," she said, her eyes filling with tears. "They were at the festival."

"Do they know you're here?"

"No," Ursula said. "They said there was no time to tell them. There was… there was a lot going on."

"What's their names?" Stewart said from the doorway… "Perhaps we could see if we can find them."

Ursula looked at him and swallowed.

"Charlie," she said, "Charlie and Louise."

"We'll go up to Ambrell," Dennis said. "See what we can do."

"They're in a brown tent," Ursula said. "An old army one. And Charlie, my dad, he's in a band. Everyone knows him. It's called *Artaois.* It means bear," she added.

"Righto," Dennis said. "Got that. Artyo. Got it."

From the corridor, the sound of a woman's voice cut through the quiet hush of the hospital ward.

"I don't care how many visitors she's got," it said. "I want to see my daughter!"

Katie slid up the bed as a woman with curly hair wearing a white winter coat and holding a triangle shaped handbag appeared from behind the curtain.

"Bloody hell," David said, knocking over the bucket chair as he stood up.

"Mum!" Katie said, clambering out of bed. "Mum!"

Two Weeks Later

Chapter 101

"Why is Lady Caroline Oxley sitting in the dock of my Court?"

The Judge peered over his half moon glasses and stared at the police officer standing in front of him. The Court rustled and murmured and shifted in their seats and the onlookers in the public gallery leaned forward.

"Lady Caroline was arrested for breach of the peace and other matters," the police officer said. "A title does not make someone above the law as I am sure Your Honour will appreciate."

Judge Calder stared at him.

"Indeed," he acknowledged. "Officer I have been up half the night reading the witness statements and I have to say this is the sorriest lot of evidence I have ever had the misfortune to consider. You might think the police had better things to do than arrest a butler and a member of the titled classes. I see that one of your officers was bitten by a dog. I'm surprised you didn't arrest the dog officer. Your men seem to have been very thorough."

The officer squirmed a little and shuffled his papers and faint laughter rippled through the public gallery.

"How many are waiting downstairs?"

"Three hundred and sixty suspects were arrested in total your Honour. Fifty of those were remanded in custody."

"Including Lady Caroline Oxley?"

The officer shook his head.

"No Your Honour. She was released from the police station on bail."

The Judge stared at the papers before him.

"I see," he said. "So in relation to the other defendants, why has it taken two weeks to bring them to Court?"

The officer looked up and although his voice stayed strong, the papers shook slightly in his hand.

"They refused to give their details Your Honour."

"So you sent them to prison?"

The Judge took off his glasses and squinted at the papers in front of him.

"To HMP Armley?"

"That's right your Honour, yes. It is common practise for remanded defendants to be kept in custody if bail can't be granted."

"You don't need to remind me of the machinations of the law officer," the Judge said sharply, dropping the papers and replacing his glasses. "It's just a pity you didn't spend those two weeks making sure the evidence was up to scratch. I have statements from the public who were attending the festival. They say that most of the occupants of the travellers' field went peacefully when asked to do so. That seems to be completely at odds with what your officers are saying in their statements."

The officer looked up at the Judge.

"Some of them did disperse when requested to do so," he said. "Others were more, shall we say, resistant."

Silence hung in the Court for a moment before the Judge spoke again.

"Who wrote these statements officer?"

The officer looked down and coughed before answering.

"The arresting officers your Honour. That is usually the case."

"One officer or more than one officer?"

"There were several officers I believe. I was not present at the time of arrest or when the statements were written."

"No you clearly weren't," the Judge said. "Because if you had been you might have noticed that they are all the same or, to put it at its kindest, remarkably similar."

The police officer scratched at his neck and slid a finger under his collar.

"Shall I read them out?" the Judge said. "Shall I let the Court judge the similarities for themselves?"

"I'm not sure that's necessary Your Honour."

"But you have read them haven't you?"

"Yes. I've read them."

"And did they not strike you as remarkably similar?"

"I am not at liberty to say sir," he said. "My role is to prosecute. What the arresting officers write in statements would be from notes taken and kept in their pocket note books."

"Do we need to see those do you think? The notebooks?"

"No Your Honour. I don't think that will be necessary."

"Hmm..."

There was silence in Court for a while and then the Judge raised his pen.

"Dock officer please release Lady Caroline Oxley and Mr Xavier Sowcroft from the dock. All charges against them are dismissed. And once you have done that, please bring up the rest of the defendants."

There was a murmur at the back of the Court as the dock officer unlocked the door and let Lady Caroline and Sowcroft out of the dock.

"How are you feeling Lady Caroline?" the Judge asked kindly, looking down at her. "You've been through quite an ordeal have you not?"

Lady Caroline smiled up at him.

"Well at least I wasn't sent to prison," she smiled. "But it's been quite an experience."

"You are free to stay or leave as you wish," he said. "If you stay I am sure that members of the learned legal profession will move along to make way for you and Mr Sowcroft on the benches."

The lawyers dressed in their black robes shuffled along the wooden benches and stood up to let them pass and sit down.

"How is the Earl these days?" the Judge asked as they waited for the dock officer to return. "Keeping in good health I trust?"

Lady Caroline sat down on the bench and looked up at the Judge.

"He's as well as can be expected your Honour," she said. "He has good days and bad days."

"Hmmmm..." the Judge said. "That's to be expected. That's to be expected."

Noise from the dock indicated that the defendants were coming up from the cells underneath.

"Do give him my regards when you see him."

"I will your Honour. Thank you."

The defendants flooded into the dock through the door at the back, blinking at the sunlight flooding into the Court from the high windows. There was hardly enough room in the dock for fifty men and women and they stood squashed together like a puzzled and startled flock of sheep.

"Good morning," the Judge addressed them amiably. "I won't keep you long. Now I suppose we need to address the question of bail. Do we have bail addresses Mr Marshall?"

The prosecuting police officer shuffled his papers.

"I have no information that we do," he said. "The police are opposed to bail Your Honour and wish to apply for a further remand into custody."

"I'm sure they do," the Judge said. "But I will decide what happens in this Court. Now," he said, looking over his glasses at the men and women in the dock. "There are an awful lot of you aren't there? Perhaps one of you might wish to act as a spokesman otherwise we are going to be here all day."

A man with long grey hair and bandaged wrists came forward to the front of the dock.

"I'll speak your Honour," he said.

"What happened to your wrists?" the Judge said.

Grendo looked down at his hands.

"There was a fire," he said. "I helped some people to get out."

The Judge stared at him.

"And did you receive hospital treatment?"

Grendo held his gaze.

"No Your Honour," he said. "That didn't appear to be available."

A murmur rippled through the public gallery.

"I hear you all refused to give your names and addresses when you were arrested," the Judge said. "Do you intend to continue with that stance?"

"No Your Honour," Grendo said, shaking his shaggy head. "We had reasons to do that at the time but we're in Court now and the rules are different in Court."

The Judge raised an eyebrow.

"How different?" he said.

"Well for one we're not being manhandled," Grendo said. "Or beaten up."

"Are you saying you've been assaulted?" the judge said. "By police officers?"

"I am Your Honour," Grendo said, his chin raised. "But I doubt you're going to believe us."

Another ripple ran through the Court. The Judge picked up his papers.

"You've been in custody for what, two weeks?" he said.

"That's right your Honour," Grendo nodded.

"And the marks on your face. Did you have those before you went in?"

Grendo subconsciously raised his hand and touched his face.

"Just a few knocks and bumps your Honour. Nothing serious."

"And this fire?" he said. "Were many hurt?"

Grendo cleared his throat and looked over at the police officer standing in the front row.

"It was them what did it," he said, nodding at the officer. "Them who set the straw palace on fire."

The Judge raised his eyebrows.

"Is this true officer?"

The prosecuting police officer shuffled his papers and pulled at his collar.

"I don't have any record of a fire in my papers," he said. "All we are interested in is the charges before the Court."

"This man says there was a fire," the Judge persisted. "Is it true that the police set fire to a straw palace? That people were hurt?"

The prosecuting police officer looked down at his papers.

"As I said Your Honour. I have no record of it."

The Judge sat back and stared out at the Court.

"I have a woman and a butler arrested at a festival," he said slowly, after a pause. "I have statements that aren't worth the paper they're written on. I have a man in front of me who is wearing bandages on his wrist for injuries he says were sustained in a fire caused by the police and yet the police know nothing about it. Tell me, officer, what do you think I should do?"

The police officer looked up at the Judge.

"Do, your Honour?"

"Yes officer, do. Because what you are putting to me today raises questions of serious concern."

"Yes Your Honour," the police office nodded.

The Judge paused again and then leaned forward and picked up his fountain pen.

"All cases dismissed," he said scratching something on to the paper in front of him.

A gasp of disbelief rippled through the Court.

"Your Honour…" the prosecutor started.

The Judge looked up and glared at him.

"You heard me officer," he said. "All charges are dismissed. The defendants are free to leave."

A cheer erupted from the dock as the Judge rose to his feet. He said no more as he disappeared through the door at the back of the Bench leaving bewilderment in his wake.

The prosecutor turned to the dock officer who shrugged back at him and unlocked the door of the dock. The group of men and women glared at the prosecuting officer as they left the dock and filed into the Court room.

"Bastards!" someone shouted from the public gallery. "Go and get a job!"

Grendo raised his head and looked up at the man who had shouted. And then he looked away and walked quietly and with dignity out of the Court room.

Chapter 102

Lady Caroline stared at the newspaper Sowcroft handed to her.

> "500 police swooped on the camp of an evil drug pushing cult in the grounds of a stately home yesterday. Local people had complained festival goers were walking around naked in the grounds of Ambrell Priory and openly selling drugs.
>
> "People were frightened to leave their homes," a spokesman for the West Yorkshire Police said. "So we waited until the festival had ended before we carried out the raid which was essential in order to protect the public. A large quantity of weapons were seized including machetes, axes, spears and knives and 360 arrests were made. Yorkshire Police want to give a clear message to the members of the Peace Convoy that this sort of anarchic behaviour will not be tolerated."

Caroline put down the paper and sighed.

"Any sign of Munro?"

Sowcroft shook his head.

"I am afraid not my lady," he said. "I have made enquiries in the village but no one appears to have seen him."

Caroline turned her head and stared out of the window.

"How can an Irish wolfhound go missing?" she said. "I mean he's hardly going to blend in with the landscape is he?"

Sowcroft remained standing, his hands clasped in front of him.

"Munro is a very intelligent canine," he said. "I have no doubt he's safe and is biding his time before he comes home."

Caroline kicked her legs off the couch.

"But he's still a dog Sowcroft," she said irritably. "He needs food and shelter."

Sowcroft nodded.

"That may be so m'lady but he is also an intelligent dog, one who will come back when he's ready."

Caroline sighed and picked up the paper again.

"And as for this," she said, dropping it dismissively on to the floor. "They're making us out to be some sort of Columbian drug cartel. I suppose all they're interested in is selling newspapers. And a butler driving a forklift truck towards a group of police officers probably sells a lot of them."

Sowcroft's lips twitched.

"It was quite an experience m'lady. Although not one I intend to repeat in the immediate future."

Caroline walked to the window and gazed out across the garden and fields beyond.

"You were very brave Sowcroft," she said. "The Earl would be proud of you. It's just the sort of thing he would have done had he been here."

Sowcroft bowed.

"Thank you m'lady."

Caroline sighed.

"I wish Munro would come home," she said. "I do so miss him."

Chapter 103

Shepherd stared at the scene before him. Carnage was the only word he could think of. Smoke was drifting into the sky from some of the burned out vehicles and everything else was covered in dull grey ash. Doors of the vans and trucks hung open by their hinges and windows had been smashed out by police batons and metal rods. Debris and broken glass littered the ground and there was a strong smell of diesel where the police had emptied the tanks of fuel onto the earth. Gone was the green and pleasant field that had been home to the Peace Convoy for the last three weeks. He could hardly bear to look at Idlewild with her smashed windows and broken door.

"Come on then," Grendo said, rallying the troops. "Let's see what can be salvaged. There's always something to be salvaged. The pigs want us to lie down and die and that's exactly what we're not going to do. We have a right to live as we choose to live not the way Society dictates."

Despite the dreadful scene in front of them, Shepherd couldn't help but smile. Grendo had that gift of raising spirits even when they were as low as they were now. Given a different life, a different path, he could have lead men into battle, he could have changed the world.

Shepherd stopped suddenly, putting his hand to his brow to shade the sun from his eyes.

"What's that?" he said. "Over there?"

Grendo stopped and squinted into the distance.

"Well if it's the pigs coming back for more we're ready," he said, picking up an iron bar and tapping it against the palm of his free hand.

It was difficult to see, looking into the sun, and all they could make out was a line of men coming up over the hill with the sun behind them, turning them into dark shadowy shapes.

"It's at times like this I wish I had a cannon," Grendo muttered. "So I could blast those bastards to kingdom come."

"Wait," Astrid said, her young baby strapped to her chest in a sling, her feet bare despite the debris on the ground. "It's not the police. Unless the police have started wearing donkey jackets."

They stared into the sun as the group approached, getting larger as they did so and as they came closer, one of the group broke away and strode towards them.

"I'm looking for a man called Grendo," he said, stopping about two feet away. "Is he here?"

Behind him the advance of men in donkey jackets stopped. Shepherd thought there were maybe fifty of them but who they were and what they wanted he didn't know.

Grendo tapped the iron bar against his leg.

"I'm Grendo," he said. "Who wants to know?"

"I do," the man said, holding out his hand. "I'm David. David Crawford. You rescued my daughter Katie from the fire."

All eyes turned to Grendo waiting for him to lead, waiting for him to say something.

"We're miners," David continued. "We heard what the police have done to your vehicles. We've come to help. I think you've already met John and Danny and Marko."

The three men stepped forward and Grendo dropped the iron bar and stepped forward.

"Good to see you man," Grendo said, as he wrapped John in a bear hug. "Good to see you."

"This is Davey," John said, as they separated. "You rescued his daughter Katie from the fire."

Davey stepped forward and held out his hand. Grendo shook it.

"Thank you," David said. "Thank you."

"How is she?" he asked.

"Getting there," Davey smiled. "Without you I don't know what would have happened to her."

"Aye well, it was the least I could do," Grendo said. "Kids shouldn't have to see things like that. I'm glad she's ok."

John turned and nodded at the wreckage that surrounded them.

"They did this?" he said. "The pigs?"

Grendo cleared his throat.

"Aye," he said. "Aye. Did a good job didn't they?"

John's face darkened as he surveyed the scene.

"Bastards," he muttered. "Bastards."

David and some of the other men stepped forward.

"We've come off the picket line," he said. "We've brought tools and diesel."

Grendo stared at the men who stepped forward holding canvas bags and metal cans in their hands.

"And food," a woman with curly hair said, stepping forward and holding out a Lipton's carrier bag. "We thought you might be hungry."

More women stepped forward holding out dishes covered with tea towels.

Grendo looked at the people standing in front of them.

"That's right kind of you," he said. "Right kind."

"So shall we see what we can do?" John said. "We can't dig coal so we might as well help you."

Grendo smiled.

"Aye," he said, clapping him on the upper arm with gratitude. "Aye. Thank you."

As the men moved towards the devastated wreckage, Shepherd saw Caroline hurrying across the field from his left. She was no longer using crutches and her blonde hair was covered in a headscarf. She was dressed for autumn in a waxed Barbour jacket and black Wellington boots.

"You're back," she said, smiling as she stopped in front of him. "It's good to see you all. I wanted to say that you're welcome to stay with me," she said. "Until you get everything sorted."

Grendo turned and looked at her.

"We don't take charity," he said.

"Well you should," she said, in a brisk business like tone as a light wind tugged at the corner of her headscarf. She clamped a hand to her head and looked at him. "But if you wanted to pay your way, you could dig the kitchen garden and help out about the place. I don't mean to insult you," she added softly. "But there's a big old house over there and I can put up about ten of you if you don't mind a leaking roof."

Grendo looked at Shepherd and Shepherd shrugged.

"Why not?" he said. "It means we could stay close while we try to sort this mess out."

"Who are the men?" Caroline said, watching as the miners spread out across the field, picking up debris and shouting suggestions to each other.

"Miners," Grendo said. "We helped them out a while back. Now they're helping us."

Caroline's blue headscarf fluttered in the breeze and a strand of her hair escaped and blew across her face. She caught it with her hand and pushed it back under the fabric.

"Life has a funny way doesn't it," she said, fishing in her pocket and taking out a bulky brown envelope. "I want you to have this."

Grendo stared at the envelope she held out to him.

"Well go on, open it."

Grendo unfolded the flap and stared at the wadge of bank notes lodged inside and thrust it back at her.

"We can't take this," he said. "We don't need your money."

"Yes you do," she said, pushing it back at him. "I was keeping it to repair the house but I think your need is greater than mine at the moment."

Grendo raised his head and looked at her.

"We won't forget this," he said. "How do we ever thank you?"

Caroline smiled.

"You don't need to thank me," she said. "But if you could find my dog I'd be grateful. I haven't seen him since the night of the raid. And after that, well maybe you could make a start on the kitchen garden."

And then she turned and walked back across the field.

Chapter 104

Sometimes in the night, Katie woke up trembling from a dream where she was trapped in a burning house and couldn't get out. And sometimes, when she opened her eyes she thought she was still dreaming because her mum was sitting by the side of her bed holding her hand and telling her it was only a dream and that everything would be alright.

It had been two weeks since the fire, since the man had picked her up under one arm and Ursula under the other and walked through the flames to deposit them safely in the field away from the burning straw. He had gone straight back in to rescue others as paramedics rushed to attend to Ursula who had blacked out. Katie had watched the gigantic flames leaping and flickering towards the dark night sky sending showers of sparks across the grass and people running and screaming and shouting. Someone put a blanket around her shoulders and she was terrified that her new found friend was going to die and then a man gave her a cup of tea and Ursula sat up and asked where her dad was.

And now, she woke and found her mum in the quilted dressing gown with the poppies on sitting by the side of her bed.

"I used to hug that when you were gone," Katie said. "Your dressing gown. Every night. I used to hug it before I went to bed."

Agnes smiled at her daughter, her eyes bright with love.

"I'm back now love," she said. "And I'm not going anywhere. Try to get some sleep. We've got a big day ahead of us tomorrow."

Katie smiled and drifted back to sleep and this time, this time her dreams were softer.

Three Weeks Later

Chapter 105

Lady Caroline looked out of the window at the men working in the kitchen garden. They had been working on it night and day for the last two weeks and now she hardly recognised it. The knee length weeds were gone, the earth was freshly dug and the red brick walls surrounding the garden glowed in the fading light of the late September sun.

Sowcroft cleared his throat and she turned.

"Mr Shepherd is downstairs m'lady," he said. "He wants to know what to do about the wheelbarrow."

Caroline looked at him with irritation.

"Mr Shepherd isn't usually announced Sowcroft," she said. "Why doesn't he just come up like he usually does?"

"I don't' know m'lady," Sowcroft said. "He said it's quite an important matter."

"About a wheelbarrow?"

"Apparently so m'lady."

"Oh for goodness sake," Caroline said, crossing the room and passing him in the doorway.

Caroline hurried down the stairs and at the bottom she stopped. For standing in the doorway was Shepherd. And sitting beside him on a makeshift rope lead with his tongue hanging out was Munro.

Caroline rushed to him and fell to her knees, tears spilling from her eyes as she embraced her Irish wolfhound. Munro barked and wagged his tail as she kissed him and spoke to him softly and stroked his ears.

"How…" she said, looking up at Shepherd. "Where…?"

Shepherd grinned down at her, reaching down to release Munro from the rope he had used as an impromptu collar and lead.

"He was in the boathouse," he said. "I took my guitar along there earlier to get some peace and quiet and there he was."

"But we searched everywhere!" she said. "We've put notices out, Robert said he'd checked all the outhouses and barns and…"

"Well," Shepherd said. "That's where he was. That's where I found him."

Caroline got to her feet holding her hair behind her neck with one hand to keep it from swinging across her face.

"Come on darling," she said to Munro as he looked up at her with bright eyes and a wagging tail. "You must be sta.rving. Oh my darling darling Munro! I can't believe you're home!" and she leaned forward and cupped his ears in her hands and kissed his head.

"Why don't you come up?" Caroline said over her shoulder as Munro bounded up the stairs ahead of her. "Come and have a drink. You've all been working so hard."

"We're nearly done now," Shepherd said. "The vehicles are pretty much back together and you'll be growing the biggest marrows ever next year."

Lady Caroline smiled at him.

"Does that mean you're ready to leave?" she said.

"Pretty much," Shepherd said, following her up the stairs. "Time to get on the road again before we get too used to bricks and mortar."

Caroline felt her heart drop. It would be strange not having them around. Over the last few weeks, she had enjoyed the sound of their voices and laughter in the house and the way they'd all crowded around the dinner table in the evening. She hadn't even minded the muddy boots in the hall or the razors propped on the side of the sink in the bathroom. Man's things sometimes made a house a home.

"Gin and tonic?" she said brightly as they entered the drawing room.

"I'd prefer a beer," Shepherd grinned at her. "I might have been sleeping in luxury for the past few weeks but I'm still a travelling man at heart."

Caroline smiled at him. Yes, a travelling man. That was exactly what he was.

Chapter 106

He had a bloody nerve, really he did. Coming up the stairs without even being invited and now he was standing in the living room like nothing had happened. He must have seen Sowcroft drive off to the village to get the weekly groceries and chosen to come in when she was alone.

"Well well Rex," she said. "Fancy seeing you here."

Caroline lit a cigarette and blew the smoke up at the ceiling.

"I thought you might have got a job as a police informer."

"And what exactly is that supposed to mean?" Rex glared at her.

"Exactly what you want it to mean," Caroline said. "What do you want Rex? I can't say it's a pleasure seeing you. Do you know what problems you caused? Do you know that you got me arrested? *In my dressing gown?"*

Rex stared at her and then looked away.

"You shouldn't have stolen my grandmother's ring," he said petulantly. "That's called theft where I come from."

Caroline stared at him.

"Where did you come from Rex? Did you crawl out from under a stone? Do you realise that I could have ended up in prison because of what you told the police? Why did you tell them I had anything to do with drugs when you know perfectly well I can't stand the things?"

Rex shrugged.

"You invited a group of drug taking hippies to a festival," he said. "That's as good as being involved in my book."

Caroline moved a step closer to him. Had she really spent so many years with this smug, weak man? Had she really once been engaged to him? Slept with him? The thought made her feel sick.

"But it's not the same is it Rex? It's not the same at all. And telling the police lies about me could have ended up with me going to prison."

"Well it's a good job your Godfather was the Judge then wasn't it?"

Caroline shook her head in disbelief.

"Yes wasn't it Rex? Wasn't it just? Because if he wasn't where would I be now? Do you know that the people who did get arrested spent two weeks in prison on remand? If I didn't have this title, if I wasn't who I am, that could have happened to me!"

"Oh for God's sake stop being so dramatic," Rex said. "You seem to forget that you sold my grandmother's ring. All you have do to is give me the money. And compensate me for the digger your butler trashed."

"Oh I do do I? Well let me exactly what I've done with your precious money Rex de Beaufort…"

There was a noise behind them and Caroline turned to see Grendo standing in the doorway of the living room.

"Is there a problem Lady Caroline?" he said.

Rex turned and stared at him.

"Who the bloody hell are you?" he said rudely. "One of these bloody hippies she's so keen to save?"

Grendo took a step forward. He towered over Rex and stopped feet away from him.

"I'll tell you who I am," he said. "I'm a man just like you're a man except I don't have a title. A man who deserves respect. Would you like me to get rid of him Lady Caroline?"

Caroline stubbed out her cigarette and lifted her chin to blow the smoke up at the ceiling.

"Do you know what Grendo," she said. "I'd absolutely love you to do that. If it's no trouble of course."

Grendo seized Rex by the arm.

"Absolutely no trouble at all," he said. "In fact it would be my pleasure."

Caroline turned away as Rex protested at being dragged out of the room and down the stairs. She heard the front door bang and then some time later, heavy footsteps on the stairs.

"You won't be getting any more trouble from him," Grendo said, breathing heavily as he came back into the room.

Caroline smiled.

"Thank you Grendo," she said. "Would you like a cup of tea?"

Chapter 107

As the lights went up, David poked his finger in his left ear and wiggled it.

"I'll probably be deaf for the rest of me life," he said.

"No you won't dad," Katie laughed. "It's only a concert."

A man with shoulder length dark hair jumped down from the stage and headed towards them. He still had his guitar strapped to his body and sweat dripped from his brow.

"Katie?" he said. "I'm Charlie. Ursula's dad. You must be David."

"Aye that I am," David grinned, as they shook hands. "Where is she? Ursula? Katie hasn't stopped going on about her all night."

"She's just gone back stage," he said. "We're having a little party. To thank you," he said. "For what you did that night. If you hadn't rescued Ursula from that fire…"

"It weren't me who did that," David stopped him. "It were Grendo from the Peace Convoy. All we did was find you afterwards and tell you where she was."

"Even so," Charlie said. "You still played your part. It's a night we won't ever forget."

"You can say that again," David nodded. "You can say that again. But you're alright now Katie love aren't you?"

David looked at his daughter and smiled at her.

Katie rested her head against his arm.

"Yes dad," she said. "I am but could we go back stage now? I really really want to see Ursula."

Charlie and David exchanged a smile over her head as a woman came to join them.

"Sorry," she said, holding out her hand to Charlie. "There was a queue for the Ladies. Agnes," she said. "Katie's mum. Where's the famous Ursula?"

"Here I am!"

Katie turned as she heard her friend's voice behind her. Her face lit up and the girls giggled and hugged each other.

"Look at you!" Ursula said, leaning back to look at Katie. "You've got stars and glitter on your face!"

Katie smiled and flushed red.

"I was copying you," she said. "Although my mum wasn't that keen."

Ursula grinned and squeezed her hand.

"Come on," she said. "We've got cheese and pineapple on sticks and everything back stage."

Katie looked back at her parents as Ursula dragged her forward by the hand.

"We're right behind you love," Agnes said. "We're right behind you."

Chapter 108

The curtains were drawn against the autumn evening and the men and women of the Peace Convoy were gathered around the long trestle table in the dining room. Caroline couldn't remember when it had last been set with silver cutlery and sparkling wineglasses and smiled to herself at what her ancestors would think about the assembled company tonight.

She carried the gravy boat into the room as Sowcroft, walking behind her, carefully set down two serving dishes on the table.

Caroline took her place at the side of the table and Grendo sat at the head. She had insisted on the seating being that way so that she didn't look like the lord of the manor.

The atmosphere was warm and noisy and Grendo leaned forward, closed his eyes and inhaled the warm steam rising from the serving dishes.

"Sausage mash and gravy," he said. "Food of the gods."

"It's what you asked for," Caroline said, smiling as she sat down. "Although Sowcroft wasn't too sure were you Sowcroft?"

"Well m'lady," he said. "I have never been entirely sure about sausages."

Laughter rippled around the table as Grendo spiked the sausages with a fork and dropped them onto plates while Caroline dished out mounds of mashed potato.

"A toast," Grendo said when their plates were full and swimming in thick brown gravy. "To peace, love and unlikely friendships."

Grendo raised his wineglass and everyone copied him and repeated the toast.

"To unlikely friendships," Caroline said, standing up and raising her wineglass. "And thank you, all of you, for what you have done. It won't be the same without you here."

She sat back down and chairs were pulled in to the table. Cutlery clattered on plates and the warm buzz of conversation filled the room. It felt like Ambrell was a home again, Caroline thought, instead of a falling down mansion that she rattled around in most of the time in solitary confinement. Munro sat on a chair next to her with a jaunty red neckerchief tied around his neck.

"So where are you off to next?" Caroline asked Shepherd, raising her wineglass to her lips.

"Molesworth," Shepherd said, his cheek bulging with food. "Cambridgeshire. There's a peace camp there so we'll lie low for the winter and start the round of festivals again come Spring."

"Don't you ever long to stay in one place?" Caroline asked tentatively. "To put down roots? To sleep in the same bed every night?"

"No," he said, spearing another sausage. "Not any more."

They exchanged a look.

"We have to think about the pigs… I mean the police… too," Shepherd said. "They'll be after us as soon as we drive out the field."

"Surely they won't," Caroline said. "Surely what happened here was just a terrible mistake. Surely they've learned lessons after what the Judge said to them in Court."

Shepherd smiled.

"You saw them that night," he said. "Judge for yourself."

Caroline held his gaze for a moment and then looked away. She would never forget that night. If it hadn't been for her position and title she could have ended up in prison. She still had nightmares about it. And as for her blue silk Parisian dressing gown, she had thrown it in the dustbin, unable to wear it ever again.

Caroline dabbed at her mouth with a crisp white linen napkin and changed the subject.

"Do you think you'll be coming back this way again?"

Shepherd swallowed and shrugged.

"That depends," he said. "On whether the landlord holds another festival next year."

Caroline looked down at her plate. As much as she still hoped festivals might attract Tim and bring some much needed finance to Ambrell, she didn't think she'd hold another festival. Not after what had happened on the August bank holiday. It was too much to think about. People in the village were already avoiding her when she drove in to buy groceries or muttering as she walked down the High Street. She didn't much care for their slights and accusations but what she did want was a peaceful life.

As the evening drew on, the Peace Convoy retired from the table and headed out to their newly repaired vans and lorries. Shepherd hung back.

"Can I help clear up?" he said.

"I've got a butler for that," Caroline said, removing plates and napkins from the table. "Why pay a dog and bark yourself?"

"Give him the night off," Shepherd said, taking the plates out of her hand. "I'd like to spend some time with you."

Caroline searched his face.

"Alright," she said. "But he won't be pleased."

After they had sent Sowcroft to bed early and washed and dried up, Caroline and Shepherd sat on the sofa with Munro lying at their feet.

"What will you do when we've moved on?" Shepherd asked her.

Sade's LP, *Diamond Life* was playing softly in the background and candles set in a silver candelabra flickered on the mantelpiece.

Caroline lit a cigarette.

"There's always plenty to do round here," she said. "I'm going to get the garden room re-built and then of course there's my father to keep an eye on."

There was a moment's silence between them. One of the candles sputtered and outside, there was a distant rumble of thunder.

"Looks like we're in for a storm," Caroline said, getting up from the couch and pulling back the curtain to look out at the dark sky. "I loved watching thunderstorms when I was a little girl. I used to go up to the attic just so I could hear the rain on the roof."

A thread of white lightning fractured the sky and Shepherd got up from the couch to stand beside her.

"And now?" he said softly. "Would you like to do that now?"

He lifted up a strand of her hair and hooked it behind her ear. He was so close she could see the blue of his eyes and the stubble on his top lip. They stood looking at each other as another flash of lightning lit up the dim room. Caroline leaned towards him and closed her eyes.

"Hello Shepherd," a voice said from the doorway, breaking the spell.

Chapter 109

Shepherd hadn't seen Caroline since the night of the storm, not since Rose had unexpectedly made an appearance. That was a week ago and Rose had spent most of it bemoaning the loss of her treasured possessions in the police raid and moving things around to how they'd been in Idlewild before she left. Shepherd found it difficult having her here and it made him feel low. So many times he had willed her to walk in the door and now that she had, it wasn't how he'd imagined it would be. At night they slept on the edges of the bed with distance between them. Rose was still trying to work things out in her mind. She wasn't ready for intimacy.

And now they were all packed up and ready to get on the road again.

"I'm not sure about joining a peace camp," Rose said when she heard that the Convoy was heading for Molesworth. "I've heard the women can be pretty bitchy."

"You don't have to come," Shepherd snapped, the words out before he could stop them.

Rose turned and looked at him in surprise. Tears hovered in her eyes.

"You don't want me here do you?" she said. "I've felt that ever since I got back."

Shepherd sighed.

"Don't be daft," he said. "I'm glad you're back Rose. Really I am."

He put his arms around her and pulled her into him.

"Do you still love me?" Rose said, her voice muffled against his chest.

Shepherd hesitated just a little too long.

"Of course I do," he said, holding her away from him by the upper arms and looking down into her face. "You know I do."

"You seemed pretty close to that woman in the big house," she said.

Shepherd shrugged.

"Caroline?" he said. "She's just a friend. There's nothing between us.

How could there be? We come from different worlds."

"But what if you came from the same world?" Rose persisted.

Shepherd rolled his eyes.

"Well we don't," he said, picking up his guitar. "So there's no point thinking about it."

Rose watched him as he headed to the door and opened it.

"Where are you going?" she said.

Shepherd looked back at her over his shoulder.

"I won't be long," he said. "I'm just going to say goodbye to the river."

Rose smiled.

"Ok," she said. "Shall I make us some fairy cakes to take on the road? You always liked my fairy cakes."

Shepherd smiled but it didn't reach his eyes.

"Aye," he said. "Aye I did."

Outside Idlewild, the field was a hive of activity. Other members of the Peace Convoy called out to him as he walked and he raised his hand in greeting. From inside her bright orange van, Astrid held her baby to her chest and waved at him from the window. It was amazing how they had got the camp back together after the raid. He never thought he'd see Idlewild restored to her former glory. He had the miners to thank for that.

Shepherd crossed the field and headed towards the lane which led to the river. Tomorrow they'd be miles away, in another time, in another place and now it was time to say goodbye.

Shepherd walked down the lane which bordered the kitchen garden. He stopped as he saw Caroline bending over, tying up a trellis. The autumn sun caught her hair and Munro sat up and barked. Shepherd opened the little iron gate that they'd fixed so that it was no longer obscured and obstructed by weeds and ivy and Caroline turned and smiled when she saw him.

"We're heading off soon," Shepherd said a little awkwardly. "I've come to say goodbye."

"With your guitar?" she said. "Were you planning to sing your goodbyes?"

Shepherd smiled. He had got used to her dry sense of humour and he'd miss it.

"If you like," he said. "I could play Goodbye Norma Jean."

"Or maybe that would be just a little too cheesy," she smiled.

Shepherd moved from one foot to the other.

"Have you got a minute?" he said. "I was going to the boathouse."

Caroline was wearing combat trousers and a white cotton shirt. Even when she was gardening, Shepherd thought, she still looked like she'd stepped off a yacht in Monte Carlo.

"I'm not swimming today," she grinned at him, peeling off her gardening gloves.

Shepherd smiled at the memory. It was one he would take with him wherever he went, an image burned into his mind.

Caroline walked out through the gate with Munro trotting at her heels.

"Are you all ready to leave?" she asked him as they fell in step and headed towards the boathouse.

"Pretty much," he said. "The Convoy moves at lunchtime."

"How long will it take?," she said. "To get to Cambridge?"

Shepherd shrugged.

"Grendo reckons maybe a day or so. We'll stop on the way. If the police don't stop us first."

They walked on in silence until they reached the boathouse and Caroline went ahead of him and pushed the door open… Munro stayed outside, sitting on the ground with his pink tongue lolling out of his mouth.

"It's quite a special place this," Shepherd said as they stopped at the door and looked inside. "It's where I first met you and where I found Munro."

"Yes," Caroline said. "As a child I always believed it was magical. I used to dream of lying on a barge like the Lady of Shalott with my hair spread out across the water. I used to pretend that a knight in shining armour riding a frisky white horse would come up the path and rescue me."

She gave a little snort of laughter and went inside and sat down on the bench.

"It's funny what we dream of when we're little," she said.

Shepherd sat down beside her and set his guitar on his knees, draping his arms over the top of it.

"All I dreamt of was staying in one place," he said. "And now look at me. I can't stay in one place longer than a few weeks."

They both sat for a moment thinking their own thoughts.

"Are you going to play something?" Caroline said. "Or did you get me here on false pretences?"

Shepherd smiled at her and lifted the guitar. He bent his head and looked at the strings as his fingers started to coax them into life. He caught the scent of her perfume. He didn't even know its name.

"Look," he said. "About the other night… when Rose appeared."

Caroline shrugged.

"You don't have to explain anything to me," she said. "She's your girlfriend. You must be pleased she's back. I could feel how much she hurt you."

Shepherd stared at the door.

"But what if she hadn't come back?" he said. "What if we'd…"

Caroline sighed.

"It would probably be something we'd live to regret," she said. "Life happens. It happens. Don't dwell on it."

Shepherd swallowed.

"I know we're from different times, different places, different worlds," he said. "But I wouldn't have regretted it. I could never regret any of the time I've spent with you."

He let go of the guitar and took her face between his hands.

"I'm no fucking good with words," he whispered, his eyes troubled.

Caroline raised her hands and placed them over his.

"It's why you sing," she smiled, tears in her eyes. "It's why you sing."

Shepherd lifted a strand of her hair and tucked it behind her ear.

"You're the only man who's ever done that," she said.

"What?" he said.

"That," she said. "That thing with my hair. It's gentle, it's special, it's you."

Shepherd leaned forward and gently kissed her on the lips and then pulled away to look at her.

"Men should always treat you gently," he said. "Never accept anything else."

Shepherd took his guitar by the neck and stood up.

"I best be off," he said.

Caroline stayed where she was and looked up at him.

"Will you be back?" she asked. "One day?"

Shepherd smiled and placed his hand on the door handle.

"Aye," he said. "One day. We've got a debt to repay, remember?"

Chapter 110

Commander Taylor was pissed off. They'd mounted a successful police raid, kicked those hippy bastards into shape, only for the Court to dismiss all their hard work in minutes and screw up all those months of careful preparation and planning.

He sat back in his chair and surveyed the ceiling. At least he was back in London although his wife wasn't talking to him again and he didn't know why. He never knew why.

There was a knock at the door and Ray Peters walked in.

"I got you the list you asked for Sir," he said, standing just inside the door holding a red file in his hand.

Taylor leaned forward, stubbed out his cigarette in the ashtray and reached out for it.

"You've got the names?" he said. "All of them?"

Peters nodded, handing the file to him.

"Good," he said. "I'll pass this on to English Heritage in the morning. Those bastards might think they've won this time but the next time we'll win Peters. We'll win."

"Yes Sir," Peters said. "Yes sir we will."

Taylor glanced at the file, put it inside the drawer of his desk and closed it.

"Well off you go then," Taylor said. "Haven't you got a home to go to?"

Peters smiled.

"It's good to be back in London isn't it Sir?"

Taylor grunted.

"Get out of my sight," he said. "I've spent so much time with you these past few months I feel like I'm married to you."

Peters left the room, closing the door behind him. Taylor opened the drawer and slid the list of names of those arrested at Ambrell out of the file. 360 of the little bastards. They might have got away with it this time but next year, next year they wouldn't be quite so lucky. Once the names were sent to English Heritage, injunctions would be sought to stop the bastards going to any festival in England next summer.

Taylor smiled to himself, replaced the list, put the file back in the drawer and locked it. He stood up, crossed the room, unhooked his raincoat from the hatstand and gave one last look around his office before turning out the light.

Outside the police station, Taylor stopped and looked up at the heavy grey clouds. His wife might not be speaking to him but there were plenty of girls hanging around Praed Street who'd be willing to do more than speak.

Taylor hurried down the stone steps, turning up the collar of his raincoat as the first drops of rain began to fall.

Author's Note

British Summer Time is a work of fiction but is loosely based on what happened at the music festival held in the grounds of Nostell Priory, Yorkshire, during the August Bank Holiday weekend in 1984.

Scenes have been created and characters invented and most of it is the product of my imagination. For example, there was no straw palace at Nostell but the support striking Yorkshire miners gave to the Peace Convoy is true. The police raid, the arrests and the paranoia which followed the Peace Convoy around the country are truthfully replicated in accordance with the accounts given by those present at the time.

It was the legacy of the UK's 1960s housing policy which led to many young people living in squats: empty houses where families unable to afford their own houses, lived together as a community. In 1977 it was estimated that over 1,800 properties owned by the Greater London Council (GLC) were occupied. Squatters and the free festival scene of the 1970s were intrinsically entwined and the first free open air music festival was held at Windsor Great Park in 1972. The first free festival at Stonehenge followed in 1974.

Changes to legislation in the mid 1970s resulted in many evicted squatters taking to the road where they lived in communities of caravans and buses. The most well known of these was dubbed "The Peace Convoy" which emerged from the UK free festival scene in the late 1970s: a nomadic community of approximately 600 people travelling between open air music festivals in over 140 vans, trucks and converted buses. The Peace Convoy travelled all year round, not just during the summer festival season and their name was given to them after they added the women's peace camps at Greenham Common and Molesworth to their travelling itinerary. Between 1979 and 1982/3 the number of people living in vehicles on the road was estimated to be doubling every four years.

Margaret Thatcher's government viewed the increasing travelling community as a serious threat to the stability of the United Kingdom. Of particular concern was the Peace Convoy which she called "The Enemy Within". As it moved around the country, it was followed by the police and regularly monitored by planes and helicopters. The Daily Mail was quick to label the Convoy as an "evil drug pushing cult" and frequently published articles which portrayed them as a movement that threatened the very fabric of British Society.

It is important to place this reaction in the context of the times. The 1980s in the UK was dominated by a culture of fear: fear of nuclear weapons, fear of revolution, fear of unemployment and fear of the IRA. There was also a war with the Argentinians over the Falkland Islands although this was often viewed by the public as something far removed and a long way away from the shores of the British Isles unless you were a soldier or came from an army family.

What happened at Nostell and at the Battle of the Beanfield the following year, when one of the largest number of mass arrests of citizens took place since World War II, had enormous consequences for the liberties of the British people. The 1986 Public Order Act gave the police the power to break up any group of 12 or more vehicles and in response to an open air "rave" at Castlemorton Common in 1992, the Criminal Justice Act 1994 extended the powers of the police, allowing them to stop and search a person without having reasonable suspicion if approved by a senior police officer. That Act also tightened the laws on trespass, anti-social behaviour and unlicensed groups of people listening to music. In 2012, the Legal Aid Sentencing and Punishment of Offenders Act (LASPO) made squatting a criminal offence.

The Trade Union and Labour Relations (Consolidation) Act 1992, introduced to manage picket lines, is relied on in our current climate by councils and corporations to obtain injunctions against those who protest in the name of climate change or who object to corporations, councils and developers removing street trees in Sheffield, building the HS2 railway line or building extensive housing developments on green field sites.

What happened at Nostell is an important milestone in the social history of Great Britain. For ever since the early 1980s, the response of successive governments to perceived unrest or potential revolution, has been to repeatedly and consistently issue punitive legislation resulting in a continuous incursion into the rights and civil liberties of the British citizen.

Liz Gwinnell

June 2023

Acknowledgements

Ukrockfestivals.com

History-is-made-at-night blogspot

Andy Worthington

Tales from the Big House: Nostell Priory by Michael J. Richford

Printed in Great Britain
by Amazon

26957413R00179